THE AND CLOUDY SKIES

Jenny Maxwell

WARNER BOOKS

A *Warner* Book

First published in Great Britain in 2001
by Warner Books

A CIP catalogue record for this book
is available from the British Library.

ISBN 0 7515 3060 3

Typeset in Palatino by M Rules
Printed and bound in Great Britain by
Clays Ltd, St Ives plc

Warner Books
A Division of
Little, Brown and Company (UK)
Brettenham House
Lancaster Place
London WC2E 7EN

www.littlebrown.co.uk

For Milka Russell
who never gives up, no matter what the odds.

1

We went on the same bus, he said, and I knew him from that. It was the number seventeen, from Tyecroft to Witham, with twenty minutes at the station when some of them would get off for a cup of coffee or tea at the stall. Or to buy a paper.

I stayed on the bus and I looked out at the big buildings with their glass windows, which were black and shiny. In the winter the driver left the engine running for the heat, so I could listen to the engine and look at the black glass, and I liked it.

It was the number seventeen bus, but I didn't bother looking at the numbers. In the front seats were the three women from the home, going to the depot at Witham where they worked. Make-work, Annie used to say, for dumbos who had to be locked up in that place because they were too thick to look after themselves.

Look out, Dozey Joan, they might take you and lock you up in that place and make you work in the depot.

I'd been frightened when she'd first said that, but Rita told me not to bother about Annie. Spiteful, she said. You're all right doing the shelves now, aren't you? Have you on the checkouts next, you'll see. You're all right, Joan.

I'm not stupid, just because I'm not on the checkouts. I don't need to look at the numbers on that bus, if the three women are on it. That's not stupid, knowing who's on the bus, and looking at them instead of the numbers. Maybe it's stupid looking at numbers when you know the man with the black coat goes on that bus and you can look at him instead.

I told Annie, all right, bloody clever, what colour boxes are free-range, then? Clever, what colour? Blue, she said, and she was wrong. Blue's farm-fresh, free-range is brown.

All right, bloody clever, on the checkouts. Wrong, then.

Blue egg boxes and brown egg boxes and careful with those boxes, Dozey Joan, eggs are fragile, yes Mr Evans. They chuck out the broken ones, so Carol said, crack some, Joanie, take some home for your mum, they won't care, they all do it. The butter with the silver stripe on the left side of the shelf, the gold in the middle, up there, and the orange and white underneath them. Don't have to read the names. Silver stripe, gold, orange and white.

You crack one more of those eggs, you stupid cunt, and you're out, yes Mr Evans. Oh, don't cry, I didn't mean it. Give us a cuddle, then, come on. Closer, right. I didn't mean it. Lovely bum you've got, Joanie, give us a feel.

Yes Mr Evans.

Davie. Call me Davie. Give us a rub, then. There's a nice bit of pork not gone through the computer, Joanie. Give us a rub, then.

Oh *ho, Mister* Evans. Dozey Joan calls our Davie *Mister* Evans, what does our Davie call Dozey Joan?

Knickers off Dozey, come and work on my meat section.

You be careful, Joanie. David Evans isn't a very nice man.

Yes, Rita.

But my mum said the leg of pork on Friday was nice, and the eggs. She didn't like the orange and white butter, she wanted the one with the silver stripe. Why's the wrapping torn, you drop this, Joan?

No, Mum.

You be careful, Joan.

Yes, Mum.

But they don't let you have the butter unless the wrapping's torn. They can sell it. Customers won't buy it with the wrapping torn, so we can have it. Davie says I can have it, don't let on, Joanie.

He was on the bus, the man, and I knew him, knew the way he looked, but I didn't think, because I only looked for the three women. He wasn't at the front where I could see when the bus came to the stop. He was halfway down, by the window, looking out when I went past. I liked it at the back. I could see everybody, and nobody thought I was staring. It's rude to stare. I didn't stare, I just watched, and I listened.

Talking about the television, and the shops, and what somebody had said, and do you like my hair this way? Thought I might have it coloured. Did she really say that, then? I told her, old cow, I goes, I don't buy my clothes to come to work in, I buy my clothes to go out in, I says. She turns round and says, feel like that about work, you could start looking for somewhere else. Like my hair like

3

this? See that programme about the strippers? Laugh, I did laugh. I don't go there any more, somebody said they had the rat-catchers in. Not very nice, is it? Not where there's food. Oh, well, here we are, back to the grind. See you, love. Give my best to your gran.

But he never said anything. He was on his own.

Sheila didn't go on the bus. Her boss picked her up on his way to work, pulled up outside the door and sounded the horn, and Sheila pulled back the curtain and waved, and then she put on her coat and kissed our mum, and said, bye Joan, nice day, and off she went.

Sheila's a hairdresser. She's nearly qualified. She'll have a diploma. Her boss says she's really good. She does my hair for me, and our mum's, and she says I've got nice hair, all thick and springy and shiny.

But I wanted it blonde, not all dark.

You leave it like it is, said Sheila, and come Christmas I'll do you some highlights.

If the Good Lord meant you to be blonde He'd have made you blonde, said Mum, and Sheila laughed. Meant *you* to be a redhead and forgot, did He?

Don't you be cheeky, my girl. But Mum was laughing, took a swing at Sheila with the frying pan, they were both laughing and screaming, so I was laughing too. And I know what henna's for, in the green paper packet in the bathroom. It looks lovely, Mum's hair, when Sheila's just done it. Looks like it's on fire, all sparks, like as if copper got exploded into tiny little bits and there was a bonfire behind it.

You're daft, said Mum, but Sheila looked at me and said, that's good. That's not daft. Put you on the telly, advertising it. What was it you said? About the copper exploding?

4

But I couldn't remember when I tried to think. I'd just said it.

Come Christmas, said Mum, they can't sack our Joan. Been there a year then.

It was the Christmas rush, why I got taken on at Fletchers. Night work, filling shelves, because it was so crowded in the day there wasn't room for the cages. Just boxes, fill up as you go, quick quick quick. Night work, and can you stay on, Joanie? Only a couple of hours, never seen such a rush. Good girl, Joanie.

Joanie, then. Good girl, Joanie. Not Dozey Joan when they wanted me to stay on in the day, after I'd been working all night.

Make yourself ill, said Mum. But the money's a help. You're a good girl, Joan.

They call me Dozey Joan, I said, and I was tired, so I started to cry.

Feel better after a nice cup of tea, said Mum, and never you mind about them. They're only teasing. They wouldn't tease you if they didn't like you.

Annie doesn't like me. At break she spat in my coffee and said it was extra cream, drink it up. Some of the others laughed. Rita knocked it over and it splashed on Annie's skirt.

Clumsy fucking senile old cow, Annie called Rita.

Just leave her alone, said Rita. It's only a little splash of coffee. A bit of *spit* will bring that out.

I was doing all right through Christmas, even if I was tired, but I knew where everything went. I was as quick as any of them. Mr Kennedy said I was doing all right, and Rita told me he never says that about anybody, so I must be good, for him to notice.

Then in January they changed everything round. All

5

the Christmas things went in bins at the back of the shop, special offers, and it was all new places and different boxes.

'For God's sake, girl, *read* the damned thing. Look, where it says on the shelf, Hartley's, see? You've put Robinson's. You've got to *read* it. I suppose you *can* read, can't you? And it's lemon *curd*, not lemon marmalade.'

I can read. I'm not stupid, I went to school. But it was all different, everything in different places, and they still said I had to hurry up. Come on, Dozey Joan, be here all night at this rate. Reading made it slow. I had to read on the box, Lemon Marmalade, and I had to look on the shelves, look for where it said Lemon Marmalade, and there's twenty-five yards of shelves for jams and things.

Some of the writing was funny, too. An L is supposed to be two straight lines joined down at the bottom in the corner, not all curly bits. It wasn't proper writing, like it was in school. It was all wrong, some of it.

'Can't have this, Joan. Nearly fifteen minutes, and you haven't even opened the box. What have you been doing?'

Looking at the labels, looking for where it said Lemon Marmalade. Strawberry Preserve, Extra Fruit, that was all curly bits, didn't even have a picture of a strawberry, took ages, reading that one. Frank Cooper's Orange Marmalade. I read that one again, because of the marmalade, I knew the M, but it wasn't lemon. Chiver's Thick Cut.

Fifteen minutes, and I hadn't found the right place. But I'd been working, I had. I'd been reading the labels, looking for the right place.

'Here,' said Carol. 'See? Lemon Marmalade. Only got to ask, Dozey.'

6

Christmas, it had been easy. Boxes of mince pies under the big cut-out of Father Christmas, crackers on the racks by the cigarette kiosk, all the same things, all in the same places.

I'm not stupid. Mum says I've got the best memory of anyone she's ever known. Carol only had to show me once, I knew where it went after that. And the one with the green lid, next to it, just under where the strip light starts.

'Can't have this, Joan. Got to work faster than this. Plenty of girls looking for work.'

'Carol?'

'On the shelf over the meat freezer where you put the beef sausages last week. Next to the ones in the square jars.'

Brown bread in brown wrappers, white bread in blue and white wrappers, and the half loaves in the middle.

'Take the yoghurt up at the same time, Joan. Don't go up with half a cage.'

'No, Mr Kennedy.'

Time to go home, and Mr Kennedy told one of the girls not to come back next week. Extra pay instead of notice, goodbye, don't come back, no reference either. A couple of tins, I'll turn a blind eye, but not cigarettes.

Lying bastard, she said, I never.

One more word and I'll have the police. Get out.

Spring sales, and night work again, just for a week. Can you work on, Joanie? You're a good girl.

I know where everything goes now, so it's good girl, Joanie. Something new, I ask Carol, and she tells me. She's my friend. I bought her chocolates at Easter, and she said I'd make her fat and spotty.

Wish I had your figure, Joan. Wish I had your skin.

Look in the mirror. Should be blonde, have big tits and a tiny little waist and a curvy bum to be pretty. I'm not like that, I'm not pretty. Dark hair, not long and straight like the models, not blonde. No tits to speak of. A bit thin.

Carol's my friend. We go to the pictures sometimes, and I like that. But I don't like it afterwards, because Carol wants to go for a drink, and I don't like it. I don't like the pubs, all smoky and the men pushing around and buying drinks and saying drink up and have another. What's your name, then? Come over here and sit on my lap. Come on out the back.

No, I say, but Carol goes, if it's someone she likes, she goes out the back, and then I'm on my own.

What's your name, then? Where's your friend? Oh, yes, gone with Eric, has she? Lucky old Eric. Going to make me lucky, Joanie?

Carol goes out the back if it's someone she likes, but the man behind the bar, he got angry once. Get this place a bad name. What comes next?

An extra tenner in my purse comes next, Carol said on the way home when I told her. An extra tenner never comes amiss. We'll go to the Black Dog next week, make a change, give old grumpy time to cool down.

But I did like going to the pictures, and Carol's my friend.

Sheila asked me, do you know what they do out there? When Carol goes out with the men, and I laughed. Of course I know. Everybody knows, even rabbits know that. We had those sex awareness lessons at school, but there wasn't much we didn't already know, except all that about love and what they called stable relationships.

They didn't teach us about prices, did they? asked

Carol. Saw this on the telly, this woman, she got a thousand pounds a night. A thousand bleeding pounds! Got this flat in London, in Mayfair or somewhere, all done up like a palace, and the men, they come in the evening, and they stay all night, and it's a thousand pounds.

'Try asking Eric for a thousand pounds,' I said.

'He'd have a fit. More than he earns in a month. Not counting tips.'

I did go out with Bob from the grocery section. We went to the pub, because he was playing in a darts match. He didn't win, so he wasn't in a very good mood when we went home.

'Going to ask me in?'

'My mum's asleep. We'll wake her up.'

'I can be quiet. You might make a noise. Most girls do.'

I pushed him away, and he shoved his hands into his pockets and kicked at the gatepost.

'Don't do it on the first date, that it?'

He sounded angry, so I went into the house and shut the door before he could come through it.

Carol said he was bloody cheeky, who did he think he was? A girl's entitled to say no. All they ever think of is sex and football. Might as well get the money out of them, it's all the same either way.

Sometimes it seemed to me all anybody ever thought about was sex, not just the men. Annie was on about it at break, sounded like boasting to me, men won't leave her alone, always trying to get into her knickers. I thought, if it wasn't so dead easy to get into your knickers you probably wouldn't have so much trouble. Most men will leave you alone, if you say no.

I wished I could work somewhere else. I wished I

didn't have to wear that overall, only thin stuff but it made me sweat. Nylon does that, said Rita. I wished I could listen to people talking about nice things, even if I didn't understand all of it. I wished I didn't have to drink my coffee out of a plastic cup and chuck it in the bin on the way out of the canteen.

Why's that cheaper? I wouldn't mind washing up a cup and saucer and a teaspoon. All those long packets of plastic cups and the poly bags of plastic stirrers, not even proper spoons, we could keep cups and saucers in that cupboard, wouldn't take up any more room.

But I never asked, they'd only have laughed at me.

I bought myself a cup and saucer. It was antique. I'd seen it in the shop window, near the bus stop where I got off to go home, and I stopped and looked. It was on a shelf with a lot of other things. I wondered what it would be like, to drink out of a cup like that. Not very big, only an ordinary shape, but special, somehow. It looked the way a person looks, when they're too important to need to make a fuss. Just there, on that shelf. So I stood and looked, and I wondered.

They kept me late at work next day, so the shop was open in the morning when I got off the bus, and I looked in the window again at the cup and saucer. Pale blue, with birds painted on.

I went into the shop, and asked to see it.

'Seven pounds fifty,' said the woman. 'Mind you don't drop it. It's bone china.'

It was so thin I could see my fingers through it when I held it, and not even up to the light, just the lamp from behind the desk was enough. And the birds, all painted on so beautifully, and a tiny thin line of gold round the rim.

There were people who had whole dinner sets like this, not just teasets, and never thought anything about it.

I could do shadow pictures through that cup. I moved my fingers to look at the shadows, and it was so smooth, and so light, it was lovely.

'You going to buy it or play with it?'

I only had three pounds to last me till Friday, and the bus fares took half that.

'Keep it for me?' I asked. 'Friday?'

I had to give her two pounds, and she said if I didn't pick it up Friday it was on sale again, and I wouldn't get my deposit back.

Mum said I was bloody crackers, all that money on a cup and saucer, I'd be wanting silver spoons next, and she was right. I had to walk back from work Thursday morning because of the deposit on my cup and saucer, but it was worth it.

On the Friday the woman was nice about it. She wrapped up the cup and saucer separately, in tissue paper, and put them in a box, and smiled at me.

'Look after them,' she said. 'Leave those to your kids. Be worth ten times what you paid for them by then.'

I didn't think they'd last that long, but they did. Mum was careful with them. She knew I liked them. She put them in the corner of the cupboard where they wouldn't get chipped when she took the other stuff out, and anyway they were stronger than they looked.

So when I got home from work I had my tea in a proper cup, with a saucer, and it felt special. I got to going upstairs and washing and changing before I had my cup of tea, so I could sit down in clean clothes feeling all fresh and nice, because of my special cup.

11

Daft, said Mum, but they're dead pretty, Joan. Ought to be in a cabinet.

I bought a little silver spoon to go with them. The woman in the shop said it was plate, I mustn't polish it too much. I nodded, but I didn't understand. What did she mean, plate? It was a spoon, not a plate.

'Only silver on the outside,' said Sheila when I asked her. 'On the inside it's ordinary metal. If you polish it too much you rub all the silver off.'

I thought about it, and I wasn't very happy. It didn't seem right. It was like it was fake, not good enough for my special cup and saucer.

'Real silver?' said the woman in the shop. 'Real, solid silver? Better start saving your pennies. Cost you, that will.'

'How much?'

'At least a tenner. Maybe more, depends. Want it to go with the Coalport, do you?

I wanted it to go with my cup and saucer, but I didn't say anything. It's better not to say anything when you don't understand what somebody's talking about. Not until you know them well enough to ask, like Sheila, or Carol.

'I haven't got a single in stock,' said the woman. 'Only a set in a box, and that's a hundred and sixty. But I can get one. Do you want me to?'

She was smiling at me. I knew it was because I was a customer, not real friendly, just pretend, but it was nice.

'A tenner?' I asked.

'If that's your limit, I can get one for a tenner. I'll keep it for a couple of weeks, if you like. Pound deposit?'

It was daft, I knew it was, a tenner for a little spoon, just to stir in the sugar, but I wanted it to be right. I earned the money, why shouldn't I have a silver spoon? But I wasn't daft right through.

'Take the plate one back?' I asked, and the woman started to laugh. This time it was real friendly, not pretend, so I laughed too.

'Have you in the trade soon,' she said. 'Okay. Paid a pound for it, didn't you? Right, bring it back, then. That's your deposit.'

Mum asked if I was planning to start up a collection, things I couldn't afford and didn't need, but she wasn't being nasty. I didn't want anything else, only my nice cup and saucer and the spoon that was right to go with them.

It did make me feel special, drinking my tea out of that cup.

One of the women from the home wasn't on the bus the day after I got the spoon. The other two were dead quiet. I wondered what had happened. Usually they were talking, sometimes daft things, but they were just talking, no harm. It wasn't the first time there were only two of them. Anybody can get a cold, but I knew there was something wrong this time.

I didn't go to the back of the bus. I sat two seats behind them, so I could listen, in case they said something. It was the one with the curly hair who was missing. I wanted to know why.

I felt anxious about her. I didn't know her, never even said good morning, but I was worried. I wished I had said good morning to them. Been going on the same bus for months, why not?

So I sat and tried to listen, but they didn't say a word. Dead silent the whole way.

Other people were talking, didn't seem anybody else

13

had noticed. Where's the one with the curly hair? The one who bought a little pot of scented hand cream for her mum's birthday present last week, where is she? Why are the others so quiet?

See that show on the telly last night, that man won nearly fifty thousand. Wonder what he'll do. What would you do, if you won fifty thousand? He says, twenty-five quid just for the brakes, like I'm supposed to care, like I don't have to go on the bus every day, come rain, come shine. Every shop in the town, couldn't find one to match, then when I goes home I finds it in the back of the washing machine. Your gran comes out next week, doesn't she? Give her my best, when you visit.

Where is she? Why are they so quiet?

When we got to the station I got off that day. I thought, cup of coffee, why not? Never done that before, stupid little thing, but it made me nervous, getting off the bus for a coffee. I wanted to walk past them, so I did it.

'Good morning,' I said, and they both looked at me. I tried to smile, but I was nervous about getting off the bus and buying the coffee, so it didn't come out very friendly, or I don't think so. Just, my lips moved a bit, not a proper smile like I meant it.

'Morning,' said the little one with the blue headscarf, and then the one in the brown coat nodded her head at me, but she didn't say anything.

The coffee was horrible. It was all gritty, and they hadn't rinsed the cup properly, so the rim tasted of soap. I only drank about half of it, and I kept worrying, have I got my handbag? Have I lost my ticket, in case the inspector comes? I shouldn't have got off the bus. I should have stayed safe where I was. How much longer before it goes? Will it look stupid if I go back now, and sit and wait, instead of out here with the others?

'Haven't seen you out here before,' said the woman whose gran was in hospital, and I was a bit surprised. She'd never spoken to me before, but it was friendly. I didn't know what to say, so I shrugged and turned away. Then that seemed rude, so I looked back at her and nodded.

I went back to the bus.

'Where's your friend?' I asked. How else could I find out, without asking? I was anxious. I wanted to know.

They both looked at me. Then the one in the brown coat started to cry, not like people usually cry, a bit at a time, building up. Not a sniff, and then a little sob, and look in a bag or a pocket for a tissue.

This was all at once. She opened her mouth and she wailed, really loud, and there were tears all down her cheeks and snot out of her nose, and a terrible noise, all sad and wild.

The one in the headscarf patted her on the knee, didn't look at her. It was like she was used to it.

'Gone to Jesus,' she said to me, but she didn't cry.

I knew it wasn't because she didn't care. It was because she cared too much, she couldn't cry. It's like when you get hurt. If it's not too bad you say something, ouch, or maybe you swear, or even cry. But when it's really bad you don't do anything, you just wait, like you're stunned.

The one in the blue headscarf, she was just waiting for that terrible pain to go away.

I sat down on the seat across from them, and I looked in my bag for my packet of tissues. It was a new one, not even opened, but that was right. You wouldn't want to give a present of something you'd used. I gave it to the one who was crying, and she took it and ripped it open. But it was the one in the blue headscarf who was hurting so much who took the tissues out of the packet and wiped her friend's face, and held one to her nose and said blow, and then wiped her face again.

There was a little ring with a glass stone in the bottom of my bag, it came out of a cracker at a Christmas party and I'd forgotten it. I found it while I was getting the tissues, and it was in my hand. I gave it to the one in the headscarf and she took it.

'Present,' I said, meaning it had been one, and then I thought, no, give it to her; give her a present.

'Present,' I said again, and made like a shooing sign at her, meaning, take it. Take it.

'Pretty,' she said, and it was. It didn't matter it was only cheap metal and glass, it was pretty.

She put it on her finger, on the left hand, like it was an engagement ring, and she held it up to the light. The one in the brown coat wailed again, but there wasn't anything I could do. I'd given her the tissues, I hadn't got any more.

They were all coming across from the station, all the passengers, so I had to go back to my seat.

'Your friend,' I said, and they both looked at me. I'd meant to say, look, her nose is running again, it needs wiping, but it hadn't come out like that. It sounded as if I was talking about the one who was dead.

'I'm sorry,' I said, and then, 'she was nice.'

But I didn't know. I'd never spoken to any of them, until that morning.

I went back to my seat and I looked out of the window, as though nothing had happened, as though it wasn't anything to do with me, the noise and the mess on the woman's face. When they came past some of the passengers said things to each other, oh dear, what's stirred her up them? Poor little soul, can't help it. Not nasty, but as if they couldn't understand so it didn't matter, what was said. Even if they heard, they wouldn't understand, so it didn't matter.

But I knew it wasn't like that. They could be hurt by what they heard. They knew they were different. Some of the time they hoped nobody else knew, or nobody had noticed. Words like that told them everybody knew, and everybody had noticed.

I felt sad for them. Not for the one who was dead; it had been not knowing that had worried me. Now I knew, it didn't seem to matter any more, about her. But the other two, especially the one in the blue headscarf, I did feel sad for them. I wished there was something I could do to make the pain go away.

In the coffee break I told Carol. One of the women on the bus from the home, she's dead, I said. That was quick, said Carol, and I thought, she's right. That one who's dead now, she was there yesterday. But how did Carol know it was quick? Had I said they were all there yesterday?

There was a new line in cakes that day, so I was worried, I didn't know where they went. Carol was working over on the dairy section. I had to read the boxes. It made me slow. I didn't have time to think about the woman on the bus, but I must have been worrying, because halfway through the morning I got really upset, and I put the boxes down and I ran through the shop to where Carol was working.

'Can't do it,' I said, and it felt as if I was shouting, but the words came out quiet. 'Bloody boxes, all little

17

writing.' And then, 'How did you know it was quick? The woman on the bus? I didn't say.'

'Give us a hand with the marge, then,' said Carol. 'Old Kennedy's got a right temper on today. Give us a hand.'

So we put out the marge, that was easy. The shelves weren't empty, just had to look for the same packages and fill them up. It was the new stuff I couldn't do, I wished they wouldn't give me that. I wished they'd let me do what I knew. I don't mind the work, when I know what I've got to do. I hate that new stuff.

'Don't get the miseries then,' said Carol, but I was in a state by then. Mr Kennedy was wandering around the place. If he found I'd left all the boxes of cakes he'd be angry. If he found me working on the dairy.

'Come on,' I said. 'Hurry up.'

He was standing by the cage when we went back, and he started right away, where do you think you've been? Slacking off like that, why aren't these cakes on the shelves?

'You lay off,' said Carol. 'It's not her fault you're not getting your oats,' and he stopped and looked at her as if she'd hit him. And I thought, oh *ho*.

I felt ashamed then, as soon as I'd thought it, those two silly words, not even proper words. That's what that nasty slag Annie would have thought.

Got to get out of here, or I'll start being like Annie.

Stupid, that. Where else can I work, that wouldn't be the same? Only without Carol or Rita to help.

Mr Kennedy walked away, he didn't even look back, and Carol winked at me. But I didn't want to think about Carol and Mr Kennedy, because somehow it seemed dirty, much worse than going out the back of the pub with the men.

18

'How did you know about the woman on the bus?' I asked again, because I wanted to think about something else.

'My auntie works there, in the kitchens. Vicky got bronchitis.'

Vicky. She knew their names. I'd never known their names, and Carol did, because her auntie worked in the kitchens at the home.

You don't die of bronchitis, do you? A bad cold, a nasty cough, bronchitis. You don't die of that.

She was so quick, reading those labels. One look, then slice open the cartons with the Stanley knife, check down the length of the shelves at the plastic labels, and she knew. So quick, it was like magic.

I watched her, and when she opened the next carton I was ready. She pointed at the shelf.

'Next to the blackberry and apple pies,' she said. 'Other side of the rail.'

I could stop worrying. Now I knew, I wouldn't forget. Green and yellow box with the red lettering and the picture of the little pies, next to the blackberry and apple pies the other side of the rail. And the next lot, they had dark green lettering, that was on the bottom shelf, leave room for the iced tarts, those had white lettering, and they were the other side of the rail too, underneath the first lot.

'Bronchitis?' I asked. Dead from bronchitis in one day, it didn't seem right.

Carol sighed, but she didn't stop working.

'Takes them like that, some of them. Weak chests. She'll be sad about Vicky, my auntie.'

Mr Kennedy walked past the end of the row, he looked at us, he didn't stop. He hadn't really got anything to complain about. We'd done the marge, we were nearly done with these cakes, so we'd been quick enough. It was only what Carol had said.

I thought, I'd better be Dozey Joan around old Kennedy for a few days, maybe he'll think I didn't hear, or didn't understand. Then it'll be all right.

I thought about weak chests, those women on the bus. I wondered if they all had weak chests. Maybe they weren't stupid at all. Maybe they were ill. If you can have a weak chest, and be on the bus one day and dead the next, maybe there's something in their heads that's the same. Like a weak brain, that catches something easy, a germ, and for them it's bad. Much worse than for us.

I thought about it all the rest of the day, trying to make sense of it, but I didn't know enough about it. I didn't know very much at all. Not enough to make sense of Vicky dying like that.

'There's books,' said Sheila that night when I told her about Vicky. 'You can find anything, in books. If you know where to look.'

'Read it to me?' I asked, and she laughed. I had been joking. I've seen those sorts of books, they had them on the shelves at school. Big and thick, with small writing, hundreds of pages, some of them.

I lay awake until nearly daylight, wondering how bronchitis had killed Vicky, and how you can find out about things if reading takes a long time.

20

2

I said good morning to the two women when I got on the bus the next morning, and I smiled at them. They smiled back, and they both said good morning. The one in the brown coat who'd cried the day before, she smiled with her mouth wide open, like a child. It looked a bit funny, but it was nice. It was a real smile, she meant it, it wasn't just polite and pretend.

I didn't go to the back. It seemed a bit rude, to go right to the back of the bus that day, after we'd said good morning. I went two seats behind them, but on the other side, and then I saw him. He'd been there every morning, I knew that. Looking out of the window, he'd never turned his head when I went past. Now, when I sat down opposite him, it was like he waited for a moment, and then very slowly he turned towards me and he looked at me.

I didn't say anything. I knew he was looking at me, but when men look at you, you don't say anything, you pretend you don't notice. I went on sitting quietly in my new seat, two back from the women, looking ahead out of the front window, watching the wipers going backwards and forwards, even though it wasn't raining very much. They made a squeaking noise.

He was a bit older than me, but not much. He had brown hair, sort of straight and floppy, and he seemed to be sitting very, very still.

What's he looking at? I wondered, and then he nodded, not at me, but like somebody had answered a question. That's right, he seemed to be saying when he nodded. That's right, that's the answer.

The two women were quiet, not talking like they had when there'd been three of them, but not dead silent, like the day before. Now and then the one in the blue headscarf would say something like, there's that shop where we got the birthday card, and the other one would say yes, that's the shop. We got the birthday card there, didn't we? But then they'd be quiet again, nothing to say. It was as if they wanted to be nice to each other, even though they were so sad about Vicky.

When we got to the station I didn't want to get off the bus. I didn't want that horrible coffee again. Everybody started to get off, and the woman who'd spoken to me the day before asked me, coming for a coffee, love? I shook my head. But then there weren't many people left. Me, and the two women, and the man who'd looked at me and nodded in that funny way, and the man in the black coat at the corner in the back, reading his paper, and coughing, and shaking it out so it folded exactly like he wanted.

I went to the front of the bus, and I sat down opposite the two women. I didn't say anything. It was enough, sitting there. That said it, it said enough. I'm here, I'm sorry about your friend.

They both smiled at me, and the one in the blue

22

headscarf held up her hand so I could see the ring I'd given her. She'd kept it on her left hand, on the ring finger, like an engagement ring, and it still looked pretty, even though it was just a piece of cheap glass out of a cracker.

'Pretty,' she said, and I nodded.

'What's your name?' she asked.

'Joan. What's yours?'

'Sarah.'

And the other one said, 'I'm Diane.'

Then she cleared her throat, and sat up very straight, and patted at her coat where it lay tight across her thighs.

'Nice weather we're having for the time of year,' she said, in a different voice.

It was raining quite hard. There was a greasy mark across the front window, where the wipers had scraped off on the dry glass, and on the side windows the rain was making pattering noises and running down.

She was looking at me, a bit nervously, a bit hopefully, her mouth open and her head forward.

'Very nice,' I agreed, and she sort of sighed, as though she'd been holding her breath.

We didn't speak again. I was thinking about what we'd said and done, and I thought, it's all right. We hadn't needed to say anything else. We could have talked about the television, and clothes, and boyfriends, and even politics, but we wouldn't have said anything more, no matter how long we'd talked. I'm me, and you're you, and that's good.

I went back to my seat when the others came out of the station and started to walk across the road to the bus, and we smiled at each other. I went right to the back this time, so I could hear what people said. It wasn't rude this time, going to the back. I thought, I can do that every day. Start off sitting two seats back, so we're not far away and it's friendly and polite, and then, after the station, go to the back so I can still listen.

Then I looked at the man again. He hadn't moved. I thought, it seems as if he hasn't moved a muscle, not once, ever since he nodded in that funny way. He's just sat there, with his elbow against the side of the window and his chin propped on his hand, looking out at the rain and the people and the big buildings, and he hasn't moved.

It wasn't natural.

The man in the corner coughed, and shook out his paper again, and I thought, showing off. I'm reading a paper, I am. Look at me, reading my paper.

A woman got on the bus with two children and a pushchair, there was scrambling and noise, and one of the children was whining, so I looked at them, and I didn't think about the man with the paper again.

Or the one sitting so still, looking out of the window.

There was trouble at work. One of the girls in the storeroom said Mr Evans had assaulted her, put his hand up her skirt when she was on the stepladder. The boy who did the greengrocery cages said he'd seen it too, but nobody believed him, or cared if he had or not. He was always trying to make himself important, pretending he knew things about everybody. In the canteen at the lunch break, he was always saying, if I was to tell what I know there'd be some heads rolling.

But the girl was upset. She was crying. Rita took her up to Mr Kennedy's office, and told Mr Evans to stay right away from her. He was shouting, he kept saying the ladder was wobbling, he thought she was going to fall, he'd been trying to stop her falling off the ladder.

I just went on putting the boxes of washing-up liquid on the cage and I didn't look at anybody. I hoped they wouldn't ask me. I knew what David Evans was like when there was a girl on the stepladder, because I'd been the girl often enough. He used to wait until I'd got a heavy box in my arms, and then he'd be up behind me, and it wasn't just a hand up my skirt it was a finger inside my knickers, and I couldn't do a thing, because I had the box in my arms and I was balancing on the ladder.

'Come on, then, Joanie. Come on down the ladder, then.'

I'd just stand there and wait, and he'd be waiting too, with his finger just there and ready, and that box getting heavier and heavier. But if I tried to come down the ladder, he'd win. You can't keep your legs pressed tight together when you're coming down a ladder.

'How's that, then, Joanie? Don't you wish it was the real thing?'

I didn't go up the stepladder if he was around, not unless there were other people there. Sometimes he'd come back before I could get down. Or he'd say, get that carton down, Joanie. There's the stepladder, up you go.

'We don't need olive oil, Mr Evans. There's two boxes in the cage.'

'Davie. Call me Davie. And do what I tell you.'

Rita was gone a long time with the girl, and Mr Kennedy's office door was shut, like it is when he wants it to be private. Mr Evans was going all round everywhere telling everybody it was a misunderstanding, he'd been trying to stop her falling, and she'd misunderstood.

'Ask anybody,' he kept saying. 'Ask anybody. I wouldn't do that. Don't even fancy her, spotty little cow.'

Mr Kennedy sent the girl home in a taxi, and Annie said she bet he'd bought her off. A few quid extra in the pay packet, keep your mouth shut and your legs crossed, or else.

'I don't think so, my girl,' said Rita, and she sounded so angry everybody looked at her in surprise. It was as though a friendly old tabby cat had suddenly barked at you. 'Hazel wasn't the first, as we all know. If I have anything to do with it, she'll be the last, at least in this place.'

'What we need in this dump is a union,' said the boy from greengrocery, but nobody took any notice. We were all still looking at Rita, but she didn't say anything else. She just finished her coffee, threw the cup in the bin and went back to work.

They kept me on late that evening, so I missed my bus home and there wasn't another until seven. I didn't mind. It was an hour and a bit overtime, and Mr Evans wasn't there. I hadn't seen him go, and nobody said anything, but everybody seemed to know we wouldn't be seeing David Evans again. Rita had meant what she said, and even though she's a very nice person she can be dead stubborn. You wouldn't think, to look at her, with her grey hair all wispy and her not being very big, but she's got quite a temper, our Rita.

'You all right down here on your own?' asked Mr Kennedy, and I jumped, because I hadn't heard him coming.

'Yes, Mr Kennedy.'

He was standing there on the concrete floor under the

strip lights, looking all around, a bit curious, and somehow as if he was a bit disgusted, too. It was like he was searching for something, as if there were clues on those racks of boxes and crates.

'Should have come down here more often. I'm sorry if you've had trouble, Miss Ferguson. It won't happen again.'

I didn't know what to say, so I just shrugged, and wondered if it would be rude to go on with my work while he was standing there.

He went away, walking across the concrete, and he called back over his shoulder, almost as if he was angry.

'You could have said. I can listen. Somebody could have told me.'

He believed it, but I didn't think he would have listened to me, if I'd said anything about Mr Evans. He had to listen to Rita, because she would have stood there in his office telling him what she knew, and she wouldn't have moved until he did listen to her. Either that or pick her up and throw her back down the stairs.

Rita's been there longer than anybody, and she's not a troublemaker.

I told Sheila about David Evans that night after we'd had our tea. I was tired and I wanted to go to bed early, so she said I should have my bath, and go and get into bed, and then she wanted to talk to me.

She sat on the edge of my bed, and she told me I was dead pretty, and I laughed. She laughed too, but then she went all serious, and told me she meant it. It was nice, me being pretty, but it meant I had to be more careful than girls who weren't.

'You're daft,' I said, and she sort of punched me on the arm. It was like she was saying, all right, I don't mind some fun, but you listen to me all the same, because I mean this.

'You're not stupid,' she said. 'Just because you're not very good at reading doesn't mean you're stupid. You mind what I say, our Joanie. You don't let yourself be alone with dirty bastards like Evans. I know you, keep out of trouble, keep your mouth shut, never say boo to a goose. Men like that Evans, they reckon that's a come-on. Of course, buggers like that reckon it's a come-on if you kick and scream too, so you can't win. Just mind, Joan. You are dead pretty, even if you don't believe me. You be careful.'

I thought about what she said before I went to sleep, and I thought, it's a bit funny. In the pubs with Carol, the men are after sex, and it's right there in the open. They want it, and if you're not giving it, somebody else will. It's not a big problem. I didn't like it, the way they kept asking if you'd go out the back with them, but it wasn't frightening. But sometimes in those storerooms at work, when I was just trying to earn a living, I was listening out for Mr Evans and I was frightened. He was dead nasty, that man. I really didn't like it, working there with him around. I hoped he wasn't going to come back.

I thought, now Rita's told Mr Kennedy about him, maybe if I say something next time he comes up behind me when I'm on the stepladder, maybe Mr Kennedy will believe me, too.

Then I remembered Carol telling Mr Kennedy it wasn't my fault he wasn't getting his oats, and I thought, no point in telling him. Even if he did believe me, he wouldn't think it mattered. It's only sex, what's the big deal?

When I got on the bus the next morning I smiled at

Sarah and Diane and I just went the two seats back, to where I'd been the day before, because I wanted to be friendly. I didn't think about the man.

He was staring at me. It wasn't like yesterday, when he'd looked, and I'd pretended not to notice, until he'd given that funny sort of nod and turned away. This time he was watching for me when I got on the bus, and he went on looking at me as I walked down to my seat. He was looking straight at me, right into my face, and it was like a dare. It wasn't friendly. It wasn't like men look when they think you're pretty either, even though that can be like a dare, too. This was nasty. It was as if I'd done something bad.

I tried to pretend not to notice. I tried not to look back at him, but I couldn't help it. I wanted to ask, what's the matter? Why are you looking at me like that? I felt my face getting hot and red, and I wished I'd gone on walking down the bus to the back, where I'd sat before, so I wasn't so close to him. But it was too late by then, I was sitting down. It would have looked funny if I'd got up and gone to the back of the bus.

Even after everybody had sat down and the bus started, I could still feel he was looking at me, staring at me, like he was angry with me. I felt my chin lifting, and I put up a hand to touch my cheek. I knew it was red, and it felt hot. It felt as if it had been slapped.

Why was he looking like that?

The women behind me noticed, too. I felt them lean together, and one of them whispered to the other. I couldn't hear what she said, but the other one laughed and whispered something back, and then they both settled in their seats, and a moment later the man turned away and stared out of the window, just like he'd done the day before, his arm resting against the side of the window, his chin on his hand.

I wanted to get off the bus and get away from him. He'd quite frightened me, looking at me like that. I told myself I was being stupid, to feel scared just because somebody looked at me. It was because of Mr Evans, and what Sheila had said the night before when she told me to be careful. There was nothing really wrong. It was all my imagination.

At the station I went forward again and sat opposite the women. They both smiled as though they were really pleased to see me. We said hello to each other, then we just sat and talked a bit, not about anything important, and I tried not to think of the man two seats back, looking out of the window with his chin in his hand. I looked at the rain falling on to the pavement; not hard like it had been the day before, just falling gently, and there were still dry patches close to the walls.

When the people started to come back from the station I stood up, but I didn't want to walk past the man looking out of the window. I didn't want to be close to him at all.

I didn't know what to do. I looked down, and I brushed at my skirt, as if I'd seen something on it, while I tried to think. I could stay where I was, there was no law that said I couldn't stay sitting in the front, opposite Sarah and Diane, but it would seem funny. It wasn't where I usually sat. It was where the married couple sat every day except Friday. People would notice.

The other man in the corner shook his newspaper, and then there were people on the step and coming in, so I straightened up and I marched right past the man at the window with my nose in the air, and I didn't even look at him. I don't know whether he looked at me or not, because I was staring out of the back window, as if the bus coming in behind us was really interesting. And then I sat down on the back seat, and I was shaking.

Stupid, I said to myself. Don't be so stupid.

But I wasn't only frightened, I was muddled and angry. I couldn't put my feelings into words, not even in my own mind. Too much was happening. I had to think about too many things: Mr Evans, and what to do if he came up behind me on the stepladder again; Rita, suddenly not just showing the little bit of temper, gone in a flash, that we were all used to, but really angry and facing up to Mr Kennedy; what Sheila had said, and whether it mattered; her daft idea that I was pretty, so I had to be careful.

Then I started wondering if the man on the bus had read my mind, and knew I'd been told to be careful, so that was why he had looked at me in that way. It was such a silly idea I got even more cross and muddled, and I didn't even know where to look, out of the window, or at the other people, or just down at my hands. I nearly missed my bus stop, and I would have done if the woman behind me hadn't leaned forward and said, 'Isn't this your stop, lovey?'

I jumped up and I dropped my bag. It was the nice driver, not the grumpy one, so he laughed, and he waited while I picked it up and ran down to the doors. I didn't look at anybody, I just got off the bus and walked away towards the alley down the side of the supermarket. I walked as quickly as I could, because I was almost frightened. The road where the bus stops is quiet and usually I like it, but this time, when I came out at the other end of the alley, I was glad the street was so busy with people who'd come into town early to do their shopping. I didn't want to be quiet, and on my own in the little alley, or in the road where the bus stops.

I thought, this is a horrible day. This is going to be a really horrible day, and I wish I'd stayed at home. Something's going to happen.

Carol caught up with me as I got to the door.

'What's up with you?'

'Don't know.'

She pushed the door open and we both went through together, squashing against the frame.

'Ouch,' I said, even though nothing had hurt, and she grinned at me.

'PMT,' she said, and I wondered, can that be it? Might be. Bit early, but it might be.

'Want a coffee?'

'Yes.'

'You pay, then. I'm skint. Buy you one Friday, okay?'

Carol was always skint, I never knew why. It didn't matter. I put the money in the machine and we sat at the table. We'd have to drink it quick, it was nearly seven.

'What's upset you, then?'

'Don't know.'

A man gave me a dirty look on the bus. Vicky's dead, and I don't see how she can be dead of bronchitis in one day. I want to find out and I can't because of reading, it takes too long.

'Davie Evans?' suggested Carol. 'How about that, then? Rita up on her high horse, just because of that stuck-up bit Hazel.'

'She's not stuck-up,' I said. 'She's just young. First job, first day.'

'He was chancing it a bit,' she agreed. 'Still, that's life,

32

isn't it? Be a boring old scene if they never tried it on. Not that I could fancy David Evans, not even on toast with tomato sauce.'

He wasn't there. He wasn't in the storerooms or anywhere. Halfway through the morning Mr Kennedy came down and asked if we could manage all right. Any problems, he said, come up to his office and ask him. Meantime, just take a look through the shop, see what's getting low, top it up.

'Isn't Mr Evans coming in, then?' asked the boy from greengrocery, all polite and smarmy, and Mr Kennedy snapped at him.

'Over my dead body, he comes back. You get on with your work, Freeman. This doesn't affect you. What are you doing in here anyway?'

I went up to the shop and I walked along the rows, looking. I could see what was getting a bit low, like Mr Kennedy had said: granary loaf, Marmite, brown sauce with the green label, fruit pickle, so I went back to the storeroom and put them on the cage and took them up.

It was dead easy. Was this all Mr Evans had ever had to do? Walk through the shop and see what was getting low and then come down and tell us, so we loaded up the cages and took them up to the shop? Was that it? Just that, and we had to call him Mister, and do what he said, and he got to wear a smart blue cotton overall and got extra money and be part of the management team?

I could do this in my sleep. Anybody could do this. He'd had his stupid clipboard, with a dinky little pen and lots of rows of squares, and he made marks in them. I didn't need a stupid clipboard with rows of squares, I knew, I could remember. There weren't much more than about twenty things running low on the shelves.

33

I got to feeling angry as I went on doing my work that morning. It wasn't fair, him getting all that extra, and being Management just for doing so little.

'You *are* in a bloody temper today,' said Carol. 'What's the matter? You missing our Davie?'

'No, I'm bloody not. Do his job, do it standing on my head. What do we want him for? What's he do that's so special?'

'All right, keep your wig on. Not me that's stuck my finger up Hazel's fanny, don't get on at me.'

'Him and his stupid little clipboard,' I said. 'What's so special, then? Just tell me, what's so special?'

I hadn't heard Mr Kennedy, didn't know he was there until I looked at Carol and she was standing up and sort of grinning, and then I turned round and he was looking at me.

'Managing all right?' he asked, as if he hadn't heard what I'd said, and I nodded. Of course I was managing all right, what was there to manage? Just a few things running low, did he think I was stupid, that I couldn't manage?

He sort of sighed, and looked around the storeroom at all the racks with the cartons.

'Have to do an extra stock check,' he said. 'Make sure we don't run out. Oh, hell. If you spot anything running low, make a note.'

'Marmite, small size,' I said. 'Fairy washing-up liquid, own-brand brown sauce, Livio olive oil, middle size, Mr Kipling Bakewell tarts, Hovis . . .'

'Not on the shelves,' he interrupted. 'I mean down here in the store.'

'I know what you mean,' I said, and I was so cross I snapped at him. I'd never spoken to him like that before, everybody was staring at me. But it was all too much, the man on the bus, and finding out just how little Mr Evans had had to do to be in charge of us and be more important, and even Carol being skint again so I'd had to buy the coffee, she'd never paid me back for the last time, either. It was all too much, and I was angry.

'I'm not stupid,' I said. 'It's down here I'm talking about, too. I know what's running low, I've got eyes in my head. I told you, Marmite small size, Fairy washing-up liquid, own-brand brown . . .'

'All right,' he said. 'All right. Very good. That's good. Just write me a list, I'll put in the order. Very good, Joan.'

And he walked off, and I watched him go, and I sighed.

Write me a list.

Carol was looking at me as if I'd grown an extra head.

'Bloody hell!' she said. 'You *are* in a funny state, talking to him like that. Do you really know what's running out? All in your head?'

What's so funny about that? I wondered. It was easy. You just thought about the racks, and then you knew where there weren't enough boxes. What was so special? You knew how many boxes there were supposed to be, and if there weren't that many, then you were running low. You didn't have to be a genius to do that. Anybody could do that.

Write me a list, he'd said.

You didn't have to be a genius to do that either. Anybody could do that, except me.

Forget it, I thought, and then, I can't. Mr Kennedy told me to write him a list. It'll take me all day, and he'll laugh at my writing.

I can't do it. I can't write it out.

35

'Joanie?'

'Help me with the list?' I asked, and Carol nodded.

'You tell me, I'll write it. But you leave me to do the talking. Okay?'

I wouldn't have known what to say anyway.

We went into the office where Mr Evans had sat when he wasn't pretending to be busy, and Carol picked up a pencil and told me to go ahead. I thought about the racks, and I remembered where there weren't enough boxes, and I started to say the names.

It didn't take long. There'd been a delivery only two days before, most of the things on my list hadn't come with it. The suppliers had run out, or something.

'That the lot, then?'

I didn't want to go up to Mr Kennedy's office, but Carol pushed me out of the storerooms.

'Go on,' she said. 'He won't bite. Well, not in his office, he won't. Back of his car up on the downs he might, but that's different.'

I shouldn't have done, but I had to laugh. Even so, when she knocked on the door and went in without even waiting for him to say so, I didn't like it. I'd never been in that office since I'd had my interview for the job.

'That the list?' said Mr Kennedy, and he reached out his hand for it.

But Carol stepped back and held it high over her head as if he was trying to grab it from her, even though he hadn't even stood up. He was just sitting there behind the desk.

'Not so fast,' she said. 'What's it worth?'

He looked at her, and for a moment he seemed as if he was going to laugh. I thought, she's used those words before. Maybe in the back of his car up on the downs.

He didn't answer. He waited for her, waited to see what she'd say, and I thought, he's clever. He knows whoever talks first has to do the arguing, and he'll let it be her.

'Joanie can do old Stinkfinger's job standing on her head,' said Carol, and Mr Kennedy looked over to where I was standing, sort of half hiding behind her.

'Who wrote that list?' he asked, and he wasn't being nasty. He knew by then I was no good at reading and writing, and even if Mr Evans was stupid he could read and write, at least well enough for his job.

Carol wouldn't answer, not for a moment. Just one question, and he'd won. It wasn't a serious argument anyway.

'Job sharing,' said Carol. 'How about that then? Me and Joanie, split the extra pay three ways, you, me, and her.'

He really did laugh then. He said it would be about two quid each at that rate, and maybe she'd like to try and fiddle it through the accounts, and were there any more extra perks we wanted to discuss while we were about it?

'Cotton overall,' I said, since he was being nice and friendly, and they both turned and looked at me.

I remembered in the Falklands war when one of the ships had got hit and some men had been burned. I remembered them saying they'd been wearing nylon overalls, and it made the burns much worse. Somebody in the navy had decided it was to be cotton overalls from then on. There'd been a picture of one of the men, the burn all down his chest and his arm. I've never forgotten, and I've never liked nylon since then. Not just because it makes you sweat, but because I remembered the men on that ship, the way the nylon had melted on their skin and made the burns so much worse.

'You want Mr Evans's overall?' asked Mr Kennedy, and he sounded puzzled. 'You can have it if you like.'

I shook my head, feeling a bit silly. That wasn't what I'd meant.

Carol understood. 'These bloody things make you sweat,' she said.

'Company policy. Sorry.' And then, 'Come on, Carol, hand over that list. There'll be overtime on both your pay packets next week.'

She didn't argue any more, or even hesitate. She knew he'd be fair. He looked down the list, and he nodded, and he told me I'd done well. Give him a list every afternoon until there was a replacement store manager, he said, and we wouldn't be sorry we'd helped out.

Carol was so pleased with herself she was jumping around as we went back down the stairs to the storeroom. She was trying to work out how much we could earn every day until they found a replacement for Mr Evans, but I didn't see much point. Mr Kennedy hadn't said.

'Fiver a day, you reckon? Hey, Joanie, that's twenty-five a week! Let's go out tonight. Let's celebrate.'

'We haven't got it yet.'

'Good as.'

'You said you were skint.'

I didn't want to go out. I wanted to go home and have a wash and change into something clean, and then sit down and have a cup of tea in my special cup. Then I wanted to tell Sheila about what had happened with the lists, and Mr Kennedy being nice, and ask her what she thought.

After that, I reckoned I could get it straight in my own mind. If I talk to Sheila, it seems things get simple and clear, because she knows me so well it doesn't matter if I don't remember the exact words. She knows what I mean. Sometimes she doesn't even have to talk to me about it. Just telling her helps me understand, and then I know what to do.

So I told Carol, no, I haven't got enough money to take us both out. I've got to save up for my mum's birthday. At first I thought she'd sulk about it, like she does sometimes when she doesn't get her own way, but she was so pleased about Mr Kennedy giving us overtime for five minutes writing down a list she just laughed and said we'd paint the whole bloody town scarlet after next pay day, nobody had better try and stop us.

That afternoon she said we had to do another list. He'd said every afternoon, hadn't he? Right, and we hadn't done one, not that *afternoon*, the one we'd done was this morning's. But I wouldn't. I said we'd been lucky enough. Push it, and he'd do it himself, it was only looking at the racks, anybody could do it, it only took a minute.

'I can make him do anything,' said Carol. 'Anything at all. I bet I could make him take two lists a day. Even three.'

I didn't answer her. There'd been a coachload of tourists in, Rita said they'd been like a flock of locusts. Running short of everything, she said. Get those cages moving, Joanie, there's a love. She'd had all she could take of people asking for things, and her taking them round and finding empty shelves.

So there was no time for arguing with Carol. I wanted to get home, so I worked as fast as I could so nobody would ask me to stay on late. It was nice, working by myself, taking up a cage and filling the shelves, looking down the next rows to see what was short, not being told, just doing it. I liked it. And I thought, when I went down for the last time that evening, I know what to put on the order list, too. Each time I'd loaded up the cage, I'd thought, getting low on Walker's Shortbread, nearly out of Rose's chocolates. So it was going to be easy, the next day.

Funny, I thought as I put on my coat, I'd thought today was going to be horrible, and it's turned out just fine. You never can tell.

So I was really happy as I walked down to the bus stop. I was going home to a cup of tea in my special cup, and when Sheila came in I'd have something nice to talk about, and she'd be pleased for me. Mr Kennedy had said I'd done well, and there was going to be extra money for a while.

I hardly even noticed when I got to the bus stop. Nobody else was waiting there, no queue, but that's usual when you start work early. Just somebody by the wall with his back to me.

And then he was beside me, and I still hardly noticed.

And then he said, 'Come with me,' and something hurt me, and I looked down, and there was a knife.

3

I thought, this is stupid. It doesn't happen like this. I thought, it's broad daylight. I thought, it's a joke, he can't mean this.

Then I thought, it's the man from the bus. It hurts, it's a real knife. He does mean it. It's not a joke.

'Come with me,' he said again, and he pulled my arm.

'Don't.'

'Come with me.'

His voice was quite quiet, almost respectful, but that third time it was harder. It was as if he was saying, I mean this. He hadn't moved the knife, but his hand on my arm was beginning to hurt.

We walked along the pavement. He was holding my arm close against his side, and the knife was still pressing into my ribs. I thought I could feel some blood running down. As we walked the knife moved, and I told him he was cutting me. He looked at me, frowning a bit, and then pulled the knife back. I could still feel it, but it wasn't against my skin any more.

I looked around to see if anybody had seen what was

happening, but there was hardly anybody in the road. There were two women with pushchairs coming towards us, and a man on the other side of the street, lighting a cigarette. The man with the knife didn't seem to notice them.

I wondered if I could get away from him, but it was as if he knew what I was thinking. The grip on my arm got tighter, and I thought, he's much too strong. I couldn't get away.

The women were nearly beside us.

'Help me,' I said. 'Please.'

I didn't know what else to say. They looked at us, as if we were a bit funny and they shouldn't stare, and then they looked at each other, and one of them shrugged.

'Please,' I said again, but they only smiled, and walked on down the pavement. I could feel them looking back at us.

He didn't say anything. I couldn't even feel the knife, but I knew it was there. Perhaps if I tried to get away he wouldn't hurt me.

Then the knife cut into me again.

How did he know what I was thinking?

The man with the cigarette was watching us, but not as if he'd seen anything wrong.

'Help me,' I called, and I felt the man beside me smile. He knew nobody would take any notice. What could people see?

I wanted to tell the man who was watching us that there was a knife, and it was cutting into my ribs. I'm being kidnapped. Please, stop him. Please, help me. Can't you see what's happening?

'Help me!'

He flicked ash off his cigarette, and looked down at it as if it was interesting. He wouldn't look at us any more, just down at the pavement, at that little bit of grey cigarette ash.

We turned the corner into another road. There were houses all in a row, all the same. Old red brick and pointed roofs, and the pavement was broken. I tripped on the edge of a kerbstone, and he caught me, as if he was helping me. We stopped walking for a moment.

'Are you all right?' he asked. His voice was really polite, as if it mattered if I'd hurt myself.

We walked on, until we were nearly halfway down the road. I'd seen nobody. There was a baby sleeping in a pram in one of the front gardens, a dog lying beside it. I remember thinking it was dangerous, now, to leave a baby alone in a garden. That was why the mother had a dog: not because she wanted a pet, but because she needed a dog to guard the baby, if she wanted to leave it in the garden. But that's new. Mothers used to leave their babies in prams in the gardens, and nobody ever thought it was dangerous. Babies need fresh air, and a little sunlight, so long as it's not too strong.

I should have had a dog.

I'd only been waiting for my bus. That's not dangerous, waiting for a bus, in the middle of the afternoon after an early shift at work. That's not dangerous, I shouldn't need a dog.

'What do you want?' I asked him, but I thought I knew.

We stopped at a gate, and he looked at me. Then he opened the gate, very quickly, with the hand that held the knife. I saw it flash, but he was too quick. And his other hand was still holding my arm, not so tightly that it hurt, but I knew he was strong enough to stop me if I tried to get away.

'Come on,' he said. 'In here.'

'I don't want to. Please, let me go. I don't want to.'

'In here.'

There was a path with smooth round little stones that rolled under my feet, like walking on a beach. They were noisy.

He didn't bother with the knife when we got to the door. He took it away from my ribs, and I saw it clearly for the first time. It was a big pocket knife, with a red handle. He pressed the back of the blade against the door-frame to close the knife, his hand spread wide as it began to move. It snapped back into place, and he dropped it into his pocket and took out a key.

'I don't want to,' I said again, and he looked at me, and then put the key into the lock and turned it.

'Come on.'

There was a tiny little hallway, dark even though it was painted white, and a staircase leading straight out of it to the side. The stairs were steep. They were painted white too, with bits of carpet nailed to them. It was all clean, but the paint was chipped, and the carpet was old. It was thin at the edges, and I could see some of the nails, just a little gleam against the brown carpet. There was a door in front of us.

He couldn't stand beside me in the hall; it was too narrow. I remember thinking, what would you do if somebody came to visit you, and you wanted to ask them in? They couldn't walk past you. It must be difficult; you'd have to turn your back on them and walk ahead, and that's a bit rude, or come right out into the garden to let them go in first.

He was behind me. He let go of my arm as I went through the door, and I heard him close it behind me. I heard bolts, two of them.

'Up the stairs,' he said, and then, 'Go on. You know the way.'

'I don't,' I said, and then I began to cry. 'I don't. Please let me go.'

'Up the stairs. Please don't be difficult.'

When I still stood there at the bottom of the stairs, crying, he put his hand on my shoulder, quite gently.

'If I have to carry you I might hurt you. The stairs are very narrow, you see. I might hit your head against the wall.

I went up the stairs slowly, trying to see what he was doing, but he was only following me a few steps below. I wondered what would happen if I tried to kick him back down the stairs, and he stopped, watching me.

I remembered. He can read my mind.

I went on up, and there was a tiny landing, with two doors leading off it. The brown carpet was nailed to the white-painted floor, the gleam of the nails showing through it. The doors were painted white too, and each one had a step up to it. Under the white the wood was worn down so the step sloped.

'The back room,' he said, as if it was something he'd said before, as if I should have known.

I turned the handle, and I went into the room.

The glass in the windows had been painted. It was like tiny white stars, so from the outside it might have looked like net curtains. It had been done carefully and must have taken a long time. The frames of the windows, and all the other wood in the room, was white, just like in the hallway and on the stairs. But this wood wasn't chipped. The paint in this room was all new and shiny. There was linoleum on the floor, and it was new, too. It was dark red with black lines, so it looked like marble. The walls were all dark blue, just paint over the plaster, and I could still smell the paint, it all smelt new and fresh.

No curtains, no furniture. There was nothing in that room except the linoleum and the new paint and a bare light-bulb hanging from the middle of the ceiling. But everything was clean and fresh.

He came in behind me and closed the door. He didn't try to lock it, but he stood in front of it. He was smiling, just a little, and then he seemed to remember something, and he frowned.

'Where were you yesterday?' he asked.

I looked at him. I didn't know what he meant, and anyway, the room had muddled me. I'd thought there'd be a bed.

'You were supposed to come yesterday,' he said. 'You gave me the signal and you didn't come. Where were you? What happened?'

I couldn't understand anything he said. I went on looking at him, and I wondered what he would do next, and I was crying again. I could feel the tears on my cheeks, and my breathing getting heavy and deep and hard, and I thought, will he kill me? Afterwards, will he kill me? Or might he let me go?

'Why didn't you come?' he asked. 'I waited for you. Why didn't you come?'

Perhaps if I talked to him he might like me. Then he might not want to kill me, he might let me go.

What was he asking me? He'd waited for me yesterday, he wanted to know why I hadn't come.

'I had to work late,' I said.

He seemed to think about my answer, as if it was very odd, something very unusual, that somebody might have to work late. It took him a long time, thinking about what I had said.

'Weren't you in control?' He was frowning again, watching me.

In control? How could I be in control? I was only a shelf-filler, I couldn't be in control. Even Carol, laughing about making the lists and how she could make Mr Kennedy do anything, she was never in control, and she was twice as clever as me.

It was such a funny question I couldn't think of an answer. I stood in the middle of the room, under the bare light-bulb, crying, and waiting to see what he would do.

After a while he sighed, as if the problem was too difficult for him, and he looked around the room.

'It's not much,' he said, 'but I made it clean. Do you want to go now?'

'Yes,' I said, and I felt so relieved. 'Oh, yes, please.'

He smiled at me, and it was a very kind smile, sort of caring.

'I'll try not to hurt you,' he said, and he took out the knife.

I screamed.

I backed away from him, until I felt the wall and part of the window-frame pressing against me, and I screamed again because I couldn't get any further away. He stood in front of the door with the opened knife in his hand, watching me, looking amazed.

'Be quiet,' he said. 'What's the matter? You said you wanted to go. Now, please, be quiet.'

I stopped screaming, but I was so frightened I was shaking, horrible little jerks as if I was a puppet, and I couldn't take my eyes off the knife. The blade was shining, but there was a sort of shimmer on the cutting edge, and I knew, almost as if I'd seen him do it, that he'd spent a long time sharpening it on a stone. It was very, very sharp.

'You said you'd let me go.'

'No. I asked if you wanted to go. To go *back*. Don't you understand?'

There was a brass catch on the window. It was an old-fashioned window, and there was a catch, holding the top window closed against the bottom one. I wondered if I could open it, or if he would reach me as soon as I tried. Reach me with that sharp knife.

'I didn't mean to frighten you,' he said. 'I wouldn't do that.'

'No,' I said. 'No, don't. Please, please, just let me go. Please. I won't tell anybody. I promise, but please let me go.'

'I can't do that. What's the matter with you? Why are you being like this?'

I was still shaking, and I felt very weak. I pressed myself against the wall, and I tried to look sideways, through the painted window, through the little white stars. I could just see a yard, with paving stones. There was a sloping roof. If I got through the window I might be able to get to the roof, and slide down into the yard.

But not before he reached me, with the knife.

He hadn't moved towards me. He still stood by the door, watching me, but the knife was in his hand.

I could hear myself crying. It was a moaning, wailing sound, uneven, and now and then there was a sob. I hadn't ever cried like that before.

My knees were trembling, and I thought for a moment I was going to wet myself, but instead I slid down the wall, until I was sitting crouched in the corner by the window, and now all I could see through the little painted stars was the sky of grey clouds.

He looked down at the knife, and he closed it, like he'd done at the front door when he came in, pressing it against the frame with his hand spread wide open as the blade began to move. Then he squatted down in front of the door, and put the knife in his pocket, and smiled at me.

'It's all right,' he said. 'There's no hurry, not after all this time. Just tell me when you're ready.'

Ready for the knife, that was what he meant, I knew by then. Ready for him to kill me. That was what he planned, and I didn't know how I could stop him. I didn't know what to do.

I had to get away. I had to escape from him, or he would kill me.

The catch on the window. I looked up at it, but I could hardly see it from where I was, down on the floor, and I didn't think I could move quickly enough to reach it. There was just the rounded edge of a little brass handle, and then below it I saw dents in the wood, where screws had been put in, and the paint hadn't been thick enough to hide them.

Even if I could reach the catch, I couldn't open the window.

I looked at the door. I didn't think he'd locked it. I just remembered him standing in front of it, after he came in. Was there a key? There weren't any bolts. If I ran across the room, perhaps I could . . .

He could read my mind. He'd done it before.

Don't think about it, then. Do it without thinking.

'I want to go to the toilet,' I said.

'You can't.'

'I must,' I said. 'I can't wait.'

'Oh, don't be so silly.'

He sounded tired, as if he was fed up with arguing about it, even though we hadn't said anything for a while by then.

The grey sky was darker, and there were shadows in the room, in the corners, where the little light couldn't reach. It was getting cold, too.

'Let me go.'

But he didn't answer. He was still squatting in front of the door, and he moved, stretching out his legs, one after the other, so he was sitting against the wall by the door. He crossed his legs and looked across the room at me.

'I'm sorry I spoke to you like that.'

We were level with each other now he was sitting on the floor. His face looked grey in the fading light, with dark shadows in his eye sockets and under his jaw. He was wearing a white shirt and a grey sweater, so everything about him was black and white and grey.

It didn't feel as if it was real.

I thought, I'll wake up, and he'll be gone. This is only a nightmare. How stupid of me. Life isn't black and white and grey, this is a bad dream.

So I moved. I pulled my legs back and I began to stand up.

Then the knife was in his hand again, and the handle was red.

Colour.

'Let me go,' I begged. 'Let me go.'

And then, because I really was very uncomfortable, 'I must go to the toilet now. Please.'

But he shook his head. As I sat down again he put the knife in his pocket. Black and white and grey again.

I thought, what about him? He'll have to go soon, to the toilet, or to get something to eat or drink. He can't sit there for ever. I only have to wait.

It was nearly dark before he did move. He said something, too quiet for me to hear, climbed to his feet, and then went out. I didn't hear a key or a bolt, only his footsteps on the stairs.

I stood up, and I crept across the room and opened the door. I couldn't hear anything in the little house, just the sound of a car in the road outside. But then there was light from downstairs, yellow against the corner. He'd turned on a light, and a door was open. He'd bolted the front door as we came in, I remembered that, but I didn't think he'd locked it.

If the bolts weren't too stiff I might be able to open the door, quickly and quietly, if I could get past the room where he'd turned on the light.

The stairs hadn't creaked when he went down.

I took off my shoes, and I went out on to the tiny landing. I couldn't hear him. He must have gone through the room, unless he was keeping still in there. There was probably a kitchen and a bathroom out at the back. That was where he'd gone.

I went down the stairs, slowly at first, but then I began to panic, and for the last few steps I was almost running. Then I was in the hall, and the front door was there, and still he hadn't come.

I couldn't open the top bolt.

I was crying again when he came up behind me, still

struggling with the bolt, still trying to move it up and down, and up and down, trying to free it enough to slide it across, and I heard him walking through the room, and stopping at the door, and just standing there and watching me.

'Oh, please. Please let me go now.'

He took my arm and led me back to the bottom of the stairs.

'I must go to the toilet,' I begged. 'You had to. Why can't I?'

He seemed a bit surprised, as if he really couldn't understand what I was asking. He stood with one foot on the stairs, frowning at me, and then he sighed.

'You *can't* get away,' he said. 'Do you really not remember *anything*?'

'I want to go to the *toilet*,' I shouted at him, and then he pushed me through the other door.

'All right,' he said. 'If you really insist, I don't suppose there's any harm in it.'

There was no window, and the door didn't lock. There was an old-fashioned iron latch, painted black.

I sat in there, crying, trying to think what to do next, trying to plan an escape. He hadn't hurt me. Even when he found me downstairs by the front door, he hadn't hurt me. Perhaps if I tried to fight him he'd let me go.

But he still had the knife.

I did try, in spite of the knife. When he said I'd got to come out now, when he said he'd open the door himself if I didn't, I pulled it open and I threw myself at him and tried to force my way past him. He caught my arms, and when I scratched at his face and kicked his shins he just pulled back, turning his face out of the way. He wasn't rough, not really, but he pulled me round so I had my back to him and my arms were behind me, held tight.

'Don't do that,' he said.

Not surprised, not angry, just reasonable. Don't do that.

There was no point. He was by far the stronger of the two of us.

At the bottom of the stairs he let go of my arms and I went up on my own, still crying. He followed a few paces behind me, too far back for me to be able to kick him, and so, as I reached the landing, I ran into the room, I ran across to the window and I smashed the painted glass with my hand and screamed through it.

'Help me! Somebody, please, help me!'

He took me away from the window, quite gently, and he looked at my cut hand and shook his head.

'This is so silly,' he said. 'Why are you doing this? Look, you've hurt yourself. It's silly.'

One of the cuts was deep. He held it up to the faint light from a street lamp outside, and he seemed quite worried. He shook his head slowly, and pressed the two edges of the cut together, holding it until the bleeding stopped. It took a long time.

'Should be stitched,' he said, as if he was talking to himself. 'Now what?'

He turned my face up towards his and looked down at me.

'I'll have to dress that,' he said. 'Will you please stay here quietly until I come back?'

'Yes,' I said.

Would he have to go to a chemist? If he was out of the house I could escape. I could break through the window and climb out on to the sloping roof, and then I'd be down in the yard. There'd be a gate, or I could scramble over the wall. I'd be free.

'Oh, I wish you wouldn't be like this,' he said.

He used electric flex to tie my wrists together behind my back, and he made me kneel down, and then he tied my ankles with the same flex. He put a handkerchief in my mouth even though I fought him. He held my head as still as he could between both his hands, and he pressed his thumbs against the back of my jaw until it really hurt.

'Open your mouth. I don't want to do this, it's your own fault. Open your mouth.'

At last I did, and then he pushed the handkerchief in and taped my mouth, I think it was masking tape. I couldn't open my mouth, I couldn't scream. I had to breathe through my nose, and I thought he'd block my nose, or put tape across it, and then I'd suffocate. I found that idea more terrifying than anything else.

While he was gone I heard people in the road outside, a group, talking and laughing. I wondered if I could reach the window and break another bit, so they'd hear the glass shatter, and perhaps come and help me. But the two women in the street with the pushchairs hadn't helped me when I'd asked, nor had the man with the cigarette. I'd often heard breaking glass and I'd ignored it. Somebody dropped a milk bottle? Anyway, none of my business. I'd had other things to do.

Nobody would come and help me. I was alone.

Mum would be wondering where I was. Two hours, she'd think, they've kept our Joanie late again. But this long, I'd have phoned. She'd be worried. She'd have phoned the shop, and been told, Joanie? Joanie Ferguson? No, she went at the usual time. Three, wasn't it, today? Wasn't she in early this morning? That's right, then. Three.

What would she do?

Our Sheila, she'd be home by now. She'd have called the police, but they wouldn't do anything. Twenty, isn't she, your Joan? Well, then. Gone out with friends.

What could they do?

He was going to kill me, and nobody knew where I was. Nobody could find me. How could anybody find me here?

He wasn't gone very long. I'd tried to wriggle my hands free from the flex, but I'd only opened the cut again, and the more I struggled the tighter it got round my ankles. It was really hurting by the time he came back, and when he came in he shook his head at me, and said I'd been stupid. Why was I being like this? he asked. Couldn't I remember anything? Why had I let myself get so involved down here?

He pulled the tape off my mouth, and it hurt, but I spat out the lump of cloth and I swore at him. Fucking bastard, I called him, let me go, you fucking bastard.

He was going to kill me anyway. At least I could swear at him.

'Hold out your hand.'

He'd brought a little bottle of disinfectant and some lint and bandages, and a roll of plaster. He did quite a neat job, bandaging my hand and taping down the ends after he'd knotted them round my wrist.

He untied my ankles, and rubbed at the red marks where the flex had bitten in as I struggled. I knew by then he was mad. He was going to kill me, but he was worried about the marks on my ankles from the flex and about a cut on my hand. He wasn't like the women on the bus, who were just slow, needing a bit of help with their lives; he was bad, this one. He was going to kill me.

I began to cry again, but I don't think he noticed. I thought of the times I'd wished I could work somewhere else, with people who talked about interesting things, so I could listen, even if I didn't understand. And I'd have given anything just then, while he was rubbing the marks on my ankles, to have been sitting in the canteen, listening to Annie talking about the back seat of Glen's car, how the springs dug in, how some nosy bugger had come round with a torch and couldn't see through the steamy windows. I'd have given anything.

'Let me go.'

There was no point in saying it. He didn't bother to answer.

I thought about my cup and saucer with the beautiful little birds, and my new silver spoon that the woman in the shop had said was about the same age. They looked so nice together. Mum had polished the spoon. I thought about how the stainless steel ones were a sort of grey silver, but my spoon was a yellow silver. There was some yellow in the pictures of the birds.

'Are you sure you wouldn't like to go now?' he asked, and this time I knew what he meant.

Shall I kill you now? Would you like me to kill you now?

I didn't know how to answer him.

The counterpane on my bed at home was blue, with little yellow flowers printed on in bunches. It was cotton. It creased if you didn't fold it properly when you got into bed. Mum had tried to find some curtains to match, but they were a different blue and the flowers were different, too. She couldn't change them because they'd

56

been in a sale. I didn't mind, I thought they were nice. Sorry, our Joanie, she'd said, I thought they were the same. I don't mind, Mum, I like them.

New carpet next year, she'd promised. Or this year, if the lottery comes up.

New house, new car, new holiday. You can't drive, Mum. I can learn, can't I? Just see me in a Jag. That'd make them look. And I'd have plastic surgery, get rid of them lines in my neck, say nothing about the ones in my face, so I'd look about eighteen.

Get yourself a toy boy, said Sheila, and Mum laughed. You bet. A twenty-five-year-old hunk with muscles like bricks, hung like a donkey. And Sheila pretended to be shocked. Don't know what the older generation's coming to.

I'd give anything, I thought, just to be in that kitchen now, listening to them, laughing at them. I'd give my right hand, sticking plaster and all. My cup and saucer and the silver spoon. And I hadn't got anything else to give.

'If I give you money, will you let me go?'

I hadn't got any money. Just a few pounds in my purse, maybe two or three. It was only Tuesday, I wouldn't be paid till Thursday evening, I only had enough for bus fares, and a little bit in case I wanted a coffee. And Carol owed me a bit for coffee, but she wouldn't pay me back. If I gave him money, would he let me go? Could I steal some?

I couldn't fight him. He was too strong, and he knew what I was thinking. Offer him money? Offer him sex?

'Are you going to rape me?'

He laughed, a short laugh a bit like a cough, and gave me a funny look.

'I wish you'd make up your mind,' he said. 'We haven't got all that much time, you know. Now I suppose I'll have to tie you up. I never thought I'd have to do that.'

It was the flex again, around my wrists, but he made me stand up, and he tied it to the light hanging from the ceiling. When he went out I tried to jerk it free, thinking it was only a bit of electric cable, it would only be tacked up, not meant to carry weight; not strong. But it didn't move. I jerked at it again, and then I swung from it, feeling as if I was going crazy as I pulled and swung, and jerked at it.

The flex around my wrists slid down the cable and reached the light-bulb. I jerked again, and the end of the cable broke free. The bulb fell to the floor. It didn't break, but it rolled on the linoleum.

I pulled the tape off my mouth and I used my teeth on the flex to free the knots. I knew it was hopeless. He'd be back before I was free, and I'd hardly started on the knot when he was there in the door again.

'What on earth's the matter with you? You never used to be this stupid.'

'What do you want from me?'

He made me stand up again, and this time he knotted the cable through the flex on my wrists, a tight knot, and he pulled the end of the cable as hard as he could. I couldn't reach it, not with my fingers, not with my teeth, and even if I could, I knew it was too tight for me.

'What do you want?'

As if you didn't know, he seemed to say as he looked at me. But then he said, just as if I was a little kid and he was playing a game we both knew, 'You are the Empress of the Dark Universe, and I have to take us home.'

4

Every time he left the room he tied me up. At first he only tied my hands behind my back when he went out for a short while, but I knew he wouldn't kill me if I tried to escape. I went to the window and I screamed through it.

'Help me! Somebody, help me! Please, somebody, come!'

He didn't believe anybody would come, but he got angry with me. He said I'd disturb the neighbours with all my noise. I was being stupid. Why was I being so stupid?

'Leave the window alone. You've already broken it once.'

Surely somebody must have heard? Wouldn't somebody call the police? But how would they find me? One window in a little house, one little house in a row of little houses, one street just like the others all round it. How would they find me?

I sat in the corner of the room and I stared at him as he squatted in front of the door, and I pictured it, as I'd seen it on the telly in police stories. Two coppers at the door of the woman who'd telephoned. She'd heard somebody screaming for help, from somewhere over there. All right, Madam, we'll take a look. And the car, driving up and down a few roads, nothing to report. Roger, Tango Charlie Three, disturbance at Red Lion, can you attend?

'I want to go to the toilet.'

'You've only just been.'

'I *want* to go.'

There was a draught from the broken window. It started to rain, and drops blew in against my cheek. He watched me for a while to see if I'd say anything about it, but I didn't, and his head dropped again, so he was looking at the floor.

'I'm not the Empress of wherever you said.'

'The Dark Universe.'

'I'm not. I'm just ordinary. I work at Fletchers, in Friar Street. I'm not an empress.'

He tied my hands again, and he went downstairs. I went to the window, and I screamed for help. If it happened again and again they'd know something was wrong. Tango Charlie Three, another report of screaming.

He came back and pulled me away from the window.

'Stupid! It's so *stupid*! Please, do try to be sensible. You never used to be like this.'

He had a sandwich in his hand. I could smell fish paste, or sardine.

'Please let me go. You've got the wrong person. I'm not the Empress.'

He looked at his sandwich.

'Are you hungry?' he asked. 'Would you like some?'

'No. Thank you.'

60

Mum and Sheila would be sitting at the kitchen table. Mum might be crying. Sheila might, too. They'd be really worried by now; they'd know something was wrong. Mrs Paliedes from next door would have come in to sit with them. She was a kind old woman, but very nosy. It would be all down the street the next day. Joanie Ferguson's disappeared, never came back from work yesterday. Nobody knows where she is. Shocking, isn't it?

It was getting light outside. I could see grey in the sky, the light wasn't only from the street lamp any more. It was early morning. I'd been here for more than twelve hours.

'I shall have to be away all day,' he said, and he sounded worried. 'I wish you'd make up your mind. I thought we'd be there by now.'

I watched him, and I waited. What would he do? He might kill me, but he might have to go out and leave me alone, and alive. Surely I could get away? But he might decide to kill me.

I began to feel sick.

He tied me to the flex that hung from the ceiling. He tied my wrists with the cable, tightly, so I couldn't free them, and then he pulled my hands over my head and looped the broken end of the flex between my wrists and tied it with a knot. It looked simple, a couple of loops, that was all. Then he pushed the handkerchief into my mouth, and he had the reel of tape in his pocket.

'I'm sorry,' he said as he spread it across my mouth. 'I wish I didn't have to do this. I daren't risk us being disturbed. You do see that, don't you?'

Again, I had the idea that he might put the tape across my nose, so I wouldn't be able to breathe.

He looked into my face, and he shook his head. He

61

seemed to be really upset, worried about me. I could only stare back at him.

Surely, when he'd gone, I'd be able to drag the flex out of the ceiling? Surely I'd be able to get away, when he'd gone?

I tried for two hours, and then I let myself hang until the pain of the cable digging into my wrists got too bad. I was exhausted, and I was confused, so confused I couldn't begin to think what to do next. Why hadn't I been able to free myself? It was only a piece of flex, I should have been able to tear it out of the ceiling.

My shoulders were hurting with the strain of holding my arms over my head, and when I tried to relax, to ease them, the cable dug into my wrists again.

I began to count. I'll count to a hundred, and let my arms hang from the cable, rest my shoulders. I'll count to a hundred and I'll raise my arms again, so my wrists don't hurt so much. I'll count to two hundred.

Please, come back soon. Come back.

I'm tired. I want to sleep.

If you come back and untie me I promise I won't go near the window. I'll be quiet. Come back.

Count to three hundred.

My jaw aches. This thing in my mouth, this handkerchief, if I swallow it I'll choke, and I can't close my mouth. I can't move my tongue. The tape itches. I'm thirsty.

Is that three hundred? Or was it only two? I can't remember. Start again.

No, my shoulders hurt too much. Just another hundred, and then . . .

Come back and untie me. Please, come back and untie me.

I want to go to the toilet.

If I swallow, I may choke on this thing in my mouth. I can't swallow properly, my mouth's dry. I can't.

Try to move the handkerchief forward, so it's against my teeth, so I can swallow. But it's too big. It's as if it's swollen. I can't move it. It's making me sick. I'm going to be sick. I'll choke on the sick.

Please come back and untie me.

I was almost unconscious by the time he came back, and I'd wet myself. That seemed to be the worst: worse than the pain in my shoulders; worse than my aching jaw and trying not to be sick, not to swallow the handkerchief; worse than my hands, because I couldn't feel my hands, I could only see them, and what I could see frightened me.

But when I wet myself I wanted to give up. I wanted to say, what do you want? Just do it. Get it over with, just do it. I don't care any more, I want this to be finished.

I don't remember him coming into the room, but he lifted me, and he was talking to me, look at you, look what you've made me do to you. Just a moment, let me untie your hands. Oh, your poor hands! Stand up. Come on, stand up. That's right. Oh, dear. Oh, dear.

I slid down on to the floor, and I curled myself up, pulling my knees up to my chest, trying to roll away from him. I felt dirty. I felt ashamed.

He pulled the tape away from my mouth, and I cried with the pain, even though it was nothing compared to what I was already feeling. The disgusting piece of cloth in my mouth, I spat it out, and then I turned away from him again, hid my face in my arms, and cried.

'I need a doctor.'

'Yes, yes, I know. There are plenty of doctors. Let's go now.'

He brought me food and some water to drink, and I didn't try to go to the window while he was out of the room. I was too miserable with pain to try to do anything. I don't remember even being frightened, then.

He'd brought a pane of glass for the window, the one I'd broken. I heard him working on it, but I wouldn't look at him. I lay on the floor, curled away from him, looking at my hands, wondering if the swelling would go down.

Wondering if he would tie me like that again.

When he'd put the new glass in the window he painted little white stars on it again, and I lifted my head and watched, wondering why he was doing it.

He began to talk. He told me he'd thought the little flowers would be nice for me. Star flowers, he called them, and said they grew in my garden. Did I remember? The flowers that bloomed before the leaves came out, one of the first flowers of spring in our home.

Did I remember?

He looked at me, and I turned away.

Summer in the Dark Universe, he said, summer was wonderful. The cloudy dark skies, like my hair, and sometimes you could see all seventeen moons. The smell in my rooms, the beeswax they used to polish the golden wood, and the lemon thyme growing between the grey stones. Music, did I remember the music?

The seventeen moons are sliding away, he said. We can't stay here much longer.

I fell asleep. He was still talking, about this place he called the Dark Universe, about the gardens and the forests, moons in the sky, the planets we would visit when we went back. They were waiting for us. They needed us.

I woke up while it was still very dark.

'I want to go to the toilet. I want to wash. I need clean clothes.'

He looked tired. His face was very white.

I used to swim in the pools below the house, he said. The water was clear there, although in the streams it was brown, from the peat, and the fishes looked like silver through the brown water. Mint grew on the banks of the pools, and it scented the water, and there was soapweed, soapwort, he couldn't remember which was the right name. Could I remember? Was it soapweed or soapwort? The plants with the mauve or white flowers and the leaves that foamed when you crushed them in water. Could I remember?

'I was never there. I want to go to the toilet.'

He pushed himself to his feet. I've never seen anybody look that tired.

'Come on, then.'

My clothes smelled, and I didn't like touching them. Damp. Dirty. I was dirty.

'Please, can I have some clean clothes? Can I have a bath?'

I'd only ever worn linen or cotton, occasionally wool in the winter, he said. I never seemed to feel the cold. I wore sandals or went barefoot. Sometimes people had been shocked. Strangers hadn't realised who I was. They'd thought I was a servant. I'd laughed about it, I'd never been offended. That time the warlord from the third galaxy had come, did I remember? I'd been in the garden, planting a root I'd found in the forest, wanting to know what it was, and the big man had ordered me, you, girl, where's the Empress? Tell her I'm here, and don't keep me waiting.

'Not me. I'm not her. You've got the wrong person.'

Then I fell asleep again, only just listening to his voice, as it got angry. I wasn't the wrong person. He knew me anyway. He'd have known me anywhere, and the signals had been arranged. The number of the bus, seventeen for the seventeen moons, the tenth seat from the front for the ten galaxies in the Dark Universe.

Just for a moment I opened my eyes and I saw him running his hands through his hair, clutching at it as he told me of the signals.

I took the bus to go to work, I wanted to say. It's the only one that goes near my home straight to the town centre.

It was daylight when I woke up, and he was standing over me with the knife and the cable.

'Shall we go now?'

'Oh, no. Please, no, not again.'

Counting, and trying to pray, remembering from school assemblies. Don't swallow, you might choke. Our Father, who art. Three hundred and ten, three hundred and eleven, three hundred and twelve. Please come back. If you come back now I'll let you kill me. I'll say yes, let's go now. Maybe it's true. Maybe there are rooms smelling of beeswax and lemon thyme, and cloudy dark skies in the middle of summer, star flowers and pools with mint and a soap plant.

I want to wash. My thighs are sore, they're stinging, they hurt.

Please come back.

'Look what you've made me do to you. Your poor, poor hands.'

The games in the summer under the cloudy skies,

when I had had to be formal and very regal, with a gold band around my head and the Star of Justice on my forehead, which I never wore in the courts. Remember the courts? The black wood, and the white marble floors; cushions scattered where people sat with the arbiters; and the last court jesters in the whole of the Dark Universe, to make them laugh together, so maybe they wouldn't have to fight. In the Courts of Justice I had worn brown linen, my hair unbound, my feet bare, and I had listened and hardly ever spoken.

'I command you to let me go,' I said, and he was pleased.

'That's better, you're beginning to remember!'

I had so enjoyed the summer games, those few days when they came from all over the Dark Universe, the evenings when the men had drunk together and chased the women and laughed and been closer than brothers, and the woman had eyed them, and smiled, and laid traps. During the days they had competed, and fought, and raced, and their brotherhood had not been even a dim memory in their determination and in the fury of their will to win.

'You wrestled,' he said suddenly after a long silence in which I almost fell asleep. 'You could have been in the team, if you hadn't been the Empress. But you said you wouldn't, you'd rather watch.'

The summer games on the grasslands, with the bright pavilions and the green trees under the dark skies. Do you remember now? You'll remember soon.

'Why don't we go now? I don't want to tie you up again.'

'Oh, no, please don't. Please don't.'

'Tell me, then. Command me.'

67

I'd thought I'd let him kill me. I couldn't stand it again. Don't. Not that, I can't. Don't.

But to say to him, kill me, then. Let's go, let's go. Kill me, I couldn't do it. Please, don't tie me. I promise I won't escape, don't tie me.

Three hundred and seven, three hundred and eight, the bright pavilions under the black sky. Relax, stand up, keep straight, it's not so bad. The Courts of Justice, black wood and white marble and people on cushions, talking. Were there others giving them food and drink? Yes, there would be. There would be kind people in my Courts of Justice, taking food and drink to those sad ones who needed help in their troubled disputes. There would be kindness, and time to listen and to understand. Five hundred, now let yourself go, hang from the cable and let your shoulders relax. One, two, three, four.

Aah, my hands. No, don't think of them. Twenty-three, twenty-four, and the cool water in the clear pools under the mint and the soapweed, the silver fish in the brown streams, and the footsteps on the stairs, fifty-six, fifty-seven, fifty-eight, polished golden wood under my clean bare feet, the smell of beeswax, and the opening door, seventy-nine, eighty, eighty-one, please come back and untie me and you can kill me if that's what you want.

'Bloody hell, what's going on here?'

The men drinking and laughing and the women watching, and it was all friendship, a memory to last a lifetime, strong arms around my waist, and a voice, it's all right, love. Bloody fucking hell, gone a bit far, haven't you? From all over the universe they'd come, in a dark blue boiler suit, lifting me, come on, love. Sorry, didn't mean that, who's done this to you? Bastard, wants bloody shooting. Can you stand up?

Smell of beer and tobacco and lemon thyme and beeswax, and lifting me off the floor, quite high now, look up at the dark cloudy sky and the broad hand wrapped around the flex, listen to the kind voices and the laughter, hold on, darling. Just hold on.

You can't. I've tried, you can't. It won't break, it won't.

Grunting, and the teeth gritted, and I'm floating because he's lifted me off the green grass and high towards the cloudy sky, and his face is red, and the veins are standing out on his forehead, and he's old, he's too old for the summer games, but he's strong, and he's got the will to win, he won't let them beat him, and it's breaking, he's broken them, there's chain on the flex.

'You poor kid. You poor little bitch.'

He's gone now, I've lost count, I can't remember where I was. Start again? Yes, start again, it doesn't matter, move my hands, lick the wrists where the cable cut in, I can lick my wrists, my mouth's free, I can move, so lick the wounds, like a hurt dog, curl up and lick, where it's red, where there's blood. See the chain on the floor, lying in the crumbled plaster, in the dust on the dark red floor, where's the green grass? Where are the bright pavilions and the dark sky?

He came, although he was too old, he came to the summer games, and he broke the chain because he was strong and he wouldn't let them beat him. He's the champion. I must give him a great prize.

I will. When these others have gone, the ones who have come now, when they have gone, I will give him a great prize. He is the champion.

5

I was in a room by myself, in the hospital, because they said I'd need to be alone. There'd be interviews, when I was well enough. People wanted to see me.

A policewoman came, but not in uniform, with questions I didn't really want to answer. But she said she'd get a statement written up, and I should read it and sign it.

'Our Joan's not very quick at the reading,' said Mum, and the woman looked at me, as though I was something unusual, but not very interesting.

The man who'd found me came the next evening during visiting hours. He was out of breath from the stairs, and he sat by the bed puffing and saying, too many cigarettes, how are you doing, they looking after you? He'd brought a bunch of flowers and some sweets. They got the bastard, he said. They got him. Just waited for him, he came back after work, cool as you please. Bloody nutter, should be locked up. Will be, too. You all right?

I wanted to thank him for pulling the flex out of the ceiling, but I couldn't think of any words. He was talking, quite a lot, once he'd got his breath back. The people who'd had the house before, they'd had a kid, hyperactive. Some medical name, well, always breaking things. Used to swing from that light, kept breaking it. So they'd fixed it with a chain, bolted it through a beam. Me, I'd have belted the little bugger, stop that bloody nonsense, but no. Fixed up the flex with a chain, so he could swing on it and not break it. Bloody daft.

'Thank you,' I said when he was leaving. And then I thought of the right words. 'I was ever so pleased to see you.'

He laughed, seemed to think it was funny, what I'd said. I was a proper strange one, I was.

Mum kept saying how worried they'd been. Couldn't think what had happened. Our Sheila had been to the police, but they'd said I was an adult, I was entitled. Sheila had told them, Joanie wouldn't go off like that. Why would she not come back, and not say anything? No reason for it. Something must have happened. They'd telephoned all the hospitals, done everything, but I'd vanished.

'Still, long as you're all right,' she said, and I looked down at my hands, all bandaged after the operation, and I thought, I'm not all right, I'm not. My hands are never going to be all right again.

'You all right?' the nurses would ask, and I'd say yes, but I wasn't. What can you say? No, I'm not. My hands hurt, and that doctor said they have to operate again, maybe three or four times, but even then with the damage to the tendons they wouldn't ever be really right again.

I'm not all right.

And where is he? What's to stop it happening again?

He wanted to kill me. What about that knife he had?

The policewoman came back, and I asked, 'What about the man?'

'Don't you worry about him,' she said. 'He won't get you again.'

There were pages and pages of the statement. She asked if I could read it. If not, she said she'd read it to me. It was going to take me hours, but I didn't want to tell her, so I said I'd read it. But after a while she started to get angry because she wanted to go. She said she'd read it to me, I'd only got to stop her if there was something wrong.

It was all wrong. She didn't know anything about the Dark Universe, they hadn't even put in about the star flowers he'd painted on the windows. It was all nasty, about the knife, how he'd been at the bus stop waiting for me and he'd cut me with the knife. How he hadn't given me much to eat, hadn't let me go to the toilet, how he'd tied me up and put the handkerchief in my mouth. There was nothing about what he'd said. It made him sound stupid, all that, as if he was just being nasty, for no reason.

There was nothing about how he'd been respectful. Even though he'd said I was being stupid sometimes, he didn't say it the way Annie called me stupid, like that was just the way I was, so let's have a laugh at Dozey Joan.

Nicholas Parry, that was his name.

'Why did he do it?' I asked Sheila, and she said, just a nutter. Been to university, had a breakdown, that's clever people for you. Well, he's locked up safe now. He can't get you again.

When he'd got a bit better, after his breakdown, he'd

got a job with an estate agent. That's how he'd had the keys to the house where we'd been, the empty house. That's how he'd got in to clean it up and paint the room. I'd just been so lucky, said Sheila. He'd been out showing somebody another house that afternoon, and the agents had wanted to check the gas. Somebody had been interested in the house, wanted the gas checked, so they'd sent Mr Carver round with the spare keys, told him to check the gas. He hadn't even been meant to go upstairs, he was snooping around. That's how he found me.

'You'll be okay now,' said Sheila, and I said yes, I'll be all right.

But I wasn't. My hands weren't going to be all right. How was I going to manage, with my hands not working properly?

Everybody at work sent a card and a big bunch of flowers. Everybody had signed the card. Even Mr Kennedy. 'Best wishes, Neville Kennedy.' Carol brought it round, and she was really angry. Annie had been to the local paper and said she was my best friend at work, and if they'd pay her she'd give them an exclusive interview. They'd given her a hundred quid, lying bloody tart, and I didn't even like her, did I? Bloody slapper. Carol had phoned the paper and told them the truth, and she'd got Rita to say I didn't like Annie, but someone at the paper had said too bad. Only one exclusive interview with a best friend, thank you very much.

'*You* should have had that hundred quid,' I said, and Carol went a bit pink and said it wasn't the money, it was the principle.

'Hazel's back,' she said. 'Ever so full of herself for getting Davie Evans the sack. You'd think, to hear her, she'd fought him off and reported him, not just burst into tears and got found by Rita, snivelling in the ladies'.'

Then she sat back in her chair and said, now, tell me all about it. What did he do? Nothing, I said, because I couldn't tell her. It all sounded so stupid, he didn't really say he was going to kill me. He wanted me to tell him to. He never meant to do me any harm, except for killing me.

I suppose I said something like that, because Carol laughed at me.

'Just that? Just kill you? Oh, no, no harm in that. Bleeding nutter. Shouldn't be allowed, bloody maniacs out on the streets. Still, long as you're all right.'

I'm not all right. My hands won't ever work properly again, and I can't sleep, and when I do I have these funny dreams. I'm frightened, Carol, and nobody understands, because I can't say.

How could it happen? I wasn't doing anybody any harm, just going home after work, and nobody helped me, not the women with the pushchairs, not the man lighting his cigarette, and I did ask. Help, I said, help me. Nobody helped me.

It could happen again, couldn't it? Another bloody nutter, like Nicholas Parry, maybe even worse. Not respectful, like Nicholas Parry. If it happened once, it could happen again.

Don't tell me lightning doesn't strike twice, there was that man on the telly, been struck eight times. Just unlucky, everybody says, he doesn't believe it. Called the Human Lightning Conductor in the papers, maybe there'll be another one waiting for me.

It could happen, don't tell me it couldn't. It could.

Don't want to go to sleep because I'm frightened of the

dreams. My hands hurt. And I keep thinking, they all know here, they all know I wet myself. I couldn't help it, but they all know.

Mum knows, and Sheila, because they took my clothes away to wash them. Maybe they'll tell somebody. Everybody will know.

I didn't want to sign the statement. It wasn't right, they hadn't said any of the right things. But when I tried to explain to them it came out sounding wrong, because I couldn't find the words. He wasn't like that, I wanted to say. He didn't tie me up because he wanted to hurt me. He'd been worried and sorry about my hands.

'I can't hold the pen.'

It didn't matter. Two independent witnesses to say I agreed the statement, that would do.

'You do agree the statement, don't you?' asked the policewoman, and her voice was quite angry. Ever since Mum had said I was slow at reading she'd sounded angry when she'd spoken to me. It was the sort of voice people used to their dogs in the park. You had to speak like that to make the dog do what you wanted, because otherwise it wouldn't understand, or maybe it would ignore you. Because it wasn't very bright.

'What do you want to change?' asked one of the student nurses. 'If they've got it wrong, don't you give in. Tell them. Tell them they've got it wrong.'

But they hadn't really got it wrong. They hadn't said anything that hadn't happened. It was what they'd left out. The Dark Universe did matter, it mattered to him, it was the whole reason for what he'd done.

Paranoid fantasies, one of the policemen said they were, and we should leave all that to the shrinks. Just stick to the facts, love. Nothing you can do about what went on in his head. The main thing is, make sure he isn't let out to do it again. To you or anybody else.

There was a card that came. Lots of cards came from nice people who'd read about me in the papers. They were strangers, but they sent cards. I thought that was kind. But this card, with a rose on the front, there was no name in it. There were just a few printed words. *Nicholas is worth ten of you.*

I put the card in the drawer of my locker, because I didn't know what to do with it, or what the words meant. Mum read all the cards to me when she came to visit in the evenings, but I didn't want her to read that one. I'd just seen those few words when I opened the card with the post in the morning. So I read it myself instead of putting it with the others on the table.

Nicholas is worth ten of you.

One of the nurses found it when she was tidying up my locker, and she gave it to the policeman. Can't have that, she said. Intimidation, that is, can't have that.

She didn't ask me if I wanted her to give it to the policeman. Nobody seemed to ask me anything. They just told me.

Another operation, they said, in two days. So you can move your thumbs a bit more. Mr Jennings will do it. He's very good. When they've had a look they'll decide about carbon inserts.

They'll decide.

But with him, it had been my decision. In the Dark Universe, it was me who decided. And with him.

Sheila brought me my special cup and saucer, but not the spoon, because she said it might get pinched, being silver. All the nurses said how nice they were, with the little birds painted on the china, and they all wanted to

76

hold the cup up to the light and see their fingers through it. Shadow pictures, through my special cup and saucer.

Mr Jennings came to see me. He said he was going to do the operation. I was worried, because they called him Mister, not Doctor. I wanted a proper doctor. He looked at my hands and he asked me to move my fingers and my thumbs. He asked if they hurt really badly, or not too much now.

Then he sent everybody away and he sat on the edge of my bed, and he tried to explain about how the blood supply to my hands had been cut off by the cable, and what had happened because of that, and what they could do.

'Any questions?' he asked.

'Are you a proper doctor?'

I hadn't really meant to ask, but he'd been quite kind and I'd just said it right out because it worried me. He knew straight away what I meant. Surgeons are called Mister, he said. First you're Mister when you're learning, then when you qualify you're called Doctor, and then, when you become a surgeon, you're Mister again. Yes, I'm a proper doctor, I'm not a beginner.

He was still sitting on the edge of my bed, as though he had quite a lot of time, so I asked him.

'What do you do if you don't think the statement the police have done is right?'

'You don't sign it,' he said, straight away, didn't even stop to think. 'What's the problem?'

But there wasn't anything in the statement that was wrong. They hadn't written anything that hadn't happened.

'In the statement, the man's horrible,' I said. 'Just nothing else. Nothing about how he said he was sorry when he saw my hands. He said, "Your poor hands. Look at your poor hands." They didn't say.'

'Tell them you want that put in. Tell them you think it's important.'

There was so much more, but I couldn't explain, even to him, even though he was being nice to me. He didn't seem to think I was stupid, he just talked to me as if I needed to be told what was going to happen to me.

'If it really worries you, I might be able to arrange for you to talk to a psychiatrist about Nicholas Parry,' he said. 'It's a very complicated subject. I don't know enough. To be honest with you, I don't think anybody does. But if you think it might help, I could try to arrange it.'

But it was obvious he didn't think I'd be able to understand, so I shook my head.

Another card came the next day, with the same rose on the front, so I looked inside, and there was printed writing again: *If Nicholas Parry is locked up, you'll be sorry*.

I put it in the pocket of my dressing gown, because I didn't want anybody to find it, and I didn't want Mum to see it. All that afternoon, I thought about it, but it seemed stupid. I hadn't locked him up. There wasn't anything I could do about it. I hadn't even signed the statement. They'd said they were going to bring witnesses so I could just say it was all right, and then they'd sign the statement, or a bit on the bottom of it which said I'd agreed, but they hadn't even done that yet.

It wasn't my fault if he was locked up.

I told the policewoman I wanted her to say he'd said he was sorry about my hands, and she looked at me as if I was mad. Then she looked at her colleague. Got a right idiot here, that look said. What would you do with them?

'You can leave that to the defence,' she said. 'Not that it'll come to that. That's their job.'

'I want it put in,' I said. 'And about the Dark Universe.'

'I don't believe I'm hearing this.'

The other woman started then.

'You got any idea how long we've spent on this stupid bloody case? Think we've got nothing better to do than type all this up again? Any idea how long that would take? To put in all that garbage about his Dark Universe? Oh, yes, I'm sorry, and all that stuff about how he apologised. For crippling you, he said he was sorry. Big deal.'

They said they hadn't got time. The statement was only a formality, Joan. There wasn't going to be a trial, Parry would go to a sort of hospital, not prison. It was only paper. Like filling in your income tax form. It wasn't going to do him any harm. Honestly.

So when the two people came up from the hospital office I said the statement had been read to me, and it was all right, and they both signed it. Then they went away.

I supposed it was all right, if it wouldn't really harm him. I wasn't thinking about it by then. I was thinking about my operation, and what carbon inserts would feel like, if they put them in.

They said I'd be able to go home after the operation. Well, after another couple of days. It was my right wrist that was the real problem. I'd have to go to outpatients and see my doctor, and in a little while they'd see how it was healing up and then they'd decide what to do next.

Sheila said she'd take the afternoon off work to come

home with me. She'd stand us a taxi. Bit of a treat, like a special occasion.

I couldn't go out through the hospital doors to wait for the taxi. There might be somebody there with a knife. Why not? It had happened before.

'Wait here?' I asked, and she asked, 'Why? It's nice outside, it's sunny.'

But I couldn't. There were lots of people there, coming in and walking past us; nurses in their capes, always hurrying; cars driving around; but that didn't matter. There'd been people the time before, the women with the pushchairs, it hadn't stopped him. They hadn't helped.

'Wait here?'

'Okay, if that's what you want.'

It wasn't long before the taxi came, but while we were waiting I asked myself, how am I going to get to work? How can I manage? What am I going to do?

When the taxi came and we went out I was shaking. Sheila was carrying my bags, and she didn't notice. The driver got out of the car and opened the boot so she could put the bags in, and I got into the back seat, and I wanted to lock the door, but my fingers slipped on the button and I couldn't manage it. So I sat looking down at my hands curled in my lap, and thinking, please, hurry. Please get into the car and let's go. Please be quick, stop talking and get into the car. He might be coming.

One of the nurses came to the taxi window, and I nearly screamed when her shadow fell across me. She was smiling at me, and I tried to smile back. Good luck, she was saying. Take care, and good luck.

Then Sheila climbed into the car beside me, and the driver said something to the nurse, and all I could think was, hurry. Please, hurry. He might be coming. Somebody might be there with a knife.

It's happened before. It can happen again.

How am I going to manage when I go back to work?

I asked Sheila, can we lock the doors, and she nodded and leaned forward and asked the driver. She didn't ask why. I think she was starting to understand.

Some of the neighbours had come over to meet us when we got back, and a photographer from the local paper. He asked how I felt.

'All right,' I said.

He wanted a picture of me standing by the door, and the neighbours round the taxi.

I just wanted to go indoors, but it had been kind of everybody to come and meet me, so I went where he said, and I smiled at everybody, but I was looking all the time in case there was somebody who might have a knife; in case there was somebody I didn't know.

Sheila and Mum were there, they would have helped me. If somebody had come with a knife, they would have helped.

When the photographer went away we went indoors, and Mrs Archer came in with a cake she'd made for me. Poor lovey, she kept saying. Never you mind, sweetheart, you're home now.

And at least he didn't do anything nasty.

People came in to say they were pleased to see me home again. Cup of tea, Mum would say, Sheila, put the kettle on. How are you feeling now? Poor love. Well, you're home now. At least he didn't . . . you know.

How does it feel to be home, then, Joanie? Glad to be out of hospital, I bet. Hate hospitals, I do. I remember when I had my gall bladder. Glad to be home, I expect.

Mind you, the nurses. Oh, yes. Mrs Archer make that? Oh, well, just a small slice, then. Just a sliver. Just to be friendly.

We were *ever* so worried. When we heard. Couldn't think what could have happened. Talk of the street, you were. Well, there's fame for you, Joanie. Anyway, you're home now. All's well as ends well, as I always say. And at least he didn't.

I think they meant to be kind, but they all said that. I got quite upset, even though I smiled at them.

'He was going to kill me,' I said to Sheila that night when I was in bed and she came in to kiss me goodnight and say it was nice to have me home again. 'And all they could think was, he didn't do anything. Like, he didn't rape me. He was going to kill me, Sheila.'

I started to cry. I just wished somebody would understand. He had meant to kill me. I'd thought he would. For all that time I'd thought I was going to die, and all they could think was, at least he didn't do anything.

My hands were never going to be right again. Mr Jennings had said that. I'm doing my best, he'd said, and I've talked to some colleagues in Belfast. I've been reading up on the subject, too.

Just for me, I thought. He's been doing that just for me. Talking to other surgeons and reading.

'You'll learn to manage, but they're never going to be as good as they were. The thumb of your right hand is the biggest problem. I don't think there's much more I can do about it. Exercise will help a bit. I want to see you again in a few weeks.'

'You're all right now,' said Sheila. 'You're home now.'

'I'm not all right,' I said sadly as she went out and closed the door. I was supposed to go to sleep now, because sleep makes you better, but there'd be dreams.

Some of the dreams were nice: the dark cloudy skies with the wind blowing and the green grass. And when I woke up I wondered if you could smell things in dreams, because I seemed to remember the smell of mint on water, and sometimes beeswax and lemon thyme.

But the other dreams frightened me. He was there, waiting for me, with the knife, and his polite way of asking, shall we go now?

I heard those words so often, and I'd wake up sweating and there'd be tears on my face, and my wrists would be hurting dreadfully, even though I'd taken my pills before I went to bed.

Would you like to go now? he'd ask, and sometimes in my dreams I'd say, yes, let's go now, and he'd come towards me with the red-handled knife, and the edge of the blade would glitter.

Other times I'd be walking down a long road and there'd be people coming towards me. He's got a knife, they'd say as they passed me, and they'd nod at me, as though they'd said good morning. I'd know he was behind me, but I wouldn't look round. Then more people would come, and nod at me, and smile. He's got a knife, they'd say.

The road was so long I was never going to reach the end, and the people were all friendly and smiling. He's got a knife, they'd say, but they didn't know what that meant.

In the hospital they'd said he was safely locked up. It's all right, sweetheart, they've got him locked up safe. He can't ever get at you again. Not ever. Okay?

Okay, I'd agreed, but one day I'd said, suppose there's another one? You haven't got all the nutters locked up, have you?

No, said the policewoman, but you'd have to be dead unlucky. Twice in one lifetime? Odds against that must be millions to one.

I'd never dared to ask the other question.

Suppose the Dark Universe is real, and they send somebody else to bring the Empress home?

6

Mum started saying it was time I pulled myself together. Can't spend the rest of your life feeling sorry for yourself, she said. Start getting out a bit, Joanie. Time to put all that behind you.

Dr Hastings said I should take all the time I needed. He'd go on signing me off sick until I wanted to go back to work, nobody could take my job away, I wasn't to worry. How was I getting on with the exercises?

I did them every day, but I still couldn't hold things, not small things. I couldn't hold a fork or a spoon. Sheila got me a pair of gloves and she cut slits in the palms so I could slide the handles in. She said if you didn't know you'd never think there was anything wrong.

I couldn't hold my special cup.

In the hospital I'd just looked at it, and held it in both hands, held it up to the light so I could see through it. I hadn't used it. It didn't seem right. They gave me a straw to drink through, so I could hold the cup in both my hands, just pushing together to hold it. My fingers felt stiff.

I don't know why I'd thought when I get home I'll use

it, I'll have my tea out of my special cup again. I had thought I could. So when Sheila made my cup of tea I tried, and I dropped my cup, and there was tea all over the table, and on my skirt.

It wasn't broken, not even chipped, but I felt as if something inside me was broken when I looked at it lying on the table, with the tea spilt all round it.

Can't have my tea out of my special cup any more. Can't hold it.

How was I going to manage then? How can you manage, when your hands don't work?

Putting boxes on the shelves at work, that wouldn't be a problem. They weren't small, I could move them almost with my wrists, I'd hardly have to use my hands at all.

'Wouldn't you feel better, back at work?' Mum asked. 'Moping around here all day must get you down a bit. What about it?'

Carol came round sometimes. She asked if I'd like to go the pictures with her, see the new Tom Cruise film. Dead dreamy, she thought he was. Why don't you come? Do you good to get out. Go for a drink afterwards.

'Go on,' said Mum. 'Can't spend the rest of your life in here. Get yourself out of this house. Go on.'

So I did.

'Pick me up here?' I asked Carol. I thought she might ask me why, when we usually met in town, but she didn't.

'Okay,' she said. 'You make sure you're ready.'

So we walked into town that evening, and I was watching all the people, looking to see if anybody came too near. After a while I thought, I'm waiting for somebody to say, 'He's got a knife.'

'What you looking at?' asked Carol. 'Why do you keep turning round?' She looked over her shoulder, worried. 'Is somebody following us?'

'No.'

Just people out for the evening, I told myself. Only people, walking along the pavements, just like us. No problems.

I was sweating. I was shaking. I wished I hadn't come. I didn't want to see the film, I didn't want to go to the pub afterwards. I wished I hadn't come.

Carol took my arm and she grinned at me.

'You'll be all right,' she said. 'I won't leave you alone.'

And she didn't. That whole evening she stayed with me; even in the pub, she didn't go out the back. She joked with the men, and she was kissing Eric, but she wouldn't go out the back. Not tonight, she said. Tonight's special. Tonight's Joan's first night out.

They were nice to me. They said they were pleased to see me, they wanted to buy me drinks. I kept looking around. I wanted to go home, but it seemed rude, when everybody was being nice to me, and Carol was staying with me. I could feel myself sweating and shaking, and I couldn't hold a glass. I said I wasn't thirsty, I didn't want a drink. But I was, I was dreadfully thirsty, but I knew I'd drop the glass. It was hard enough at home, when I could just think about both hands around it, and lift, and then tilt it a bit, and sometimes I hardly spilt any at all.

I didn't want to do that in the pub. And I was wearing my best blouse, I didn't want to spill anything down it.

'You back at work yet?' somebody asked, and I shook my head.

Carol said they'd got a new man in to replace Mr Evans. He was quite old, but he was all right. She said she reckoned he was a pooftah, because they wouldn't want to risk another dirty lech like Davie Evans. I laughed at her, and she grinned back at me.

'Well, he hasn't made a pass,' she said.

She'd done the lists while I was away, best as she could. It had taken her a while because she couldn't remember what was getting low, she'd had to go round checking, writing it down at the same time. She'd been right about the money. Twenty-five a week, until the old geezer turned up and took her job.

'Just for writing lists?' I asked, and she dug her elbow into my ribs.

'Yeah, *just* for that, you dirty-minded cow.'

When Eric went to the bar to buy another round I whispered to her, 'Can we go soon?'

'You tired?'

'My hands hurt.'

I was lying. They weren't too bad, but I was so thirsty, and I hated people standing behind me. I was as close to the wall as I could be, but there were seats and tables, it wasn't easy. I didn't want to sit down. I kept thinking, if somebody comes I can get away if I'm standing up. I knew it was stupid, with all those people there, but I couldn't help it.

I started to think I could hear the word 'knife'. I was wrong, most of the time. Words rhymed with it, and I was just picking up the end of the sound. 'My wife', somebody said. *My knife*, I heard. 'Night out', and I heard *knife out*. It felt as if it was echoing, *knife, knife, knife*, fading off until it was just people talking and laughing again. And then another word, 'it was a rotten bloody dive,' *it was a bloody knife, a bloody knife*, echoing again.

'Please, Carol.'

'In a minute. Promise.'

There aren't any knives here, I told myself, but there was a boy in the corner, he was cleaning his fingernails with a knife. All in black leather, and it was a big knife, but it had a black handle.

I told myself, it isn't him, and the knife's got a black handle. He wouldn't wear black leather, and his knife has a red handle.

It could be another one. It could be, he's got a knife. He's got a knife.

'He's got a knife,' I said, and they stopped talking and stared at me. 'The man in the corner.'

They looked at him, and then Eric said he'd take me home. I was looking a bit tired.

I thought I was going to cry.

Carol sat in the back of the car with me while Eric drove. She had her arm round my shoulders because I was shaking. I don't think she understood but she knew something was wrong, and so did Eric. He was very quiet, not making remarks about Carol like he usually did, no jokes about quantity discounts tonight. I'd never liked him very much, but I was grateful that night because he'd said he'd drive me home, I was looking tired. He'd seen there was something wrong. He'd been kind.

People were funny, I thought. It's not all black and white. Eric's stupid and he makes jokes all the time about women; I don't think he even likes women, just for sex, that's all. But when he saw there was something wrong he wanted to help, and he did help, he did everything right. It was kind of him. He was stupid and he didn't like women, but he was kind.

It's a bit like the way people look, I thought. That boy Trevor Freeman in the greengrocery, skinny and spotty and greasy hair, but he had really nice eyes, all clear and grey with dark lashes, and his eyebrows looked like wings over them. A bit of everything, most people. A bit of nice, a bit of nasty, a bit of ugly, a bit of beautiful. It all depends on what you're looking at, which bit you see. What they're doing, which bit comes out on top.

'You all right, Joanie?' asked Carol, and I managed to smile at her.

He'd had a knife, and he'd worried about my hands.

I was a shelf filler at Fletchers, and I was the Empress of the Dark Universe.

I shivered, and tried to push the idea away, because it was crazy and I thought, if I think crazy I might go crazy. Maybe that's how it all starts.

When we got home Eric got out of the car and came to the door with me. He said he'd sit in the car until I waved out of the window. Not to worry, Joanie. Not surprising, to get a bit tired first time out.

Kind, dirty-minded lecher, I thought as I said goodnight to him. And I went into the house and thought about other words that wouldn't make sense unless you knew people were all patches. 'Ugly glamour girl'. 'Mean little saint'. But I couldn't think of any good ones.

'You're back early,' said Mum, and I just nodded, and I pulled back the living room curtain and I waved.

Carol was in the front beside Eric, and they both waved back and then drove away.

'Nice time?'

No. It hadn't been a nice time, it had been horrible.

90

'Yes,' I said.

'Told you it would do you good to get out. What was the film like?'

Was I always going to hear the word 'knife'? I wondered. Even when it wasn't said, would I always hear it? Was I ever going to be able to sit in the cinema and look at the screen and not wonder about the people around me? Would I ever know somebody was standing behind me and not be frightened?

I went into the kitchen to get myself something to drink, but I dropped the mug, and the water splashed everywhere and the mug broke on the floor.

I started to cry.

Mum came in and she picked up the pieces. Come on, Joanie, not the end of the world, only an old mug.

'I'm thirsty.'

She got me another mug and she poured Ribena in, very strong, and she put a straw in it. It tasted really good, and it didn't matter, sitting at the table and not even bothering to hold the mug, just drinking through the straw.

She was trying to understand why I was crying, and I thought that was a bit funny, coming from Mum. She often cried, not for any good reason, and sometimes she'd say nothing like a good cry to make you feel better. It's not like that for me. Crying doesn't make me feel better, not right away. It makes me feel rotten, it gives me a headache and makes my eyes sore. It's just, when I'm crying everything seems to come out, on to the surface, where I can see it. Anger, most of it, when people have been mean and stupid. I cry, and I remember, and I'm angry when before I'd been sort of helpless, not knowing what to say, not able to get away.

91

And the feeling of being in a trap, wanting to get out, wanting to be something different, not knowing how. That comes out when I cry. And being tired, the sort of tired that's like being bored, only you can't do anything about it.

The only thing about crying is, you get these feelings, and they're out in the open and you can look at them. And sometimes change them a bit, or at least shape them, as if they were that Plasticine stuff we had at school, still the same but in a different way.

I thought, in the courts in the Dark Universe, when people cry there might be somebody who understands about crying, understands a lot more than I do, who can show people how to change the shapes. It might help.

No, I thought. Don't. I'm going crazy.

'I kept thinking there was somebody with a knife,' I said to Mum, and it was true.

'Oh, Joanie! That's just daft. He's locked up, that Nicholas Parry. He can't get at you. Ah, Joanie, come on. Poor lovey.'

I knew it wouldn't really help, trying to explain. I didn't know the words. I was just frightened all the time, and I didn't know what about. I knew he was locked up. I knew it probably wouldn't happen again. It was just, knowing it, and feeling it, wasn't the same thing.

There's two of me. This me knows it won't happen again, and I've got bad hands that won't ever really be right again. And that other me knows it can happen again, and it might, so be careful, and look out for knives, and listen to people who say, 'He's got a knife.' Doesn't matter if it's right out there in the street or only in dreams, listen to them. They know something, too.

'Go and have a bath,' said Mum. 'Make you feel better.

92

Go on, use some of my Christmas bath salts. Then come back down here and I'll make a nice cup of tea.'

It wasn't even my bath night, so it was nice of her, because we've got an immersion heater and she's always worried about the bill for the electric.

Sheila was home by the time I came down. It had been her night for practising, when students or pensioners go into the shop and she and Meg, who's learning at the shop, do their hair for nothing, just to learn. Sheila was in a good mood because it had been Mrs Young that evening, who's been on the stage and even in films, and she's always a laugh. She doesn't mind what Sheila does, what colour, what style, so long as it's fun.

'She said, give you this for a challenge, then,' said Sheila. 'Straight up in the air with a knot in the top and a bone through the middle.'

'You what?' said Mum.

'Seen it in a cartoon, she had,' said Carol, 'and she said, bet you can't do it. Paul said bet he bloody could then, long as it was a plastic bone, and of course you could. Just make a wire frame and comb the hair over it. I cut a bone shape out of a bit of a cardboard box. It looked so funny, I nearly wet myself. So did she. Laugh! Well, she only had time for a shampoo and blow dry after all that. Never mind.'

So we sat round the table having a cup of tea and talking about Mrs Young, who'd once been in a film with Sean Connery and said he was ever so nice.

I felt a bit better after a while, only I had that empty feeling where there's nothing inside except a sort of coldness. I get that when I've been crying. And a headache, but it wasn't too bad, I didn't need an aspirin or anything.

I knew there'd be dreams that night. People crowding all round me, not unfriendly, not nasty, but all knowing something I didn't know, none of them what they seemed to be, not what they looked like. All something different underneath, and they all knew it, all except me. I was the only one who didn't understand.

7

Mum stopped saying I should go back to work for a while after the night I'd gone out with Carol. She said I'd feel better soon. Not to worry, Joanie, you'll feel better soon.

Then you can go back to work, but she didn't say it.

I watched the telly. I kept the house nice, and I did my exercises, so it wasn't long before I could do the dusting without dropping things, if I was careful. Washing up was hard, with things wet and slippery. I broke a lot of things. Mum said, leave it till your hands are better, but I knew they wouldn't ever be better, not completely.

Mr Jennings said I should just keep on with the exercises, and maybe they could do another operation in a few months. I thought, he's bored with me now. He was nice, he did his best to help me, but I'm in the past for him now, he wants to do something else. So I said thanks, and bye, and I thought, well, that's it. Just what the exercises can do, and that's it.

My thumb that wouldn't go right across the palm of my hand any more, just close, but not tight. My fingers that wouldn't go straight. That's it, just the exercises now.

Oh, well.

At least he didn't *do* anything.

Dr Hastings said I could get compensation from the Criminal Injuries people. There were forms, he could get them for me.

'You'd have to go to a tribunal,' he said. 'I don't know how much you'd get. Would you like me to get the forms?'

I thought about a tribunal. Strangers, talking about me, about what had happened. Maybe they'd know I'd wet myself, while I was hanging there from that light flex. Would they ask about that?

I felt my face growing hot, and I looked down into my lap, where my hands lay, the fingers just curled. There were scars from the operations, but they weren't too bad now. They'd fade, Mr Jennings had said. In a while they'd just be thin white lines, nobody would notice.

'Would they look at my hands?' I asked, and Dr Hastings said he supposed so. They'd want to assess the damage, so they'd know how much money to give me.

I tried to imagine strangers looking at my hands. When I was a child I'd had trouble with my ears, and there'd been a doctor who'd treated me in hospital. I'd had an operation then, to clear a blockage. He'd been quite kind, that doctor, and I hadn't minded him. He'd helped me with my jigsaw puzzle, and told me about his dog. He'd said he had a daughter the same age as me. But she hadn't had anything wrong with her ears.

I hadn't really liked him, even though he'd been kind, but I hadn't minded him. I'd let him look in my ears, and there'd been tests with buzzers, which I'd done and he'd said he was pleased with me. But one day he'd come with three other people, two men and a woman, and he'd told me they wanted to play the buzzer game and look in my ears.

Play the buzzer game. I remember thinking then, that's a silly thing to say. It's not a game, it's a test, to see how well I can hear now. And I remember thinking, I can't stop them. If they want to look in my ears, I can't stop them.

So they'd looked in my ears with the lights and their things that poked down and hurt, not much, but a bit. They'd talked to each other. I'd sat on my bed looking down at the colouring book I'd been drawing in, and I'd wanted to cry, but it seemed babyish. I didn't want to be babyish, especially since the doctor had said 'buzzer game'.

They could do anything they wanted, and I couldn't stop them. If I'd said no, they'd have said don't be a silly girl. They were bigger and they were stronger, and they could call the nurses over to help them.

When they'd gone I'd coloured my picture black.

It would be the same. They couldn't call over the nurses to help hold me down, and they wouldn't say I was a silly girl. Well, they wouldn't use those words. But it would be the same. They were still bigger and stronger than me, and if they wanted to look at my hands and ask me questions, they could. And if I said no, or wouldn't answer?

Well, Miss Ferguson, I'm sorry, but since you won't co-operate . . .

Silly girl. Wasting our time like this.

Strangers, looking at my hands, telling me, clench your

fists, hold this pen, can't you do better than that? Try harder. No? Very well.

When you were in the room could you really not get away? You say you were hanging from the ceiling. Tied to the light flex.

'No,' I said.

I've heard the word 'humiliation', and I thought, that's it. That's what it means. Being ashamed, and being helpless, because they're stronger and you can't do anything, even if it isn't your fault. I'd known the word; I hadn't thought, I wonder what that means, but now I understood it. Sitting in Dr Hastings's office, I knew what it meant, because I could feel it.

'No,' I said again.

'There's nothing to be ashamed of,' he said, and for a moment I felt panic. He can read my mind, he can read my mind.

No. This wasn't him. This was Dr Hastings. I wasn't in the room with the star flowers painted on the windows, I was in the doctor's office, or surgery. Sometimes he said come into my office; sometimes, come into my surgery. There were no flowers on the window, and there were strip lights on the ceiling and a desk lamp. No flex.

After I'd had the operation on my ears they said I'd probably do better at school, I'd catch up on the reading. But they'd been wrong.

And after the tribunal, what? What then, after the tribunal?

'I don't want . . .'

What didn't I want? What could I say?

'I don't want . . . to.'

He shrugged.

'Let me know if you change your mind,' he said. 'Now, how much longer do you think you need off work?'

He's tired of me, too. Time to go back to work. Same thing, different way of saying it. Aren't you bored, hanging around here? Don't you think you'd be better off at work? How much longer do you think you need? Same meaning, different words.

'A week?'

'All right. You can have longer, if you need it.'

You don't need it. You're better. Go back to work and forget about it. Get on with your life. Don't mope about it. At least he didn't do anything.

'You aren't half getting sulky, our Joanie,' said Sheila that evening, and it felt like she'd hit me. Sheila hardly ever said anything nasty to me.

'What do you mean?'

'Long face, never laugh any more. Always used to be good for a laugh and a joke. Okay, a bad thing happened, but don't you let it spoil your life. That's like letting him win, not even putting up a fight.'

I hadn't been able to fight. He'd always known what I'd been thinking. Sometimes he'd seemed to know almost before I'd thought. On the stairs, that first time, when I'd had the idea of kicking him and when I'd looked he'd been too far back, and he'd been watching me, waiting for it. He hadn't had time to back off. He'd known I was going to think that, before I'd even thought it.

That wasn't what Sheila meant, and I knew it. Maybe she was right. She wouldn't have said it just for spite.

I tried to smile at her, and she reached out and touched my cheek.

99

'That's better. That's our old Joanie.'

A week, and I'd have to go back to work. On the bus.

It was the number seventeen for the seventeen moons that were swirling away into the cloudy sky, in the tenth row of seats for the ten galaxies in the Dark Universe until I gave him the signal that I was ready to go back. Until I'd gone and sat beside him, and he'd looked at me, and then looked away, and then he'd nodded. Right, that's the signal. She's ready to go back.

He wouldn't be on the bus any longer. Sarah and Diane would be there, unless one of them had got a bad chest and gone to Jesus, like Vicky. I could have asked about that, when I was in the hospital. Mr Jennings would have known. I could have asked him, how can somebody be well one day, and the next day be dead of bronchitis?

I hadn't thought to ask Mr Jennings; I hadn't remembered. I should have asked him. I wanted to understand it. Just a bad cough, a sore throat, and dead. It wasn't right. Somebody should have seen, seen in time to stop it getting so bad.

It wouldn't have happened in the Dark Universe because people would care enough to watch out for the signs. Vicky's coughing, don't forget her weak chest. Give her medicine, now, don't wait. Get the doctor. Do it now, because she's got a weak chest, and a cough's dangerous.

She wouldn't have died, and Sarah and Diane wouldn't have to be so sad and so silent about their friend.

He'd said there were doctors in the Dark Universe. Lots of doctors, he'd said. When people are ill you have to be quick. You have to make them better quickly. Not in a few months' time maybe we'll operate again. And all talk, let it settle down, see how it goes, do the exercises. Make it better now, not in a few months.

Silly. It doesn't happen like that. Things do take time; even if you start straight away, healing does take time. You can't be ill one moment, better the next.

Not here, anyway.

'Do you highlights in your hair?' asked Sheila, and I tried to laugh at her.

'If God had meant me to be blonde,' I said, and she gave me a big hug. That's my old Joanie, at least trying.

Cloudy dark skies, like my hair. Not blonde highlights.

'Going back to work next week,' I said.

'Oh, Joanie.' A little bit of a worried frown, I thought, but she did smile. She was trying, too. 'That's good, our Joanie.'

I polished all the wood in the house. I moved all the things off the chest in the living room, and I sprayed on the polish and then I made a soft duster into a pad and leaned my arms on it. I could have done it with my hands, but I wanted to see how it went, doing it just with my arms, and it came up much better. More weight on the duster, and it was like it forced the shine down deep into the wood. I stood over it and I looked down at my face shining back at me and the pattern in the wood. So then I did all the rest of the furniture, in the same way, except for the little bits, like the bars on the chairs and under the table. Everything I could lean on, I did, and then I put everything back as carefully as I could, and I thought, I can go on doing things like this for the whole week, and then I won't have to think.

Back at work. On the bus. And when I'm there

everybody will stare at me. She's back, they'll say. She's back. See her hands? Yuck.

She wouldn't charge him with rape. Oh, don't be stupid, three whole days? Of course he did. You ask her, go on, I dare you.

Annie would, in the canteen. Didn't he fancy you, then?

I dropped Mum's brass flower vase and it rolled under the table.

I can do the brass, I thought. After Mum's silver hairbrush and things. I can do that.

So I spread newspapers on the kitchen table and I got all the metal things in the house and then I sat down with the polish and the rags and the old blackened toothbrush and I made myself think about polishing. Getting into all the little corners with the toothbrush, and rubbing at it all as hard as I could until it was shiny. I was only thinking about that, about the black marks just under the rim around Mum's hairbrush, about that black bit in the dent on the little warming pan that hangs by the fireplace, wrap a bit of rag round the end of the toothbrush and see if you can dig it out.

But I couldn't hold the toothbrush well enough for that.

Hold it in your teeth then, and squint down until you can see the little black bit. Go on, now move the warming pan, not the toothbrush. Just wiggle it about a bit.

When I looked in the mirror there was black metal polish all over my face.

Next week. Back to work next week.

'House looks nice, Joanie. My, you have been busy. I'll say this for you, my lovey, you do your best. Cup of tea?'

'I'm going to do the shopping,' I said next morning, and Mum asked if I needed any money. She didn't seem to notice. Only Sheila looked at me, a long look, and then a funny sort of smile. Almost like, that's brave.

I don't think she meant me to see.

I hadn't been out on my own, only to Dr Hastings just down the road. When I had to go to the hospital they sent a car. They'd done that right at the start, and I suppose they'd forgotten to check.

Shopping. I didn't really know if I could do it, but I'd said I would, and there was the three pounds on the table that Mum had left. Not enough, but that was all right, because I had some money. I was still getting paid. Not what I usually got every week, because there was no overtime, but basic, I was still getting that. No bus fares. No coffee in the canteen, for me and Carol. I only had to pay what I gave Mum every week, and I hadn't spent anything. I had nearly twenty pounds. I'd only ever had that much before at Christmas, when we got our bonus, and then it all went on presents.

I had to go past the shop where I'd bought my special cup. It was closed. You never knew, with that shop, when it would be open. There'd be notices in the window and the door would be locked. I looked through the window at the shelf at the back where the woman put china. There wasn't anything I liked, and anyway, now I had my cup and saucer, I didn't want anything else.

Then I saw the woman at the back of the shop, and she waved at me, and came to the door. I suppose she saw me and thought, customer. It would have been rude to have walked away, so I waited while she unlocked the door.

'Come on in,' she said. 'You better now? I heard what happened. Bloody hell, you poor kid. Bastard, what a bastard.'

She sounded really angry as I followed her into the shop.

'Want a coffee?' she asked. 'I was just going to have one. You haven't inherited a fortune, have you? Pity. Got some crackle ware here. Well, sod it, we'll have our coffee out of it, then it can go on the shelf.'

'No,' I said. 'Cheap mug?' I held up my hands. 'Can't hold things. Might drop it.'

She didn't ask any questions, but the angry look came back into her face, the one that had been there when she'd called him a bastard.

'Right. Cheap mug. Do you know how to spell "junk"? A-N-T-I-Q-U-E, that's how you spell "junk", in this bit of the shop. Cheap mug, cheap mug, cheap mug.'

She was muttering to herself, looking in cardboard boxes, and I watched as she pulled a blue and green piece of pottery out from under a heap of picture frames, and looked at it with her head on one side and her eyes all squinted up.

'I won't find anything much cheaper than this. Worth more as broken crock in the bottom of a window box than in one piece. Hang on, I'll wash it. You haven't broken the cup and saucer you bought here, have you? What was it, Coalport?'

I looked at her, and I thought, which do I answer? If I say yes, I mean it was Coalport. That's what she called it. But she might think I've broken it. If I say no . . .

I gave up.

'I haven't broken it.'

But I had dropped it, three times since I came back

from hospital, and each time I'd thought it would break. I'd picked it up, my lovely cup, I'd hooked a finger through the handle and picked it up and laid it in the palm of my other hand, and I'd looked, and the little birds had been lovely, and delicately painted, and there were no cracks, and no chips.

'It's strong,' I said, but what I meant was, thank you.

'Don't drop it edgeways on concrete.'

She wasn't looking at me, but she was talking.

'Just instant, that all right? Do you take sugar? Where's the bloody milk? Oh, God, how old is this? Does that smell all right to you? Smoking sixty a day, I've got the sense of smell of a plastic lemon.'

She held a greasy milk bottle out towards me, and I sniffed at the top.

'It's all right,' I said.

'Just as well, that powder stuff's wearing a green overcoat. I'd have to tunnel for it. Come on, kettle. Tell you what, I could put that up as an antique. One of the first electric kettles ever made. Or maybe not. One of the slowest. Not much value in that. Want to buy it? Thought not. Pity. Is that steam, or has it caught fire? Let's risk it. Oh, bubble, bubble, toil and trouble, clean out of newts' eyes, sugar lump do instead? Good.'

She hardly looked at me all the time she was making the coffee, but she never stopped talking, and I liked it. I didn't have to answer, just listen, and it made me smile. Daft things she was saying, like Jacobean coffee with just a touch of added rust from the Queen Anne kettle element; there's a spoon here somewhere, good grief, personally designed by Isambard Kingdom Brunel just after he finished Paddington Station, or was it Euston? And all the time, 'Want to buy it? Thought not. Pity.'

It was nice. Daft, but it was sort of clever too, names I didn't know but she did. She knew what she was talking about, she could make it all into nonsense because she knew about it. I listened to her, and I thought I wish I could do that. If only there was something I knew about, enough so I could talk fast and make it all funny, so people would smile.

I was grinning by then, and she didn't seem to be thinking of anything in particular, just this quick talk, but when she'd made the coffee she didn't hand me the mug, she put it on the table and slid it across to me. Talking like that, and being funny, but she hadn't forgotten I couldn't hold things.

'Park yourself,' she said. 'Got to be a chair in here somewhere, it used to be a furniture shop. Isn't that a chair? If you're not in a fussy mood? Vague outline, isn't there? I suppose somebody must have loved it once, God knows why. Theresa, do not talk like this in front of the customers, she might want to buy it. Don't want to buy it, do you? Thought not. Pity.'

She started coughing, thumped herself on the chest and then sat down on a stool behind the table. Her eyes were watering.

'Bloody cancer. Gives me the pip. That coffee okay?'

The mug had a thick handle, but I could push two fingers through it and hold it quite steady from the other side.

Cancer, she'd said.

'You got cancer?' I asked.

'I have. Enough sugar in that? What are you doing out and about? People who've had bad experiences are supposed to spend months lying around being sorry for themselves and having counselling. Here you are out on

106

the street, even walking. Are you Superwoman or some-thing?'

'Just shopping. Back to work next week.'

'You're a disgrace, you are. You haven't even had a decent nervous breakdown. And what about all those poor counsellors, looking for somebody to patronise? I bet you never spared a thought for them. "Back to work next week", forsooth.'

It was the same sort of talk, laughing at everything, but I wanted to go home and think about it. Theresa, she'd called herself. She had a nice face, not pretty, but sort of sad and wise and funny, as if she'd known she wasn't pretty, and it had made her unhappy once, but then it had been all right because she'd found something better.

'What work?' she asked. 'What do you do? Can't they manage without you any longer? World leaders stuck for ideas for the next summit conference? Serious danger of peace breaking out in the Middle East and fucking up the arms trade if you don't get back out there and stir it up again?'

'Shelf filler at Fletchers,' I said, and I wondered if she'd stop being funny then, because maybe she'd think I wouldn't understand.

'They've been out of Patak's Garlic Pickle for the last three weeks,' she said. 'Damn right you'd better get back. I didn't know you worked there. I'd have been on at you for a staff discount if I'd known that. What have you been doing since you came home?'

She didn't wait for an answer, just went on talking, but now and then there was a bit of a pause, and I told her I'd polished the furniture and the brass and the silver, not much silver, I said and she laughed, and how I'd leaned on the duster because my hands hurt a bit by then, how the wood had come up so much better, because of the extra weight, maybe.

She said she didn't use spray on the furniture in the shop, she used a special polish with wax in it. There was a little rosewood table, look, over there, do you know, the people who'd sold it to her had painted it? Blue gloss paint? Enough to make you cry.

I asked her about rosewood, because the roses I'd seen only had little sticks of wood, nothing you could make furniture out of.

It's not from rose trees, she said. It's called rosewood because it smells of roses when you cut it. But what do you think of the little table? Hasn't it come up well?

So we looked at some of the things in the shop, and she told me a bit about them, how old they were, where they'd been made. There was a very old table, and she showed me underneath it, there was pinewood. Just cheap wood, she said, they put it there because it's softer than the oak. If there are woodworm they'll go into the pine, and leave the oak alone. Good idea, wasn't it?

'I must go,' I said. 'I promised Mum I'd do the shopping.'

'Come again. Show me how you polished that chest. Will you?'

Theresa. I wanted to read her surname on the notice above the window, but it was a long one, so I thought I'd look some other time, when she wasn't there. She hadn't treated me like a customer, she'd treated me like a friend. We'd drunk coffee, and she'd joked with me, and sworn a bit, as if we'd known each other for a long time. When she'd said come again she'd meant it, and I wanted to. Maybe we could sit at the back of that shop and polish things together.

I was watching the people in the road. I'd had the dream the night before, when they came up to me and said, he's got a knife, and I was trying to walk quickly. Now, on the road only a little way from my home, I made myself walk slowly. I watched the people coming towards me, and they didn't even look at me. But I was listening. And every few yards I'd think, I'm starting to walk fast again. Walk slowly, there's nobody behind you.

I turned round, and I looked.

Just people like me, just ordinary people. Mostly women.

Nobody was saying, he's got a knife.

Then I was in the High Street, with the big discount furniture shop on the corner, which I always hated, I don't know why. All those big posters in the window, saying 'Sale'. Always a sale. And words I'd worked out while I was waiting for the bus. 'Prices slashed'. He's got a knife, I thought, a knife that slashes.

Don't.

I walked past the bus stop, and thought, five days and I'll be standing there in the morning. Early. Early shift, so the women from the home will be there, Diane and Sarah. I'll see them. I'll say good morning to them.

I'll wear gloves.

The music shop with the same dusty drums, been there for years. Shiny brass instruments hanging from an iron rail. Dirty windows, and a box outside with sheet music in it, and a paper notice stuck to it. The laun- derette, with people sitting in there, looking at the machines as if they were watching telly, not just clothes going round and round.

Walking too fast. Slow down, there's nobody behind you. Except the two women with the pushchairs.

Help, I'd said. Please help me, and they'd just looked at me, and gone on. Two women with pushchairs, talking to each other.

I stopped, and I waited till they'd gone past, and then I looked around again.

I wish I hadn't come. I wish I hadn't said I'd do the shopping. Wish I was safe home. He could be anywhere. Him, or somebody like him. Could be watching me right now, thinking, there she is, there's the Empress, she gave the signal so it's time to go back.

He's got a knife.

I didn't give any signal. I haven't sat down, not in any seat, not near anybody, so there wasn't a signal. I don't want to go back. Where is he?

I went into the launderette. I thought, stay here for a moment. Look at the machines.

I walked up the row of washing machines, and they were all full. All moving, clothes and things going round and round, colour swirling in white soapy water. There'd been another launderette in Green Street, but it had closed down a couple of months ago, and now this was the only one, so it was always full. People had to wait for the machines.

Sit down, I thought, and then, no. No signals.

'I think I'm next, dear,' said a woman sitting on the bench with a full bag between her knees, and her voice wasn't friendly, even though she'd called me dear. She thought I was trying to take her place, but I hadn't got any washing with me, only my shopping bag. She was being bad-tempered, to show she wasn't going to be put upon, not by anybody. It was her turn next, and nobody was going to get in front of her. Oh, no.

I went outside again, and then I stood with my back

against the window of the launderette, looking up and down the street. I watched the faces of the people as they came towards me, and one or two stared back at me, but nobody spoke. Nobody said, he's got a knife, and there was no young man near me.

But if I turned my back, he might come.

I have to do the shopping. I told Mum I'd do the shopping, and she left me three pounds to buy tea, and potatoes, and milk, and bread, and something nice for afters this evening. I have to do the shopping.

There's nobody near me. It won't happen again. He's locked up, he can't get at me.

They might send somebody else.

I pressed my hands against my eyes, feeling the wool of my gloves rubbing into the skin, and I told myself to stop being stupid.

On down the street, I mustn't look behind me. There is *nobody there*. Nobody is following me. I have to do the shopping, and I want to go home, so I must get on with it now. Tea, and potatoes, and milk, and bread, and something nice for afters.

People talking at the door of the baker's. Don't listen, you'll only hear things; you'll hear things they're not saying. Don't listen.

He's got a knife, knife knife. Did you hear? Knife. Knife.

Turn the corner, and there's the supermarket, and he's standing with his back to me, looking in the window. He's there.

He's got a knife, did you hear? He's got a knife.

Stop. Wait. It isn't him, he's safely locked up, he can't get at you. It isn't him. There's no knife. Go on, go into the shop.

One step, and another, and he turned towards me and looked at me, just as he had in that little room with the star flowers painted on the windows, looking at me as if he was waiting for me to say something, as if he was waiting for me.

I took another step, and I tried to turn away, and my knees went all weak under me, so I fell on to the pavement and dropped the shopping bag. When I heard footsteps coming quickly I wanted to get up, I wanted to run away, but it was too much trouble. I'd stay where I was, then.

And I looked up into the wise and funny face of my new friend Theresa.

8

By the time I looked back towards the supermarket he'd gone. Maybe he'd never been there at all, I thought, but I knew he had. I'd seen him, and he'd seen me. But now he'd gone, and there was just Theresa, sitting on the pavement beside me as if it was the most natural thing in the world, to sit there, on the pavement a few yards from Tesco's, and I thought, I'm safe now, because Theresa's here.

'I followed you,' she said, and she sounded pleased with herself, as if she'd done something clever. Maybe she could read my mind too, because then she said, 'I thought that was quite clever. You didn't see me. I'd always thought those detective novels were crap, with people not spotting each other when they were being followed, but they're not. You didn't see me when you looked round, did you?'

I didn't want her to talk about that. I wanted to hear the funny talk she'd used in the shop that made me smile. But why had she followed me?

She stretched out her feet as if to make herself more comfortable, and a woman had to walk around us. The woman said something about it only being halfway through the morning, and Theresa gave a little sigh, but a sort of happy one, not tired or sad.

'She thinks we're drunk.'

'I saw him,' I said, and she didn't seem surprised.

'Did you? Yes. Well, I thought you might. Well, something like that. I thought, one cup of coffee isn't going to set her up for this one, not first time out. Theresa Harringdon, I said to myself, time to be a nosy parker and a do-gooder, and pretend to be Sam Spade. Where is he?'

'He's gone,' I said, and I knew she didn't believe me.

It couldn't have been him. He was locked up, he couldn't get at me. They'd sent somebody else.

Why would they send somebody who looked just the same? I'd know, wouldn't I? I'd know they'd sent him. Maybe they'd thought I'd agree to go back this time, so it wouldn't matter, if he looked the same. Maybe they'd thought it would help me; I would see him and go with him, because I'd recognise him.

No. This is crazy, thinking like this. This is how you can go crazy.

'I've got to do the shopping.'

I didn't want to. I wanted to be at home, or in Theresa's shop, not sitting there in the street and wondering about what I'd seen, and how it had happened, and what it meant.

'I suppose we'd better stand up, then,' said Theresa, but it was me who helped her to her feet. She wasn't very strong, and she seemed a bit wobbly at first. She put her hand on my shoulder, and said something about just a minute, and her head was down so I couldn't see her face.

I thought she'd say we should go back to the shop, but she didn't. We went into the supermarket, and she pushed the trolley, leaning on the handles as we went down the shelves, which looked a bit funny, like a kid playing. I knew she didn't care if it looked like that. She'd only have cared if it looked as if she was too weak to push it properly. Better to look like a kid playing, and have people think she was daft, than have them think she was weak and ill.

It didn't take long, to get just the few things Mum said we needed, and cigarettes for Theresa. It was all right while she was there, I didn't have to look around, or listen to other people.

He'd gone.

I'd have to think about it later. If I was going crazy, I'd have to think about that, too. Seeing things that weren't there. Something wasn't right.

'He wasn't wearing the same clothes,' I said when we were outside again, and Theresa was holding my arm and looking along the street. She was thinking, could she walk that far now? And I was looking to see if he'd come back. Both of us, looking up the street.

'Ah,' she said. And then, 'Now *that's* very interesting.'

We went into the launderette on the way back, and there were some chairs free, so we sat down. Theresa lit a cigarette and sat back, and coughed.

'Nice to have somewhere to go and sit down on the way back from the shopping,' she said. 'Look at the way those clothes are all cuddled up there, do you see? That shirt's got its arm round a pair of knickers. Isn't that romantic?'

She seemed to be thinking, but under the surface, so she could keep talking and making me smile even when

115

she was thinking about something else. It wasn't till we got back to the shop that she got serious.

She phoned the police. Any chance, she asked, that Nicholas Parry might be on the loose again? No blame to them, but you know the National Health Service. *Looks fine to me and we need the bed, let him go home?* Yes, there is a reason for this question. I think I saw him. Outside Tesco's in Zircon Street, if that makes any difference. Would you check? And call me back? Thank you.

'Get the obvious out of the way first,' she said, and then, as if the words tasted funny and she was trying them out again, 'Different clothes.'

The police phoned back and told her Nicholas Parry was in a secure hospital. She must have made a mistake.

It can't have been him, I thought. I suppose that means I'm going crazy.

It isn't fair.

Theresa was pushing the blue and green mug across the table to me again. Then she asked me, and she seemed very serious, why, if he was wearing different clothes, I'd thought it was Nicholas Parry.

'He looked like him,' I said, and then I thought, no, that's wrong. At first it was that, when he was looking in the window. But I knew he was locked up, so I managed that, somebody who just looked a bit like him.

'It wasn't the way he looked,' I said. 'It was the way he looked at me.'

As if he was waiting for an answer. As if he was waiting for me to speak. His head just a little on one side, looking at me from under his eyebrows. That way he held his head. But his hair was shorter, maybe not quite such a dark brown.

Oh, I couldn't remember that. The colour of his hair, I

couldn't remember. But I did think it was a bit shorter.

And his clothes, that denim jacket and the jeans, he hadn't worn them. I didn't think he would have worn denim, not jacket and jeans like that. He was the sort of man who wore grey trousers. Not so casual.

'You can be bloody convincing,' said Theresa. 'That *is* odd. Well, it's damned unlucky, anyway. That's all it is, you know, Joan. Damned unlucky.'

Was that all it was? I'd seen somebody like him, and I'd been frightened. It wasn't him, he was locked up. I knew that. But seeing somebody like him had frightened me. Just damned unlucky.

'I'm glad you were there,' I said.

I didn't say anything about it to Mum or Sheila. I kept telling myself Theresa was right. Damned unlucky, and I never said unlucky without saying damned first. It made it sound better.

The way he'd looked at me.

They'd sent somebody else to bring the Empress home, somebody who looked almost the same, so she'd know. She'd recognise him. This time I ought to go, because the seventeen moons were swirling away, and I was needed. It was time to go back to the Dark Universe, because they needed me.

But I might come back here again, and I might know about Vicky, and about Theresa. I might know how to cure Theresa.

Crazy, thinking like this. I'd just been damned unlucky, and in five days I'm going back to work. Time to stop moping around here, I'll feel better when I'm back at work. *Did you see her hands? Yuck.*

I'll wear gloves.

I'm going to work on the number seventeen bus, and

117

I'm going to sit at the back, the tenth row back. Unless I don't want to. I might sit by Sarah and Diane and talk to them, all the way to work. Not just when we stop at the station, I might talk all the way, like the two women. Did you see that on the telly about the strippers? Laugh, I did laugh.

'Can you go to the shops, our Joanie? We need milk. And what about some fish fingers tonight? Can you get chips?'

Don't look. Don't look at anybody. Theresa's shop's closed, and she's not there, I don't think, don't look. Walk, quite quickly, but not too fast, and don't listen and don't look, anybody can do this.

Milk, fish fingers, chips, not the oven chips, they don't taste right. The big bag of frozen chips, hope there's room in the freezer. Don't look at the people, and don't listen. Just walk and walk, and stop at the kerb and look and listen, like you were taught as a baby. And walk and walk, and don't look, and don't listen, only to the cars. Don't listen to the people.

I was just damned unlucky.

Never going to look at anybody again?

'Fancy going out for a drink, Joan?'

Carol, on the phone. No, thanks, Carol. I'm a bit tired.

'Do you good to get out,' said Mum.

I've been out. I've been to the shops every day, I did it, and I don't think Theresa followed me either. I didn't see her. One day I was damned unlucky. I've been to see Theresa in her shop twice since then, and we had some coffee, and she showed me marks on the backs of silver spoons; hallmarks, so you knew who'd made them, and if they were real silver. And there was a big coffee pot, it was half copper and half silver. It was plate, she said, silver stuck to the copper, but it had been polished and polished and the silver had worn away. Pity, but it was quite interesting. Somebody would buy it. Nice shape. Simple. When you're looking at silver, never mind all the twiddly bits, all the leaves and fruit and rubbish like that, it's only ornament. Look at the shape underneath all that. Is it a good shape under all the rubbish?

'Antique wax, antique wax, wherefore art thou antique wax? Where the *bloody* hell have I left it now? Oh, yes. Now, why in the filing cabinet? Never mind. Earth hath not anything to show more fair, that thing under your elbow is a box of dusters, Joan. Suspend disbelief, I mean it. Dusters, and I knew where they were. Show me this business with leaning on your arms and making the shine deeper. Let me see if I can think of a way of patenting it, and making our fortunes.'

She didn't talk about the man at the supermarket, but she didn't seem to avoid it either. It was all right.

There was a table she'd bought at an auction, and it was too big to go in the shop so it was in the yard at the back under a tarpaulin. It'll be all right until the winter, she said. Have to sell it before then. Let's see what sort of a shine we can get out of it. It's bloody filthy.

Wire wool and vinegar, she told me to get some when I went shopping. I'll show you a trick, she said. Go on, I mean it. Don't pick up anything under six foot or over forty, and bring me one while you're about it. When I came back she wiped the table with the vinegar, and rubbed it with the wire wool, and then washed it and dried it, as if it was china. Just look in that bucket, she said, and the water was black. Do that a couple of times, we'll see what we've got.

Bit of old tat, I said, because I was picking up the way she talked by then.

It was golden, that table, it wasn't black at all. We wiped some polish on, and then we spread out the dusters and sat on them and pulled ourselves up and down the table. Theresa said if my forearms could drive a shine deep into wood, think what my bum could do. We were both laughing, but after a bit she stopped because she was coughing, and it was bad. She didn't like me to notice when she coughed, but this time I brought her a drink of water. She was a funny colour and she was breathing very fast, but not deep.

'People less bone idle than me', she said after a while, 'would have stripped that down and resurfaced it and made a right good job of it. Me, I don't like hard work. If I can get away with a bit of cleaning, I'll do it. Never put off till tomorrow what you can forget about altogether.'

Tomorrow. Back to work, on the bus. Wear gloves, but I wasn't that frightened. Annie had a nasty tongue, and she'd say things, but while I was having my cup of tea that last evening, I thought about Annie and Theresa, face to face; Annie's nasty bits of spite, and Theresa. I used to think Annie was clever because she was on the checkouts. I'll never be on the checkouts, but Annie's not clever. I'm not scared of her spiteful talk, either. Theresa could chew her up and spit her out if it came to talk, and never have to be spiteful at all.

That made me feel better. They never would meet, but Annie would never make me cry again either. When she got spiteful I'd just think, I know somebody who could chew you up and spit you out. You wouldn't know what she was talking about, but you'd know you'd been beaten.

Theresa would be a wonderful arbiter in the Courts of Justice. She'd make people think she liked them, and if somebody like Theresa could like them they weren't too bad. Then they could stop feeling as if everybody hated them and as if they had to stand up for themselves all the time, like that woman in the launderette, *I think I'm next, dear*, so they wouldn't have to quarrel. They could let their disputes go away.

He'd said there were disputes, when I was in the Courts of Justice wearing brown linen and sandals, not the state robes, not the jewels. I was there, and I hardly ever spoke, but I listened.

When you listen, when you listen carefully, it makes people speak carefully. It makes them think carefully about what they're saying. Then it becomes clear. Then you can see what to do.

That's why I hardly ever spoke, but I did listen.

Theresa gives people time to think when she's talking. It's just on the surface, make you smile, make you relax, not distracting, but giving you a bit of time, to get things straight in your mind. Sitting on that pavement with the people having to walk around us, she didn't care when they thought we were drunk. Think what they like, their privilege. What mattered to Theresa was, give Joan a few moments to get herself together again.

Then after that she needed me. Just a minute, her hand on my shoulder because she was shaky, head down. Hide the pain. All right for people to think, she's drunk, she's daft, leaning on that trolley like a silly kid; but not all right for people to think, she's ill.

Stuff that, she'd say, if she said anything at all.

She'd told me she'd got cancer. Bloody cancer, she'd said, gives me the pip. I didn't think many people knew.

Telling me that, it was like she was giving me something. She wasn't looking for sympathy, never that. A secret, more like. Sharing a secret. It could have gone wrong. I could have hurt her, so in a way it showed she trusted me.

Thinking about it, while I stood waiting for the bus, I had a mixture of feelings. I was worried about Theresa, hoping it didn't hurt too much, but at the same time it made me feel sort of warm, that she'd told me something she hated people to know about.

Whenever I was out I thought about Theresa, or I tried to. I tried not to look at people and not to listen to them, so I didn't hear them saying things about a knife. So I didn't see him. If I didn't look I wouldn't see him, and then he wouldn't be there.

I wouldn't be crazy, I said to myself. The Dark Universe doesn't exist. He's locked up safely, he can't get at you. One day I was damned unlucky.

Theresa and me, cleaning bits of furniture. Vinegar, wipe it in gently with the wire wool, not *that* gently, we don't want to spend all day. Wash it and dry it and what have we got? Worth a bit of polish, or hit it with the axe and sell it as kindling?

Old glasses, don't you dare use washing up liquid on those. Do you see the way that *doesn't* shine? We call that bloom. Like you get on those dark purple plums, they call that bloom, too. It's a sign of age. On glasses anyway, I wouldn't know about plums.

'I don't like it,' I'd said. 'I like glass all sparkly.'

The bus was late. My first day back at work. Or maybe it was just me, and Mum making me go a bit early. First day back, Joan, don't want to miss the bus, hurry up. But the man behind me, he kept looking at his watch, and he was sighing. He was getting cross, so the bus must be late.

Can't be helped, if there are road works or an accident or something. It's not the driver's fault.

I had my money for the fare counted out in my pocket, so I wouldn't have to open my purse. I can't count out money with my gloves on. Mum said maybe I could buy some really thin gloves, or those fancy summer ones made of white lace with no fingers in them. I could wear mittens, I thought. My fingers don't look too bad, not if you don't look closely.

But trying to count out money, that was hard. If I just had to put the money on the little scooped-out tray, and take the ticket, I could do that. I hoped I wouldn't drop anything.

Shopping, I could hand over the notes, and then brush the change off the counter, one hand into the other. A bit funny maybe, but not really so anybody would notice, not to remember later. Not so you'd say, I saw a funny thing in the supermarket today.

The man behind me muttered something and I looked up, and the bus was coming. Number seventeen for the seventeen moons, and I will sit where I like, maybe not ten rows back for the ten galaxies. Maybe nine, so one of the galaxies might be lost, might go spinning off, away out into the dark and cloudy skies, like the moons, so I have to go back. If a galaxy is lost, I'll have to go back, for a galaxy.

Crazy talk. He's locked up safe, and there is no Dark Universe.

My money's ready and I'm going to work. *Did you see her hands?*

Gloves. They won't see.

I can see Sarah and Diane; they haven't seen me yet, but I can see them. I'll say good morning as I go past, why not? Been travelling on the same bus for months, why not say good morning? And maybe I'll come and sit near them later. There are the two women. Did you see that on the telly last night?

I've got my money ready.

He's there. He's sitting where he always sits.

No.

He's there. Just damned unlucky. Just damned unlucky.

Grey again, grey jacket. Brown hair, a bit shorter.

'Are you getting on, or what?'

Looking at me, looking at me.

'Look, love, do you mind? Are you getting on, or what?'

Get off. Turn, and . . . sorry, excuse me. Get off. Got a knife, they've sent somebody else, he's back. Sorry, I'm sorry, excuse me. Okay, love, what the hell . . . sorry, excuse me, please. It's him. It is him. Going crazy? Seeing things? It's him, looking at me. That way he looks at me. Walk away.

Can't walk. My hands are hurting. My hands. Sit down then. Think I'm drunk, don't care what they think. Long as they don't know the truth. Going crazy. It's him.

Walking towards me. He's got off the bus too. Going to take me back because the seventeen moons are swirling away out into the dark and cloudy skies, he's come to take me back.

'Told you you'd be sorry.'

Walking past me, but looking back, to where I'm sitting on the pavement. I'm going to cry. I'm going to faint. I feel sick, my hands hurt.

No.

It isn't him. He's locked up safely. Theresa phoned the police, he's in a secure hospital. It's just damned unlucky. Again. Told you you'd be sorry. It isn't him, it isn't him.

I'm going crazy. What am I going to do? Go home. Go home now. Phone, say I'm ill. Got a cold. Going crazy. I'm sorry, Mrs Lovell, I can't come in today, I'm going crazy. I've got a cold. I can't come in today.

It isn't him.

I looked along the road towards him, walking away from me, not turning back. Grey trousers, grey jacket, he used to wear those. But it isn't him, it can't be him, he's locked up, it can't be him.

Told you you'd be sorry.

'Joan? Joan? You all right, Joan? You all right?'

Diane and Sarah were standing over me, and Sarah was rubbing her hands together as if it was cold, looking down at me with her mouth open.

'You all right, Joan? You all right? You fell over? You all right?'

'We missed the bus now.' Diane was wailing, she sounded frightened. 'We missed the bus. What we going to do now?'

Sarah was looking worried too. Still rubbing her hands together, and her mouth was open, asking me, 'You all right? You fell over? What we going to do? We missed the bus.'

'Get another one,' I said. 'It's all right, there'll be another one. We can get that.'

They'd got off their bus to come and help me. It might be difficult for them, getting off at a different stop. They might not know what to do now.

I'd have to help them. We'd have to get another bus and I'd have to go with them.

I got up, and Diane brushed at my coat with her hands, all down the shoulders, even though I'd only been sitting. Sarah helped her, both of them brushing at my coat, as if it was dusty. Can't go to work with a dusty coat.

'You been ill?' asked Sarah. 'Been a long time.'

They didn't look worried any more. I'd said we'd get another bus, so it was all right. I'd said so. Don't have to worry.

'I'm all right now.'

'I like you,' said Diane, and gave me her big, open-mouthed smile. 'We been worried. Thought you were ill. We said, where's Joan? We been worried.'

'We'd better wait at the bus stop,' I said. 'Or they won't know we want to get on. The driver might not stop.'

I didn't want to go to work. I wanted to go home. But Diane and Sarah had seen me get off the bus, and when they'd seen me fall they'd come to help me. I couldn't leave them alone in a street that was strange to them, not knowing how to get to work from there. They'd come to help me, and now they trusted me to help them.

How can I go to work if I'm going crazy?

Just filling shelves. I hope they haven't changed everything around. I hope I can still find my way, with my cage. I hope Carol's there, if they've changed anything. I wonder what the new manager's like. Got to be better than Davie Evans, hasn't he?

'We get the seventeen,' I said. 'It'll go the same way. Every twenty minutes. But your bus was late.'

'Lots of cars in the road,' said Sarah, and she held up her hand. She was still wearing the ring.

'Look.' She was smiling again, not worried any more. 'Pretty.'

I'd have to look for the number. The seventeen and the fourteen and the twenty-eight all come to this stop, and now I'd have to look for the number. Other buses come down this road too, but they don't stop here. I'd have to look.

'Number seventeen?' I asked, and Diane nodded.

There's a one, which is straight up like a flagpole. Any number that doesn't start with a straight up number I don't have to look at. So, that's probably most of them. There are lots of numbers.

And I can ask, just to be sure. Does this bus go to Witham? Lots of people ask, does this bus go to? They ask, it's not stupid, just checking. Don't want to get on the wrong bus.

'Does this bus go to Witham?'

'Yes.'

'Come on then, this is our bus. Come on.'

They followed me, down to the back of the bus because there was an old man sitting on the seat they usually had. So we went right to the back, where the seats go across the back window, five in a row because there's no corridor, and we sat together. Diane pulled her coat tight across her knees, and sat holding it, gripped in her fist.

'Soon be summer,' I said, thinking she wouldn't need her coat then.

'Yes,' she said, and then cleared her throat. 'Nice weather we're having for the time of year.'

'Yes,' I said. 'Nice weather.'

9

Rita met me as I went in, and she gave me a big smile and said it was good to see me. How are you? Feeling okay now?

'Okay,' I said. 'I'm late. The two women on the bus, from the home, I had to . . .'

She patted me on the shoulder. She seemed smaller somehow, but her smile was nice. 'Don't you worry, I'll see Mrs Lovell. I reckon we can write that off, first day back.'

It seemed to be all right after that, but then in the middle of the morning I started to shake. I thought I saw him.

Up till then I'd been busy. I'd been working, and not too much had been changed around, just the cheese because there was a promotion of Dutch cheese, but Carol was doing that. So I was only doing what I always did, the cakes and the jams, and there'd be the bread in the afternoon. Perhaps it was because I didn't have to think too much, so I remembered.

I saw him. And he said, told you you'd be sorry.

But he'd never told me I'd be sorry. He'd never said that.

'You all right, Joan?' asked Carol, and I looked up at her, and she said, 'Bloody hell, you're white as a sheet, look as if you've seen a ghost.'

I felt sick.

'Come on,' said Carol, 'let's go downstairs. You need a sit down and a cup of tea. What's the matter? Your hands hurting?'

I thought, no, they're not hurting. They don't work very well, but they don't hurt much. It's just, I'm going crazy. I'm seeing things. What do you do about that? How do you make yourself well, when you're going crazy?

A couple of aspirins, plenty of hot drinks, get up when you're feeling better.

I started to cry, right there in the shop, hanging on to my cage with my woollen gloves slipping on the metal, and Carol put her arms round me and said again we had to go downstairs for a sit down and a cup of tea. I must have come back to work too soon.

Who would understand, when I said I was going crazy? They make jokes. You're a nutcase. You loony. You're daft.

It's not funny.

The new manager was called Mr Bradwell, and he was quite nice. When we got downstairs I wasn't crying any more, just sniffing a bit, and Carol got me a box of paper hankies off the shelf. He saw, but he didn't say anything. He got me a chair, and said I should just sit quietly until I felt better, and he'd get me a cup of tea.

'Can I have one?' asked Carol, all cheeky, and he smiled. But when he came back there were two paper cups, and he'd brought the sugar separately, and there were two biscuits.

'You can have ten minutes,' he said to Carol, 'unless Miss Ferguson isn't feeling better by then. Come and tell me.'

Then he nodded at me. 'You take as long as you need, Miss Ferguson. No hurry.'

Sitting on the chair in the stores, by the racks of kitchen towels and toilet rolls, all the paper things, it was all so normal. I felt safe there. I wasn't seeing things, it was where I worked, as if nothing had ever happened. And Mr Bradwell was nice. He was old, and a bit fat, and when he smiled it was just polite. He looked at your face, not up and down your body, the way Davie Evans had done.

'He's nice,' I said, and Carol shrugged.

'He's all right. Drink up your tea before it gets cold.'

I couldn't hold the paper cup. It was too small, and when I tried to grip it my fingers went jerky, and I squashed it. The tea splashed all over my lap.

I started to cry again. I hadn't thought about the paper cups, not being able to hold them. I'd only thought about filling the shelves, boxes and jars. I'd thought I could manage them, I hadn't thought about the stupid little paper cups for the coffee, nasty, cheap things. Why couldn't we have proper cups? It wouldn't cost any more.

'I'm *not* drinking my tea out of these *crappy* things,' I said. 'I'm bloody not.'

'You getting all posh in your old age? You got tea all over your skirt. What's up with you anyway?'

I didn't want to think about that. I was angry, because I'd got tea on my skirt, and I blamed the paper cups.

'Why can't they treat us like human beings? Think we're going to walk off with their bloody cups and saucers?'

'You're not. Annie is. So's Christine, so's Trudie, and I'm not that sure about me, neither.'

She was trying to make me laugh, so I smiled at her, but inside I was so angry, and it seemed to be mostly with myself, for spilling the tea.

Mr Bradwell came to the door of his office.

'Is everything all right?'

'She can't hold these paper cups. She's spilt her tea.'

He went away again, and I grabbed a whole handful of the paper tissues and rubbed at my skirt. The tea was on the overall too, but I didn't mind that. Rinse out and dry if you blow at it, that was what Rita said about the overalls, but they were nasty and cheap too, and they made me sweat. I'd forgotten the overalls, and the flimsy paper cups that seemed to be half paper, half plastic, and the stirrers, all the things I hadn't liked about Fletchers. Even if I couldn't use my special cup and saucer at home we had china mugs, or cups and saucers. I didn't know anybody who used these horrible things at home.

'I wouldn't feed animals off plastic,' I said.

When Mr Bradwell came back he had another cup of tea for me, and this time the paper cup was in a plastic holder, with a handle. It was still plastic, but I managed to push a finger through the handle, and then I could hold it, half balanced.

'Do you feel the cold?' he asked. 'Do you have to wear those gloves?'

'It's the scars,' explained Carol, and he looked a bit cross with her.

'I think you could go back to work now, Miss Crooks,' he said. 'If Miss Ferguson's feeling better.'

Carol tried to get huffy with him, said she wanted to stay with me, but he made her go. So she went back up to the shop. Carol never really minds if she loses an argument, she doesn't get snotty about it the way Annie does, and she'd never complain. She just forgets it.

'You can keep the holder,' said Mr Bradwell. 'You'll need it in the canteen.'

He looked up into the big steel rafters over our heads, as if he could see something interesting up there.

'I doubt if the scars are as bad as you think,' he said, and he sounded all vague. 'Try not to let it worry you.'

'Easy to say,' I thought, but maybe I said it aloud, because he looked at me, and then away again before he went on.

'My wife got her face burned in a bonfire accident. You hardly notice anything when she's wearing make-up. But she hates going out. It's a shame, it's spoilt her life. I don't think anybody would notice.'

I didn't know if he was talking about me or his wife with that last bit, but in my lunch-hour I went into the ladies and I took the gloves off and looked at my hands, trying to think what it would be like if I saw them for the first time. There were some scars, but it was mostly that I couldn't move them properly. When I tried to move them, they looked clumsy.

That night when I got home I didn't say anything about seeing the man on the bus. I didn't know what to say. I'd never told Mum and Sheila about thinking I'd seen him outside Tesco's. But I asked Sheila about the gloves.

'I think they make people look at your hands more,'

she said. '"Why's she wearing gloves indoors?" they'd think.'

When I'd first been in hospital my hands had been very ugly, but then they'd been swollen, the nails all blackened. My fingers had looked like rotten sausages. I suppose because I'd seen them every day I hadn't really noticed them getting better.

'I can't *hold* things,' I said, and I began to feel angry again. 'I squashed the cup when Mr Bradwell brought me some tea because I was feeling funny. My hands went all jerky and it got all squashed. Fucking paper cups, why do we have to drink our tea out of fucking paper cups?'

'Language,' said Sheila, but she was looking worried. 'Come on, our Joanie? That's easy. Take your own mug in, tell the buggers. Tell them, can't hold those bloody things, not since my . . . not since my trouble with my hands. Fletchers are being all right, aren't they? No trouble?'

Everybody had been very kind. Well, everybody in the office, in the management. Carol had said it was just my rights, but I didn't think it was just my rights when Mr Kennedy came down specially and said I should tell Mr Bradwell if there was anything I found difficult, and it was nice to have me back. It hadn't been just my rights when Mrs Lovell had winked at me at lunch so I knew Rita had sorted it out about me being late. That cup of tea from Mr Bradwell wasn't my rights either.

'Joanie?'

Trudie and Hazel had been whispering in the lunch-break, and Annie had said something about, don't you say nothing nasty, she's my best friend, and then she'd given me a big nasty smile, all sarky. I knew she was talking about the newspaper piece, when she'd got a hundred pounds for lying about being my best friend, and Carol had been angry. Rita had looked cross with Annie, but she hadn't said anything. I thought of Theresa then. Before I knew Theresa I'd have been upset about Annie and Trudie and Hazel whispering about me, but I thought, I know somebody who could chew lumps out of you three, or maybe not even notice you, not even bother. It made me feel better.

I pushed the handles of the knife and fork into the slits Sheila had made in my gloves, and I didn't look at them to see if they were staring at me.

You're just stupid, I thought.

'Why don't you take a mug in to work?' asked Sheila again, and I said I would.

'That one with the teddy bear on it,' I said.

'Isn't that a bit babyish?'

'Sod them.'

I couldn't be bothered with thinking about it. When you're going crazy you have to be careful what you think about. Maybe you haven't got very much time left when you'll be able to think at all, so you have to think about things that matter, not about three stupid tarts who think they're clever because they're on the check-outs. I bet they don't know you have to look at the shape of silver under the ornaments. I bet they don't know old-fashioned cabinet-makers put soft wood under tables so the woodworm wouldn't get into the good stuff.

Maybe when you're going crazy you use up the best bits of your brain. You mustn't waste them. You have to think about good things while you can.

Told you you'd be sorry.

I was sorry. I was sorry I was going crazy. I was seeing

things that couldn't be there. Unless maybe the hospital had made a mistake, and they had let him out, after all. Got the papers muddled up, let the wrong person out. Might that have happened?

It did happen, papers did get muddled up. Delivery notes got muddled up in the stores, so nobody knew if the right amount had been sent. Run out of Tate and Lyle, sent Silver Spoon instead, that's not what it says down here, that's not my fault, I just load up the lorry, how can I sign this when it's all wrong, that's your problem, mate.

How can we let out John Smith when it says Nicholas Parry here, that's your problem, mate.

Paperwork had happened with Dad, they'd said. A mistake on the paperwork, they'd said.

There wasn't much paper in the Dark Universe. We didn't seem to need it so much.

'You dreaming, Joanie?'

'What about gloves, then?' I said. 'What about knives and forks and suchlike?'

'Wrap a couple of rubber bands round your hands. That'll hold them.'

But I wanted to wear gloves when I went out. It was daft, I knew that. Out in the street nobody was going to look at my hands. Nobody knew there was anything to look at.

'If it makes you happier,' said Sheila.

Was I going to be seeing things again, on the bus?

'Got to go in early tomorrow,' I said. 'Early delivery, see? And they're running out of some of the stuff on the shelves. So they asked me to go in a bit early.'

If they've sent somebody else to take me back, will he know I've gone in early? Will he be on the earlier bus?

I had to look at the numbers. One and seven, that's an upright like a flagpole, and then two lines joined up making a corner. That's not so hard, I can do that. I can remember that from school, and anyway I can do numbers. It's not so hard. Just a straight up, and the two lines making a corner.

'Does this bus go to Witham?'

'It does, my love, and right out the other side, too.'

Sarah and Diane might wonder what had happened to me, but they'd be all right. I didn't think they'd worry.

I sat three seats back, alongside a woman reading a book, an old woman with an umbrella stuck between her knees. The seat opposite was empty. There's nothing with threes in the Dark Universe, and there was nobody to see a signal.

He wasn't there.

The woman with the book looked at me, and then she leaned forward and looked at the empty seat opposite, and looked at me again. She might as well have said it. Why don't you sit over there, instead of squashing up against me?

Fair enough, I thought, so I moved over to the other side and I sat by the window and looked out.

Nobody was talking on this bus. Nobody said anything. Nothing to listen to. It was boring.

But he wasn't there.

I can't always come in early, I thought. And anyway, if they've sent somebody else, it won't be long before he finds out.

Crazy.

Seeing things, or thinking things about some weird place that doesn't exist, that has dark and cloudy skies, both crazy, but if I am going crazy it doesn't matter what

I think about. I might as well think about a place where I was important, and I could do what I wanted. There were gardens and woods and green grass. Bright pavilions for the summer games. Brilliant colours, he'd said, and people from all over the universe had come to compete. I'd worn state robes then, and the Star of Justice on my forehead. I could have competed. Wrestling, he'd said, and I thought that was very odd. Wrestling? But he'd said I could have been in the team, if I'd wanted.

I didn't know about wrestling. I don't want to wrestle, all sweaty and rolling around trying to pin somebody down or hurt them. I'd seen it on the telly sometimes. Not women, though.

But the green grass under the dark skies, and the brilliant colours at the summer games, I'd like to see that. I'd like to be there then. Like a great big party, with everybody having fun. I'd like that.

If I'm going crazy anyway, I can dream about it.

'You're early,' said Mr Bradwell, and I thought, you too, then. He seemed to expect me to explain, so I told him I wanted to take a look round and see if anything had changed while I was away. So I could find things, not waste time looking.

'Excellent,' he said, and then, 'I wasn't criticising, Miss Ferguson.'

So I wandered up and down the rows in the store, just looking, and there wasn't anything much different. There was just more in the freezers now summer was coming, more ice-cream and frozen fruit.

But I can't come in early every day.

What will I do, if I come in at the right time, and he's on the bus again?

Pretend he's not there. Don't look at him. Say good

morning to Diane and Sarah, and maybe even sit near them, and talk to them. Pretend he's not there. After all, he isn't, is he? You're just seeing things, maybe going crazy.

I tried very hard not to look when I got on the bus the next day, but I couldn't help it, and he was there. He was watching for me. I said good morning to Diane and Sarah, and I walked down the bus to the end, where I'd always sat before, behind the two women, and they turned and looked at me, sort of wriggling in their seats so they could see. Then they looked at each other, and the older one nodded to her friend. Then she whispered something, and the other one nodded, too.

'I think we'd better just act natural,' she whispered.

He was different. He kept turning his head to look at me. I wouldn't look back, but every time the bus stopped, I wondered if somebody would sit where he was sitting, right on top of him, and then I'd know he wasn't there. I'd know I was seeing things.

Same clothes, though. Grey, and a tie.

At the station I walked right past him to go and sit at the front with Sarah and Diane, and I didn't look at him. Does it matter, if I look at him? I thought. Does it matter? Will he know, if he's not there?

I started to feel really muddled then, so I just sat down by Sarah and Diane.

'Did you get to work all right?' I asked, and they both said yes.

'We were late,' said Sarah. 'Twenty minutes. Mrs Arkon was waiting at the bus stop. We told her you fell over. We told her.'

'Was she cross?'

'No.' But Sarah didn't sound as if she was sure.

'You all right now?' asked Diane.

'Yes.'

He was there, and he was watching.

Somebody, please go and sit on top of him. Then I'll know. It was the worst thing of all, not really knowing. Is this somebody else? Have they sent somebody else? Or have they let him out by mistake? Or am I going crazy?

That evening I went into Theresa's shop. It was quite warm, so she'd left the shop door open, propped with a kitchen chair, but she was still wearing a sweater and a cardigan, and she looked so thin. Grey, too, even though her hair was brown. But there wasn't much hair on her head. You could see skin through it. Her skin was grey, on her face.

She'd told me her secret. Bloody cancer, gives me the pip, she'd said.

'I'm going crazy.'

It's *not funny*.

'Tell me,' she said.

I told her, he's on the bus in the mornings, sitting in the same place, and he looks at me. First time I saw him, I got off, and I fell over, and he walked past me and said, told you you'd be sorry. Same clothes this time, grey. So, I'm seeing things, because he's locked up, isn't he? Or did they make a mistake with the papers? Let the wrong one out, because they'd filled in the forms all wrong, like on the delivery notes when they send something in place of what they haven't got.

'Bloody bleeding hell,' she said, really quietly, looking out of the window with that look on her face, thinking as hard as she can.

I just sat, waiting. I didn't know what she was going to say. It didn't matter much; I was just sharing a secret, like she had with me. That was all. Because I liked her, it was a bit like a present. This is my secret.

'Did you ever see him with anybody else? Before he kidnapped you?'

It had been so long since she'd spoken I didn't understand what she meant. I looked at her, but she was waiting, so I thought, and then I realised.

'I don't know. I never took much notice of him.'

She was quiet again for a long time, and then she asked, 'Why don't you notice men, Joan? Nicholas Parry's quite good-looking, by all accounts. I've never heard you talk about men. Not even pop singers or film stars, no one.'

I shrugged, but she wasn't going to let it go, so I said, 'I don't think I ever saw him with anybody. It was only on the bus. He was by himself, unless it got crowded. Then, you know, anybody sits down. Where there's a seat.'

'Why don't you notice men, Joan?'

Because. Because what? Because they're more trouble than they're worth, always trying to get into your knickers, only think of one thing, all the things they say about men in the canteen. Only they never stop talking about men, so maybe they're not more trouble than they're worth, not if they never stop talking about them.

But I don't want to.

In the pub, when they put their arm round my shoulder, I just say, don't, and they don't. They don't any more. Just a joke sometimes. Going to make me lucky, Joanie? Lucky Eric, out the back with Carol, going to make *me* lucky, Joanie?

Don't.

Don't, Theresa. Don't want to. Don't want to talk about it, either.

Mum used to say, when I was on early shifts, poor Joan, got to get up at six. But I never minded. On the bus, when there were the three women before Vicky died, and him, and the two women who talked, and a few others, but not many. Late shift, or afternoons, it was crowded. Some regulars, I'd look for them when the bus came so I'd know it was the right bus and not have to look at the numbers. Mostly they were people going shopping, lots of people. Sometimes you couldn't get a seat until the station. Then you'd be all scrunched up in your seat because of people coming in on the trains and catching the bus, no room, sometimes I thought I could hardly breathe. Somebody fat beside you, with shopping, and people standing, all leaning over you. I hated that. I'd sooner get up early and have a seat to myself and not be squashed up into the corner, thinking maybe I'd never get out at my stop because of all the people between me and the door.

'Anything else, apart from seeing him?' asked Theresa.

'What he said. About he'd told me I'd be sorry. But he never did say that. He never did say I'd be sorry.'

Somebody came into the shop, and Theresa went out to meet her. I sat at the table, listening to her talking about bookends. Staffordshire she said, and, yes, she knew about the chip, that was why they were cheap.

Sometimes she wasn't very nice to her customers. She didn't seem to care. Going to buy it or just look at it? The ones she knew she was all right with, let them wander around looking.

'If he wants it he'll be back,' she'd said. 'If he doesn't I've stopped him wasting my time.'

'When you said you're going crazy, is there anything else? I mean, any other reason?'

So I told her about the Dark Universe, what he'd said, and how I used to think about it. I'd think about the Courts of Justice, with the people who came for help in their disputes. I wasn't sure what a dispute was, but they had to come to the Courts of Justice when they had them. It was mostly what he'd said about the Courts of Justice, and the summer games, and then at the end of the day yesterday, I'd been really tired. I'd thought about the brown pools and the silver fish, and the soapweed, because my overall had made me sweat. While I was washing my hands in the ladies I'd thought, it would be nice. The soapweed, and being in the pool with the fish. He'd said the water was brown, but I'd never thought that meant it was dirty.

'He said he'd come to take me back because of the seventeen moons. They were going away. Sometimes you could see them all, he said. But they were sort of sliding away, so I had to go back. To stop them, I suppose. He didn't say. I was the Empress of the Dark Universe, and he had to take me back.

'So sometimes I think, maybe now they've locked him up, somebody else will come to take me back. And I think about the Dark Universe. There's no such place, but I keep thinking about it. It's like, I know it's not there, but there are these pictures in my mind all about it.'

There were shadows on the table from the things Theresa had on the window ledge, and she was tracing them on the wood with her fingers. After I'd stopped talking she got up and turned on the lights, and then she came back and sat down again.

'When I was a child we used to go on holiday to Ireland,' she said. 'My mother's best friend was Irish, and she had a farm in Kilkenny. I used to spend all the year looking forward to summer, because we'd go to Ireland. Then Sally moved. She came to England, so there were no more holidays in Ireland.

'I went back about ten years ago. It took me two days to find the farm. It was much smaller than I remembered, it was full of rubbish heaps, and there was a dead cat on the wall. Horrible. A man came out and told me to go away. He wasn't Irish. Italian or Spanish, I think. I still think about the farm. I dream about it, but my dreams are what I remembered before I went back and found out the truth. Huge fields, I dream about them, not the nasty little paddocks with barbed wire and bits of old broken wood.'

She started to cough again. She'd been talking for too long.

Later she said, 'Daydreams aren't hallucinations. We'd all be in padded cells if they were.'

There were things she wanted to tell me, but talking made her cough, and coughing hurt.

'Disputes are disagreements,' she said when I was helping her put things away for the night. 'The wall in the yard at the back is mine. I have to look after it. The man next door built a cold frame against it and made it damp. Now it's got to be repaired. I think he should pay some of it, and he won't. That's a dispute.'

She'd been quite quiet all afternoon. I asked her, is something bothering you, Theresa?

'This bastard on the bus bothers me,' she answered, but then she started coughing again, and she had to sit down.

I began to feel a bit frightened. She'd never been this bad. I got her a glass of water, and she drank some of it.

She was sort of red under the grey of her skin and her eyes were watering, very close to crying.

'You got any medicine?' I asked.

'Cigarette and a taxi home.'

She dialled the number of the taxi, and I told them to come, and where to take her.

'Touch him,' she said while we were waiting. 'Tomorrow, touch him. Then tell me. Solid? Or did your hand go right through?'

'Don't talk. It hurts.'

She didn't say anything else, but she was looking at me, so I said okay, I'll touch him, and she nodded.

The idea of touching him made me feel sick, but I'd promised.

I'll brush against him, I thought. I'll pretend to lose my balance. Or I'll drop something.

What do I touch? His shoulder? His arm?

I don't want to. I don't want to.

The taxi came, so I locked up and dropped the keys into her pocket, and then I held her arm to help her get in. She was still that strange colour I'd never seen before, but she grinned at me through the window as the taxi drove away, and I think she waved, but I'm not sure.

10

I meant to touch him as I walked past him to my seat, but I couldn't. I was going to brush his shoulder with my hand, like an accident. I was going to turn round to look back down the bus as if I'd seen something, and my hand was going to swing out, and brush against his shoulder. An accident.

I had it all planned. It wouldn't be so difficult, I thought, and anyway, what could he do? I wouldn't hurt him, just brush my hand against his shoulder. Theresa had said, touch him. Solid or does your hand go right through?

'Good morning,' I said to Diane and Sarah, and they both said good morning back, smiling at me. They liked it, somebody speaking to them in that way. I knew it made them feel comfortable, and safe. It was so easy to be nice to them; just a glass ring from a cracker, sit and talk, and it made them happy.

Walk past, turn and look back, hand swing out, brush against his shoulder, and I walked on right past him, looking through the window at the back. I couldn't. Sorry, Theresa, I can't touch him. I can't do it.

At the station I walked past him again, and I told myself, turn and look back, and brush against him. I didn't. I walked on and I sat down by Diane and Sarah, and I asked what they were doing on their holidays this year. I'd been thinking, ever since I got on the bus, what shall I ask them?

'We go to Brighton,' said Diane. 'We go on a bus and we stay in a place near the sea. We go on the beach and we can swim. We go for walks.'

Can't touch him, I thought, but I was listening to them telling me about Brighton. Everybody from the home went for a week. It was their holiday. It was the same every year, and they liked it.

When all the people came out from the station, I got up and I went back to my seat. No signals, I thought as he looked at me. Don't look at him. Don't sit anywhere near him. Don't touch him, I can't.

I can't touch anybody, I thought. But him especially, I can't.

Just as the bus was starting somebody came running up, so the driver slowed, and the man jumped on. Thanks, mate, he said, and he came down the bus, and he sat beside him.

'Anybody sitting here, mate?'

I watched. Somebody else could see him. And where they sat together, his sleeve was sort of creased, crumpled up his arm because there wasn't room.

Somebody else had seen him, and touched him, and he was solid.

I thought about it all day, wondering what it meant. He'd been let out, or they'd sent somebody else.

I'd like to see the Dark Universe. I'd like to touch the star flowers, and bathe in the brown pools with the silver fish. I wondered if I'd had friends there, and what we did together. I'd never asked, and he'd never said. He'd told me things I did, what I wore, places I knew, but he'd never said anything about friends, and I'd never asked him any questions at all. I'd like friends.

We'd walk on the green grass. At the summer games we'd be in a pavilion, and we'd sit together to watch. We'd talk about things. What would the Empress talk about with her friends? I'd be like Theresa, half joking, but I might know a lot. I could talk about all sorts of things if I knew a lot. I could find out. Like the shape of good silver, and soft wood for the woodworm. I could find out more; I could talk about all that with my friends. What's the best sort of soft wood to go with oak? Is it different from the one that goes with rosewood?

Annie broke my teddy bear mug, but Rita got me another one from the shelves, not teddy bear, but with a pattern on it. Break that one, she said to Annie, and I'll get it stopped off your wages, and don't think I can't.

Interfering old bag, said Annie. Only an accident.

I looked at the bottom of the mug the way Theresa did when she had china to check, but the writing was all in a circle. Anyway, it was only a supermarket mug, not going to be Rockingham or Chelsea, was it?

Even though she broke my mug Annie wasn't worrying me much. She left me alone mostly, after she'd made the nasty remarks about the papers and being my best friend. I thought it might be because I wasn't noticing her any more, I didn't care about Annie, but Carol said, Annie's not as nasty to you as she used to be, is she? So I knew it was true. And I knew it was because I didn't care. Now she couldn't upset me she'd given up.

Carol asked me if I wanted to go the pictures that

Friday, but I said no. There wasn't anything on I wanted to see. She went on at me a bit, said it would do me good.

'I don't want to,' I said.

I was beginning to think Carol only wanted me to go out with her because going into the pub on her own was a bit obvious. Going in with a friend, it looks like you're having a drink together, just sociable. Going in on your own, unless you're meeting somebody, that's different. Either you're an alcoholic or you're looking for a man.

I felt a bit sad after I'd thought that. I'd thought Carol was my friend, and then I wasn't so sure. It's not like being a friend, when you use somebody. And I worked out that she must owe me a lot for coffee by now. You get this lot, I'll buy you one Friday – I reckon she said that nearly every week.

'I don't want to,' I said.

I'd rather spend the time with Theresa, I could learn things from her. Maybe one day I'd be able to talk like her, like I wasn't having to think at all, I knew it all so well. That would be great, to be able to do that.

But the shop was always shut when I went past in the evenings.

Every day he was on the bus, looking at me. But it got easier. I could just think, either he's there and something's gone wrong, or he's not and I'm seeing things. Nothing else seems too bad. So, might as well get on with things, take no notice.

And think about the Dark Universe, what it would be like. It's only like day-dreaming, there's no harm. I'd have friends, and they'd like me. Not just for being the Empress, they'd like me anyway. We'd go for walks together.

I couldn't really think about what you'd do with friends in the Dark Universe. He'd never said they had the pictures, or even the telly. I had the idea it was a bit like in history lessons, 'Olden Times' they used to call it. But not all like that. There'd be proper doctors, and they'd know how to heal Theresa.

Touch him, Theresa had said, but I couldn't.

It's so personal, touching somebody. I can shake hands, no problem. Somebody bumps into you, accidentally, I don't think anything about that. But reaching out your hand, and touching somebody, on purpose, that's personal. I don't like that.

I said to Sheila, 'There's a man on the bus looks just like Nicholas Parry.'

'Oh, yes?'

'Bothers me,' I said.

She asked me, 'Does he speak to you? Does he come and sit by you?'

'Just looks at me.'

'You're a pretty girl. Blokes look.'

I wanted to say, same clothes. Same seat, where he used to be. Not just a bit similar, Sheila. Could be him, it really could. What should I do?

I started to dream again, not the same dreams, but they worried me. I didn't want to go to sleep at nights. People, people I knew, all saying, 'Shall we go now? Would you like to go now? It's time to go now.' All words like that. Carol, and Mr Kennedy, in my dreams I'd be with them, doing anything, and they'd turn and look at me and ask that question. 'Shall we go now?'

What they meant was, shall I kill you now?

What should I do about the man on the bus?

Then Theresa's shop was open, and I went in and

there were two men in there. One of them looked up.

'Sorry, love, it's not open for business.

'Where's Theresa?' I asked, and the other one put down his papers and asked me if I was a friend.

'Yes. Where is she?'

'Bad news,' he said. 'Sorry. She didn't make it.'

She's dead. I only knew her such a little time, and now she's dead. My good friend who helped me, and I never even managed to touch him like she asked me, and now she's dead and I'll never see her again.

'Want to sit down?' the first man asked.

I wanted to think, and I didn't even seem to have the words for that. I should be able to think about this. I was just angry. Why? There was so much you could have told me. I could have been like you, if you'd stayed. Now I just know a little bit. I know just enough to know what I can't have.

It's not fair. I thought you liked me. I thought you'd help me.

Who can I tell about the man on the bus now?

'Sit down, love. You've had a shock. I'm sorry, I didn't know she was a close friend. Come on, sit down. Do you want a cup of tea?'

'Coffee.'

'Right. Tea's best for shock, but I suppose you know what you want.'

I wanted to tell him, the green and blue mug with the big handle, but he was being kind enough, making me a coffee. Telling him might have been bossy.

Oh, Theresa. You never said. You never said it was that bad. I didn't know. I thought you'd come back.

'That's right, love, you have a little cry. Feel better then.'

'She was telling me about things. I was learning.'

'Are you Joan Ferguson?'

'Yes.'

'She's mentioned you. She told me a bit about you. I'm her nephew. My name's Paul, Paul Harringdon.'

'Pleased to meet you.'

What was there to smile about, then? I was only being polite. He wasn't like Theresa. He was all snooty, with a posh accent, thought he was better than other people. Theresa hadn't been like that. It was me who thought Theresa's better than me. Not her. She didn't care. She told me things because she knew I was interested. Sometimes she'd say things, as if she was telling me something I already knew, maybe I'd forgotten, just for the moment. I knew, afterwards, when I thought about what she'd said, it was her way of telling me something I ought to know and didn't, without making it seem like she was better than me.

Paul wouldn't be like that. Paul wouldn't care if he made me feel stupid and ignorant. Theresa never made me feel stupid.

'She left you five hundred pounds. You can't have it right away, the will's got to be proved. But it's there.'

He looked at the other man, and said something about get on with the lists; not like he was in charge, telling somebody what to do, more like he was saying he was sorry that he wasn't helping.

I was in the way. He wanted me to go away.

I looked around the shop. I'd helped polish those chairs. I'd stuck down some of those frayed bits of rush that made the seats. Up on the shelf were the glasses Theresa had said you mustn't wash with detergent, looking sort of dusty even though I knew they were clean.

151

In that corner cupboard where the other man had put down his papers there was vinegar and wire wool, and now I knew how to clean dirty wood, so you didn't have to strip all the polish off and start all over again.

Five hundred pounds? I could hardly even think about five hundred pounds. I earned it every month, gross they called it, but what with the taxes and the money for the social, and what I gave Mum, and the bus fares and a bit every week for the mail-order catalogue we used for clothes, I never had more than a bit in my pocket. And now he'd said, five hundred pounds.

'Do you take sugar?'

'Yes, please.'

It was Theresa's own blue and white mug he gave me. I knew she wouldn't mind, she wasn't like that. But still.

'That blue and green mug,' I said. 'By the sink, that one. Can I have it?'

'For your coffee? Why didn't you ask before I made it?'

'No. To keep.'

One of his eyebrows went up. Cheek, he was thinking.

'I'll pay for it,' I offered. Theresa would have given it to me.

'I'm not sure what it's worth, I'm afraid.'

'Nothing,' I said. I was disgusted. Theresa's nephew, and he was pig ignorant. Lord Snooty, mouthful of marbles and nothing in his head. 'It came free with the mustard.'

'I beg your pardon?'

'In the supermarkets.' I'd have to explain to him, stupid berk. 'Full of mustard, see? Buy the mustard, the mug comes free.'

'Why do you want it, then?'

Because, I wanted to say. Just because. I didn't know

how to say it. Like something you bring back from a holiday, only more important. Souvenir? Sitting at this table with Theresa, looking at a vase. Cut glass, or moulded? Run your thumb down that bit. Not hard. Now, this bowl. Can you feel a difference? One feels lumpy, one feels rough. A bit like testing the blade of a knife, you now how to do that? Ah, well, what you don't do is press your thumb against it; it might be like a bloody razor and then you've got to find the plaster. Brush your thumb across the blade, lightly, and if it feels rough it's sharp. Do that with glass. Now, the bowl.

'The vase is rough,' I said, and she smiled. Cut glass, she said, the bowl's moulded.

I'm not going to tell you why I want it, Lord Snooty, I thought. None of your business, mouthful of marbles.

The other man said, 'She's right, Paul. I remember that promotion. It's only cheap Staffordshire ware. You'd get about ten pence for it.'

'Of course you can have it, dear.'

Oh, yes? Suddenly started to think I'm not bad looking?

'Mrs Harringdon did have your address, didn't she, dear? She wrote it in her will. I hope she got it right? For when we contact you about the legacy?'

Oh ho. Oh, yes. Theresa knew where I lived, but I'm not so sure I want you to know.

'Better go,' I said. 'My mum will worry if I'm late. Can I have the mug, then?'

The other man reached across to the sink and took it. He handed it over to me, just a quick, nice smile, nothing said. I wondered who he was.

'Theresa's dead,' I said to Mum as I went in, and she looked at me with her mouth open, and then started on.

Oh, dear. How sad. That was sudden, wasn't it? I didn't want to listen. And I didn't want to hear her tell me I shouldn't say 'dead' like that. It's shocking. It's nicer if you say 'passed over' or something. Say what you mean, Theresa used to say. Bugger all that faffing around.

I ran upstairs and I lay down on my bed, and I said out loud, 'Theresa's dead.' I had to make myself understand it. Not just hear it and know it, but believe it. And not feel angry about it. It wasn't her fault, why should I be angry with her for dying?

I loved you, Theresa. Stuff your bloody five hundred pounds, I wish you hadn't gone. I'd give five hundred pounds to learn what you could teach me. I'd give everything.

Who am I going to tell about the man on the bus now? Who can I tell? Theresa would have listened. Bloody hell, Joan, that's odd. That is very odd, she would have said. And then she would have thought about it.

I could have said, he doesn't just look like him, he looks at me in the same way, wears the same clothes, sits in the same seat.

Tomorrow, I will touch him. I will. I won't think about it, because I'll get all upset and worried, I'll just do it.

'Cup of tea, Joan,' Mum called up the stairs, so I called back, coming, and I thought, I should be crying for Theresa.

Hurts too much to cry. It really does hurt, like being hit with an axe, this one. When I understand it, I'm going to miss you. But I will touch him, because you said so.

I did. The next morning, I didn't let myself think about it. I remembered the time I was learning to ride my bike, when Dad said he'd only let go of the saddle when I said so. I knew then, if I thought about it I wouldn't dare.

So I said, let go then, not thinking about it, and then I was on my own, riding down the path in the park and I was hardly wobbling at all.

On the bus, don't think about it, walk along and then turn round, and my hand swung against his shoulder, and it was hard and solid. He jumped, he wasn't expecting that, and he looked up at me, almost angry.

'Sorry,' I said, and I thought, now you bloody answer. I've said sorry, you answer. And I looked straight at him, I pictured myself slapping his face because I was starting to feel angry, too.

'*Sorry.*'

'All right.'

Who are you, then? Different voice. He wouldn't have said that. He would have said, '*That's* all right.' He would have smiled, not looked away out of the window. Nicholas Parry's locked up safely, you're not Nicholas Parry.

Tell Theresa. Theresa's dead, but think about telling her as if she wasn't. If he's not Nicholas Parry, who the bloody hell is he, and what's he playing at?

He'd only ever spoken to me twice, and the first time I was so shocked I hadn't really noticed. I remembered what he'd said though. The second card that came when I was in hospital, the one I put in my dressing gown pocket to stop the nurse giving it to the police. It might still be there.

I looked for it that night. It was still in my dressing gown pocket, a bit crumpled from where I'd pushed the dressing gown into the cupboard – a card with a rose on the front, and the printed words inside.

If Nicholas Parry is locked up you'll be sorry.

Told you you'd be sorry, he'd said.

Theresa would have gone to the police. That first time she'd phoned them, she'd never even thought twice about it. She was the sort who thought, that's what they're there for. She'd think, I pay their wages. Or maybe not, maybe she wouldn't think like that. But this, oh yes. This is for the police.

They would have listened to her. She had the sort of voice policemen listen to. She knew all the words. But when I tried to think what Theresa might say I couldn't. I could think how it might sound, her talking quickly, telling them what had happened, and then I thought how it would be if I went to them and said, there's a man on the bus, and they'd look at me, and I'd start to feel stupid and not know what to say next.

Take the card.

Intimidating witnesses, the nurse had said, can't have that.

The policewoman who'd written my statement looked at the card and asked when it had come. When I was in hospital, I said, and she asked so why bring it now? It's a bit late, isn't it?

If Theresa was here she'd make her listen.

'There's a man looks like him.'

'Yes?'

'On the bus. Looks like him. Looks at me like he did.'

I could feel myself getting stupid, and getting angry. Stop looking at me like that, all bored, and like it's a bit funny. I'm trying to tell you.

'He said that. Said, told you you'd be sorry. He said it.'

'When was this, then?

Think. How do I tell her this?

'First time he was on the bus. When I fell over.'

It was no good. I tried to tell her, but she asked all the

156

wrong questions, I never had time to think. Why did you fall over? Was that the first time you saw him? What about that time at Tesco's, did he say anything then? How can you be sure that was what he said, after all this time?

I did try, but she wouldn't listen. Same clothes, I said, but Nicholas Parry only wore ordinary clothes. It's not against the law to look like him, and I'd just fallen over, I could have misheard.

'It's the way he looks at me.'

'You're a pretty girl.'

I didn't mean that, stupid. I don't mean look in *that* way. I know how men look at you when they fancy you, I don't mean that. I mean that way with his head a bit tilted, just like Nicholas Parry.

'Let me know if he does anything,' she said as I went out, but I knew I might as well not bother.

Theresa, you could have taught me how to make people listen. I could have learned the words from you. I'll never know now. Damn.

Bloody cops. Bloody fucking cops.

What am I going to do?

He had the knife the next day. He took it out of his pocket and he opened it and he looked at me to make sure I saw. Red handle, I saw it.

I asked Mr Bradwell, can I come in earlier?

'Why?' he asked, but not nasty.

'There's a man on the bus, he's bothering me.'

I can say it, if I don't think how to. It's when I think too hard I get muddled. It was like touching him. When I thought about it I couldn't do it. I can only do things when I don't think too much.

Mr Bradwell was looking at me as if he was surprised. 'Doesn't the driver stop him?'

I can't talk about this. What can the driver do? He's not breaking the rules, not so far as I can tell. There's a list of rules written up on the bus, but I bet it doesn't say you can't look like Nicholas Parry, and you can't sit where he sat and you can't have a knife like he did, with a red handle.

'I can't give you overtime. There's no extra work.'

I don't want the overtime, I thought. I just want not to be on that bus with him.

'That's all right.'

'I don't see why not then, Miss Ferguson.'

'Ta. Thanks, Mr Bradwell.'

He wasn't the sort to come breathing down your neck like Davie Evans, but Davie Evans never spotted Tracey breaking the boxes on the frozen stuff so she could have it cheap, and Mr Bradwell did. Tracey got a written warning. We didn't run out of stuff so often either, and there wasn't a muddle every time there was a coupon offer, with customers complaining about us not having them in stock like they were in other supermarkets.

When I came in early the next morning Mr Bradwell was already there, and he looked as if he'd been there quite a while. He was drawing something on squares on a clipboard. He said good morning, and he asked if I'd like to take part in a project.

I didn't know what he meant, so I looked at him, not like I was being stupid, but as if I wanted him to explain.

It was about loading up the cages so we didn't have to spend so long doing it. All the things we used most, have them nearest the door and the lift, and the things we didn't use so much, furthest away. Save time. And things like the bottles of washing-up stuff, that were heavy, shouldn't be up on the top shelves. Light stuff up on the top shelves, heavy stuff lower down, where it was easier to carry.

I thought, he's going to change the storeroom around so I'll never find anything. I'll have to read all the boxes. I can't, I'll never manage. Not everything in the stores.

'We'll do it just a bit at a time,' he said, and I thought, how is it everybody knows what I'm thinking these days? It's weird, I don't like it. Only time people don't know is when I'm trying to explain.

'What do I have to do?'

He said I should write down everything I loaded, so he could check which came most often. And anything that was difficult, or too heavy.

'Can't I just tell you?'

Davie Evans would have said no, write it down, Dozey. Do what I tell you, don't argue. Mr Bradwell said something about whichever I'd prefer.

'Olive oil,' I said. 'That's dead heavy, and the steps are always at the other end of the store. Could do with another set of steps. Takes ages, dragging them things back down here. And that bleach, Fletchers' own brand, that's heavy too, and it leaks. Get it all over your hands, there's always at least one in the box split.'

I wanted to go on telling him, but he said we should go into the office so he could write it down. It was easy, I don't see why he needed it all written down. I could remember what I had trouble lifting, what I used to think when I had to go all the way to the end of the stores just for a carton of tea bags, when we use them up every two days. And the milk, always dripping down so it ran under the racks with the toilet rolls, and you couldn't get at it to mop it up, stinks in summer, that does. And if they run out of pallets there's the toilet rolls

159

on the floor, and the milk runs into them, then there's the best part of a carton to chuck out.

He was writing as fast as he could, and sometimes he said, just a minute, Miss Ferguson. All right, go on now.

When the others came in he said I should go on with my usual work, but we'd talk some more the next day, and maybe there could be some overtime after all. He'd have a word with Mr Kennedy.

'I'm doing this project,' I said to Mum that night, 'with Mr Bradwell. So that's why I go in early.'

'All by yourselves?' asked Mum. 'What's this Mr Bradwell like, then? Dishy, is he?'

She was in a good mood. There'd been a party at the restaurant where she works, and the customer had sent back a hundred quid for the kitchen staff, to share out for helping to make it a success.

'Wish there was more like that one. Mind you, we did do well. That cake Dizzy made, that was a treat. And the salmon soufflé.'

'I'm getting overtime,' I said, and Mum said, that'll be handy. Bit of extra money never comes amiss.

Mr Bradwell told me Mr Kennedy had said the overtime was all right. Two weeks, come in early, and get paid extra. Great, I thought. Get paid for doing what I wanted anyway.

He had a big chart on his desk, all little squares, and bits of cardboard you could move around on it. He said it was a plan of the storerooms. We could move the racks if we had to, but better not, because of disruption. The pallets, that was no bother.

We'd already changed the milk and the butter around, so when the milk dripped it ran out near a drain, not under the toilet rolls. We'd put the butter where the milk used to be, and moved all the other stuff along just a bit, and it made no difference, except being easier to clean.

It was good, doing all that with Mr Bradwell early in the mornings. He was nice. If I had an idea he'd say, right, let's try it. Or if he didn't like it, put that on the spike for the moment, we'll look at that again later.

'What do you mean, on the spike?' I asked, and he told me he'd worked on a newspaper once. Putting something on the spike meant the editor didn't like it much. It didn't go straight in the bin, but on a real spike on the desk, so it could be found in case there was a gap in the paper that needed filling.

He didn't mind hard work, either. When we came to shifting the boxes of olive oil he was the one who went up the stepladder and carried it down, he didn't make me do it. He said I should clear the space ready for it, move the jars of salad cream along a bit, he'd bring the oil.

After ten days we'd got it nearly planned out, the big things we wanted to change, the way the pallets stacked up against each other so we could get the trolleys through without banging up against the wall. There was hardly any heavy stuff on the top shelves any more. Mr Bradwell said it was safer, too. Not so top heavy. One or two of those shelves, it was a wonder they hadn't fallen down, he said, could have hurt somebody. Couple more days and we should have it about right, and he reckoned we'd earned ourselves a bottle of wine each for the weekend. His treat.

It was the first time anybody had offered me a present like that, because I'd done something well, except maybe that time Carol got Mr Kennedy to say we could have overtime after Davie Evans got the sack and we did the lists ourselves. I should have remembered what happened that time. But I didn't. When I went for the bus that afternoon I was just thinking, I'd done well. I'd enjoyed it, too, working out how to make it easier for everybody. It had been good work, that, it was going to be a help.

Mum and Sheila enjoyed a glass of wine now and then, and so did I. I'd tell Mum, we might get a joint of meat for Sunday. With my overtime we could afford that, no trouble.

He was waiting at the bus stop, and I was still thinking about the bottle of wine. I was thinking, if he let me choose I'd pick that one in the funny-shaped dark green bottle, the pink one that sparkled. So I walked right down the alley and out into the road, and I was nearly at the bus stop before I saw him.

Standing right there, right by the wall, where he'd been that time before.

Looking the other way, down the road.

I stopped, and I thought, don't run, he might hear you.

I turned around, quite slowly, and I walked back into the alley, and when I looked back he was just beginning to turn his head towards me.

I ran. I ran as fast as I could, until I got into the High Street, and then I stopped, and I looked around, and I thought, what do I do now? What can I do now?

He's going to kill me, and nobody will believe me.

11

I'd asked people to help me last time, and nobody had taken any notice. He was going to follow me out of the alley, and he'd have the knife ready, and he'd take me back to the little room, or maybe somewhere else, and then he'd kill me.

'It's not him,' I said to myself, and I knew that was right. He wouldn't have looked away out of the window, he'd have smiled when I said I was sorry. Nicholas Parry had good manners. Didn't matter that he was mad, wanted to kill me, he still had good manners. This other one, he was different, but he had the knife, and he sat in the same place on the bus.

Somebody else.

I walked down the High Street, right past Fletchers, and I thought, if I walk all the way home, maybe he won't find me.

I'll go home a different way, I thought. I'll walk to the Broad Street junction, and then I'll catch a different bus. Sort you out, Mister whoever you are. I won't catch that bus ever again, nor the one in the morning. I'll find another way to get to work.

Following me round. Bastard. Same bus, same seat, now he's waiting at the bus stop for me.

I was walking very fast. I kept looking over my shoulder, to see if he was following me. I tried not to think what I'd do. All the time I was half expecting the people in the street to come up to me and say, he's got a knife. But nobody did, they didn't even look at me.

I was really scared, but I was angry, too.

You're not going to get me again, I thought. You're not.

That's stupid. It wasn't him. Nicholas Parry was locked up, safely locked up.

All the time I was walking I was trying to think what to do. I ought to be able to go back to the cops, maybe talk to somebody else, not that woman who only heard what she thought I was saying, not what I was trying to tell her. Bloody cops.

There must be somebody.

Sheila. I'd ask Sheila, she'd listen to me. Even if she thought I was going barmy, she'd listen.

She did listen, but she didn't know what to do. He looks like him, I said, dresses like him, sits in the same seat on the bus, even got the same knife.

'What's he done wrong?' she asked.

He scares me, I thought. Waiting for me.

'He's doing it on purpose.'

'Doing what?'

'Listen,' I said. 'Listen. I'm trying to tell you.'

But I couldn't. After she'd given me a kiss and said, not to worry, Joanie love, and gone out of my room, I thought of things I could have told her. The card. The way he'd said, told you you'd be sorry. The way he looked at me. And when I stopped going on that bus and got the earlier one, the way he'd waited for me at the other bus stop.

It shouldn't be allowed. Frightening people, it shouldn't be allowed.

It's not against the law to look like Nicholas Parry. Nothing he's done is against the law.

I'm not going crazy, though. I'm not. I touched him, and he's solid. He's there, I'm not seeing things. And he's not Nicholas Parry either. He's rude, and Nicholas Parry wasn't rude.

'There's a letter for you,' Mum said a few days later when I got back, and she looked really worried, I'd never seen her look at me like that before. It was a white envelope, and it felt like little lumps, the envelope, all stiff and not very smooth. Really expensive stuff.

'Why are they writing to you, then, Joanie? Look, that's from a solicitor. Oh, Joanie, what have you been up to?'

'Nothing. I don't know. Nothing.'

She was upset. That letter had come in the morning post, and all day she'd been worrying. Letter from a solicitor, what's happened? What's our Joanie been doing, to have solicitors writing to her?

'Open it, then.'

I tore it open and I unfolded the letter and looked at it. I might have read it myself, but it would have taken me a long time, and Mum was upset, so I just handed it over. She grabbed it, and started to read, her lips moving.

'Joanie! Somebody's left you five hundred pounds! Who's Theresa Harringdon?'

I thought, I told you. I told you about Theresa. Didn't you listen?

Mum read me out the letter, but I knew the most

important part. What he'd said, that snooty man, it was true, Theresa had left me the money.

Thanks, I thought. Wish I could say it to your face, but thanks anyway.

'You've got to open a bank account. Building society, that would be best, get a bit of interest. Start saving up. What do you want, our Joanie? A holiday? That would be nice, might even go abroad. Spain?'

'Don't know,' I said.

'Who's Theresa Harringdon? Well, I mean, who *was* Theresa Harringdon?' I thought, you couldn't even be bothered to remember, why should I tell you about Theresa again? But I didn't want to have a row with Mum.

'She sold me my special cup and saucer.'

'Oh, that place you used to call in on your way home? Oh, Joanie. What a nice lady, to leave you all that. Wonder why she did it. Didn't she have any family?'

I wondered why she'd done it, too. All the time I'd spent with her in the shop, didn't matter what we'd been doing, she'd never paid me. I'd done some work, but she'd never paid me. Never even offered.

Sheila didn't see that it mattered. 'Can't take it with you. Might as well give it away.'

'She had a reason,' I said. 'I know she did.'

I was feeling stubborn. I was tired, for one thing, walking to work dead early, and walking home again, three days, just as well it wasn't raining. Mum said she'd help me open a building society account, then we'd have to write and tell the solicitors, so they could pay in the money. She and Sheila had been talking about it non-stop. Five hundred pounds, what do you want to do with it, Joanie?

I told Mr Bradwell. I said, I've been left five hundred pounds, and he said, that's nice. I don't know what to do with it, I said.

Later that morning he came over while I was loading my cage.

'Are you worried about the money?' he asked, and I nodded.

'A bit.'

He stood there, waiting, and I tried to tell him, because he'd been nice to me. I said I thought there was a reason why Theresa had left it to me, but I didn't know what.

'Not just because she liked you?'

I shook my head. He was still standing there, as if he was thinking about it, but then he walked away, back to his office, and I went on putting the new delivery of bread into the cage.

That bit of my job was getting boring, loading up bread and things, always the same, but at least I could think about other things while I was doing it. I couldn't help feeling a bit angry with Theresa for dying like that, just when I was beginning to learn from her. Going off and leaving me just as I was beginning to think I might be able to be a bit like her. Knowing things, and having fun because of knowing things.

When the idea came, halfway through the afternoon, it wasn't like a surprise. I just seemed to know what she'd wanted. Find out about this man who looks like Nicholas Parry; get all that out of the way, tidy it up. Then, go on learning. Carry on where we left off.

There was another promotion on cheeses, and Carol wanted me to help. She'd been slacking off that morning, not doing so much, said she had a hangover. They had demonstrators in, standing by the chiller cabinets behind little tables, giving the customers daft little squares of biscuits with dabs of cheese smeared on them.

'If you wanted to find out about somebody, how would you do it?' I asked, and Carol said, 'Who?'.

'I don't know.'

Stupid question, I thought. If I knew, it wouldn't be so bad.

'Say, you're going home from the pub, and somebody keeps following you.'

'Tell Eric.'

It was as if Theresa spoke to me then, said, fat lot of bloody good *she* is.

'Coming to the pictures Friday? Jean-Claude Van Damme.'

I should *know* this sort of thing without having to ask. It's just *stupid*, being this helpless.

'Private detective,' said one of the demonstrators. 'Like in this old film with Humphrey Bogart,' and Carol laughed, and then made a funny noise and held the back of her hand up against her forehead.

'Bloody vodka. I swear, I'll never.'

'Have a biscuit, love. Soak up the alcohol.'

'No, thanks. I'd throw up.'

'There's Turkish baths. Saw a film with that once, all little blue and white tiles, and steam. All these fat blokes.'

Then she turned her smarmy smile on to the customers.

'Good afternoon, madam. Would you like to try the new cheese spread from Denmark? Special offer this week.'

'Who's following you, anyway? What's he like?'

Eric had been nice, that first time I'd gone out after I came out of hospital. When I'd got frightened he'd driven me home, made sure I got into the house all right. But I couldn't talk to Eric. All he wanted to do was go out the back with Carol, or take her home. I wondered if he was still paying her.

'Just a bloke,' I said.

There'd been a row with the driver from the bakery. Mr Bradwell had moved the bread store right up close to the lifts, so the driver had to carry it all the way down to the back, and he'd been shouting about it. Three more drops to do after this, no bloody consideration. But Mr Bradwell was right. We had to get that bread four or five times a day, not just once. But I was glad when he said it was his idea. Whose fucking bright idea was this, then? the driver had yelled, and I'd felt a big, cold lump in my stomach. I hate it when people shout, and it had been my idea.

'Mine,' said Mr Bradwell, 'and please don't swear in front of my young ladies.'

It was my idea, I said to him later, and he answered, a very good one it was, too, but it was my responsibility.

We'd finished changing the storerooms around. It hadn't been too bad, learning where things were, because I'd been there when they were moved. It was only once or twice I couldn't remember the new places, and it hadn't taken long to find them. Nobody said anything. It was nice, not having to carry the heavy stuff down from the high shelves.

I wondered whether Davie Evans had left them like that on purpose, so he could get us up the stepladder with our arms full and we couldn't get away from him.

Perhaps because it was too easy, I wasn't thinking, I tried to pick up a box of mayonnaise jars like I used to, just fingers hooked under it and lift, and I dropped it.

Smashed glass all over the floor, and that horrible yellowy white stuff splashed all over the place. If it had been on the top shelf I'd have thought about it, lifting it a bit slowly so it didn't tip over.

'Sorry,' I said when Mr Bradwell came out.

'Accidents happen. Can you manage, clearing it up?'

Just when I thought I was doing all right.

How do I clear up this mess about Nicholas Parry? Take more than a dustpan and brush and the bucket and mop. I don't know what to do.

I thought about facing him. Maybe take somebody with me and go to the bus stop where he'd been waiting for me. What do you want? Who are you? Why are you doing this?

'Come with me to the bus stop?' I asked Carol.

'What for?'

'There's this bloke keeps following me. I want to ask him what he thinks he's up to.'

Carol looked at me as if I'd grown another head. 'You bloody daft, or something?'

I didn't answer. A bloke following you, what do you think he's up to? Only one thing, isn't there? That's the way Carol thinks, and I haven't got the words. Theresa could have told her. Theresa could have made it so Carol would say, right, okay, let's sort him out. I'll get some of the blokes, tell the bastard where he gets off, no problem.

'Mum, this man that looks like Nicholas Parry. He's doing it on purpose, just to frighten me.'

'Ignore him, our Joanie. He'll give up sooner or later.'

'He's got a knife.'

She put down the potato peeler and looked across the kitchen at me. 'Has he said anything? Has he threatened you?'

I shook my head. It wasn't threats. It was just him being there. I didn't go on the bus any more, I walked all the way to and from work, and it wasn't too bad, not in the nice weather. But I knew he'd find me again, sometime. He'd do something else. He'd said I'd be sorry, and I wasn't sorry enough yet.

I thought, I'm beginning to forget how it was with Theresa, and even with Nicholas Parry. With Theresa, when she talked, after a little while I could talk better too. When she made me laugh, I could answer her. Not talking the way she did, but better than before, and better than I could now. She gave me that, but it's going away again.

And even Nicholas Parry, all respectful to the Empress. He was going to kill me, but he was never rude, even when he said I was stupid. It was just that he couldn't understand. Why are you being so stupid? You never used to be like that.

Dozey Joan. If I didn't do something soon, I'd be Dozey Joan again, only fit for putting things on the shelves at the supermarket, and then only when she knew just where they went. Give her something new and she's had it, take her all day, standing in front of those shelves trying to make out the stupid little bits of writing.

'Wish I could read.'

Mum was peeling the potatoes again, not really listening. Why was it when I told Theresa about the man, she listened? She looked as if she was all tightened up, really listening, and thinking. It mattered, Theresa knew it mattered, there was something going on. Whether it was Joan going crazy, or somebody playing silly buggers and dead nasty with it, it mattered. And Mum just went on peeling the potatoes.

She's my mother, it ought to matter to her. More than to Theresa.

He'd find me, and it wouldn't take him long.

'Sheila, this man who looks like Nicholas Parry, he worries me.'

'Oh, Joanie, you're not still going on about that. He's not *doing* anything, is he? Well, then.'

But I'd said to Sheila, I'd told her. He dresses like him, sits in the same seat. He worries me, frightens me. Why had she said that, about not still going on? My sister used to love me. Used to care about me.

'Sorry, Joanie. Bad day. Go on, then. Tell me.'

I didn't want to, not like that. Not, sitting at the table, only got to listen, just let her get it off her chest then she'll be okay again. I wanted somebody to tell me what to do, to have some ideas, listen to mine, talk to me and hear me, not, go on, then, tell me.

If somebody knew what to do, and would tell me, I'd do it. But I didn't know myself. I just didn't know what to do.

Mum helped me with the building society account. There were forms and things, and I had to sign my name, and they did it all in a little book on the computer. A passbook, they said, bring it in whenever you want to pay in any money, or take it out.

Mum reached out for it, and I thought, that's not right, it's mine.

'Can I have that?' I asked, and she looked all surprised, but she gave it to me, talking about it, the way she does. You take care of that, then, don't you lose it, you know what you're like.

All the way home she was saying how nice it was to have some money, and what did I want to do? I could go abroad with that. She was hoping I'd say we should both go together, have a holiday in Spain or something, but I didn't want a holiday, and I wished she'd stop talking about it. I wanted to get rid of the problem with the man, and then I wanted to learn a bit.

I didn't know where to begin.

Go back to school. When I was at school they'd had these teachers to talk to about jobs. They'd never taken much notice of me. If you can't really read there's not a lot you can do, they said. Never mind, Joan. We can't all be clever, can we? Just find yourself a nice, steady job. You'll manage.

'I've written to that solicitor,' Mum said the next day. 'Just write your name at the bottom, Joanie.'

'What did you write?'

'Only the account number and all that. What he wanted to know, so he can pay the money. Write your name at the bottom, then we can put it in the post, then you'll get your money.'

I should be able to do that for myself. I wrote my name, then I went up to my room and I sat on my bed, and I felt so angry I wanted to go and fight somebody, maybe hit somebody as hard as I could. I felt like I was tied up with ropes. Can't even write a letter to get my money.

It never used to worry me. I'd got a job, earned a bit, enough to get by. What's to worry about, can't read or write properly? I got by. I managed.

I'm getting worse again, I thought. I am, I'll be Dozey Joan again if I'm not careful, with Annie spitting in my coffee, extra cream, drink it up.

'What's up, Joanie?' asked Sheila, and she came right into my room and didn't even knock.

'Fuck off.'

'Oh, thank you. That's really nice. Came to try and cheer you up, get told to fuck off. Right, madam, I'll do just that.'

She slammed the door on her way out, but I didn't care. Before, if Sheila had been upset with me, I'd always followed her, saying I was sorry. Sorry, Sheila, I really am. I am sorry. Until she'd said it was all right, not to worry. Then we'd have a little hug, and I'd feel okay again, because she wasn't angry any more.

This time I didn't care. I didn't bloody care. Nobody listened to me, they all thought they knew what I was going to say, and they didn't. They didn't know. I want to find something out, and you could do it for me, but you won't because you won't bloody listen, so I don't bloody care. Bloody bloody bloody. Bloody fuck off.

Twelve jars of mayonnaise smashed on the floor, all got to be cleaned up. Forgot my hands don't work the way they used to. Never will again, but at least he didn't *do* anything. My friend dead of cancer, how nice, five hundred pounds. Enough for a holiday.

Want to spend that getting rid of *him*. And *he* doesn't *do* anything either. Only going to make me sorry, that's all. Not sorry enough yet, twelve jars of mayonnaise because of my hands. Bastard.

'Joanie?'

Mum was knocking on my door, and she sounded angry.

'Joanie? You answer this door, my girl. Joanie?'

It's not locked, I thought, but I didn't say anything.

'Joanie?'

You fuck off too, I thought, but I didn't say it. Our Mum's got a temper.

'You don't come out of this room till you're ready to say you're sorry. You hear me? Joanie?'

She went away, stamping down the stairs so I'd know she was angry with me. Thud, thud, thud. And then saying something to Sheila, her voice all high, and the door closing so I couldn't hear. They'd have a cup of tea, sit at the kitchen table, and they'd talk about me. *Always*, they'd say. She *always* does this. She's *always* been like that. Do you remember when? And there was that time . . .

I'm not going to say sorry. I am not.

They never listen to me. They never have. It's always my fault, whatever happens. Brought it on yourself, Mum said. She'd said that about my ears. Nothing wrong with her ears, she'd said at school, it's just she won't listen. Never has. If you don't use your ears they'll go wrong. It's like when things get rusty. There's a word for it. Atro something. Stands to reason. Brought it on yourself. If you'd listened.

If I'd listened I'd have heard Dad and Sheila.

Now she's up there sulking, they'd say. She *always* sulks when she can't get her own way.

After the operation, when I still couldn't read they'd said I was lazy. I sat in class and I didn't try. You're lazy. You're being lazy. Joan, are you listening? Yes, Miss. What did I just say? Don't know, Miss.

Can't remember. You pick on me, make me jump, I'm not used to this. Shouting my name like that, making me jump. Then these questions, when I'm all scared, that sudden noise. Joan, *Joan*, JOAN! Can't remember. Don't know, Miss. Leave me *alone*.

No excuses now, Joan. You can hear perfectly well. There's no reason why you shouldn't catch up. You

175

must apply yourself. Do you understand? Yes, Miss.

It's all noisy, shouting like that. Makes me jump. You try it, a bang in your ear like a gun going off, and right away, what did I just say? You try and remember, with that bang in your ear so sudden, before you can even stop shaking, what did I just say?

You just said bang, you bitch, scared me, made me jump. No, I can't remember, and I don't want to. Leave me alone.

We're doing our best, Mrs Ferguson, but she isn't making much progress. I'm afraid she's rather lazy. Is something at home bothering her, perhaps?

All that trouble operating on your ears, our Joan, and you still won't work. Doctors might as well have saved themselves the trouble. I'm not coming down to the school again only because you're lazy. Got better things to do.

Always got better things to do.

The kitchen door opened and Sheila came up the stairs and went into the bathroom. I sat on my bed and listened until I heard the toilet flush, and then she went downstairs again, not thud, thud, thud like Mum, but running. Like she was dancing.

Got a certificate for dancing, Sheila. In the school competition. Got her name down for the town competition, might have won a cup, but she hurt her ankle in the playground and couldn't take part. Shame.

Going to be a dancer when she leaves school, Mum said. Maybe professional. Got the legs for it.

Extra dancing lessons at Mrs Beauchamp's Academy of Dance, not cheap, our Sheila, don't you waste your opportunities. Tuesdays and Fridays after school, two hours, and do your practice every day and a bit longer at the weekends. If you're going to be a dancer you'll have to work at it.

Don't want to be a sodding dancer, said Sheila, and Mum was crying and shouting, all that money, can't get it back.

All my friends go out weekends, and Friday nights I got to stay home tap tap tapping in these sodding shoes. Stuff it.

Language like that from my own daughter, and don't think I blame your father for what happened. Oh, no, my girl, I know a little tart when I see one.

Elizabeth Carstairs got extra lessons for her reading. It's nice, she said. Just three of us sitting round a table with Mrs Inez, taking it in turns. She's ever so nice in those lessons, never gets nasty with us.

Think I'm made of money to hear you two talk. All that wasted on Mrs Beauchamp's bloody Academy of bleeding wiggle your arse, and now you on about reading lessons. You stop being lazy and you'll catch up, Joan. That's what your teachers say.

Don't you argue with me. Since your father left I'm at my wits' end, trying to make the money go round. I haven't got any more. I haven't even got the rent this week, if you must know.

Sheila, go and do your practice. Don't want to. Sheila! Mum, nobody else has to do practice every night. Whole day at school, then practice, it's not fair. Anyway, I've got homework. I've got to do my maths.

Are you going to be a dancer, or aren't you? All that money for Mrs Beauchamp. I'm doing my best for you, our Sheila. Never mind maths, with your looks and your talent you could make a fortune, dancing. If you hadn't hurt your ankle you could have won a cup by now.

Mum, listen. At Mrs Beauchamp's there's others streets better than me. I'm not that good, honest.

Mum was crying then. All that money and you won't even try. Sheila got angry, you never asked me. You said I was going to be a dancer, I never. I never said I wanted to be a dancer. I want to be a hairdresser. I don't want to practise. I don't want to do my maths homework but I'll get into trouble if I don't.

You'll get into trouble if you don't do your practice, don't you think you won't. I've had all I'm going to take of this, our Sheila. Now, get into that room and put that record on the player and start your practice, I won't tell you again.

Doors banging, and shouting, and Sheila broke the record, smashed it over her knee, and Mum hit her. Bloody little tart, leading your father on, I should have chucked you out and let him stay. That record comes out of your pocket money.

What pocket money? I haven't had any pocket money all month. And I did not lead him on. He never left me alone. Every time you went out of the house. Off with a fancy man, I shouldn't wonder, that's why Dad came after me.

Mum hit Sheila with a wooden spoon then, right across the face, split her lip and cut her eyebrow, and Sheila screamed and Mum got frightened.

They'd forgotten I was there, sitting in the corner. All that noise, all that screaming, I had my hands over my ears. So loud, it hurt. I was frightened. Everything was so loud, it kept making me jump.

I wished I hadn't had the operation. Everything was horrible, all the noises, making me jump. Made me feel sick.

They never thought of me, being there. I can hear you.

Our Joanie never listens. They say there's something wrong with her ears, but I reckon it's just she never listens.

I can hear you now.

I wish I couldn't, but I can hear you.

12

I went back to my school. I went in through the playground door, past the girls' cloakroom, and nobody
looked at me. Maybe they thought I was one of the
mothers. I thought I'd feel stupid, and I did, a bit.

Who else could I ask?

I remembered from school, sometimes somebody
would say, I went to see Mrs Gerhard and she was ever
so nice.

Mrs Gerhard was horrible. She took us for English and
Maths, and she was our class teacher. She used to go on
and on, telling me to listen. Joan, are you listening? Yes,
Miss.

There was a room they called a Careers Advice Office,
only most of the time it was full of boxes of old exercise
books. But sometimes they cleared it out and stuck
posters on the walls, and had a table and chairs, and
then there was something on the door, green if you
could go in, red if you had to wait.

I thought, if it's Mrs Gerhard I'm going right home,
I'm not going to sit here and have her being all sarky.

But it was Miss Clarkson, and she looked just the same

as ever, a bit messy and vague, and always fidgeting around, as if her underwear was uncomfortable. She used to tell us not to fidget.

Carol Parkinson, stop fidgeting, she'd say, and there she was, wriggling around like she wanted to scratch but it was unladylike.

'Yes?' she said. 'Can I help you?'

Didn't remember me. Didn't know who I was.

I shouldn't have come.

I stood in front of the table and I put my hands behind my back, as if I was a kid again, and then I thought, I'm not.

'Don't remember me?' I asked, and I tried to smile.

She looked at me and her eyes screwed up, and then she knew.

'Joan!'

'Yes, Miss.'

'Joan Ferguson. Well, how nice. This is nice, Joan. Sit down. I've only got a couple of minutes, but tell me what you've been doing.'

I sat down, but I couldn't think what to say. Only got a couple of minutes. I couldn't ask her in a couple of minutes, not what I needed to know.

Oh, please, Miss. You used to be ever so nice. You never shouted. Miss Clarkson, please, I need more than a couple of minutes.

Please.

I looked down at my hands lying in my lap, and there was a little splash on my thumb.

Cry-baby. Stupid Joan Ferguson's a cry-baby. Can't even read, stupid Joan Ferguson.

'Oh, Joan, my dear! Whatever's the matter? Here, have a hankie. Oh, goodness, where are they? Just a moment,

I think there are some . . . yes, here we are. My dear, what's the matter?'

'It's okay,' I said. 'Sorry.'

'I heard about that dreadful incident. You poor girl. I suppose I should feel sorry for that young man, too, but I can't. Mentally ill, I understand. Well, he'd have to be. It must have been absolutely ghastly for you. I think I'd have died of fright. How long were you in hospital? Operations on your hands, wasn't it? Did they help? Are your hands all right now?'

I nodded.

'Not too bad, Miss.'

I wasn't crying any more. She'd talked so I didn't have to say anything, gave me a bit of time. I was all right then. Didn't matter what she'd been saying.

Couple of minutes. Better go, I thought, so I stood up.

'Joan, dear, it's only a five-minute interview I've got now. Well, I'll see to it that it's only five minutes, then I've got a coffee break, I'm thankful to say. Please, my dear, do stay and have a coffee with me. Can you spare the time? It would be nice.'

She was looking at me as if she was really asking, please have a cup of coffee with me, like she really wanted me to.

'All right.'

And it was five minutes, or only a bit longer, and I went back in and she made some coffee, and it was in a cup and saucer. Tiny little handle.

I looked at it.

'Can't hold it,' I said. And I held out my hands, because I didn't know how to tell her. Look, they're sort of curled. You have to look, or you don't notice, but they're not right.

'My *God*.' She sounded angry. 'Can't they do better than that for you? What is it, shortened tendons? I thought they could put in carbon inserts these days. In fact, I *know* they can. I wish I knew more about it.

'Well, never mind that for now. What do you usually use for a drink? Oh, I know. There'll be some straws in here somewhere.'

She was muddling around looking in the drawers of the desk, just like she used to in the classrooms, never could find the chalk for the blackboard. It made me smile, thinking about that, and she looked at me and laughed.

'At least I haven't changed, have I? Even if you have. Don't tell me you weren't remembering. That poisonous little brat Sophie Barratt used to hide the chalk, didn't she? I was sure it was her, even if I couldn't prove it.'

I was glad I'd come. She was being so nice. She'd always been nice, but now it was different, we could have a laugh together.

'Tell me why you came,' she said when she'd found the straws.

It took such a long time. I kept talking about the wrong things, because I was trying to explain. I wanted to say, there's this man, following me, but then I had to tell her about Theresa, and the money she'd left me, and what I thought she wanted me to do with it. And I told her about the man with the knife, how I was scared, but he hadn't done anything wrong, he just looked like Nicholas Parry. I didn't know what to do, and I'd thought I was going crazy, until I'd touched him.

Miss Clarkson had another appointment, but she said I should come for lunch, school dinner again, disgusting, she said. Spaghetti and tomato sauce.

183

'Got to go to work,' I said. 'Afternoon shift.'

'Oh, damn. What time do you finish? No, I can't. Not tonight. Not with thirty putrid little efforts on the Industrial Revolution to mark.'

But I went back two days later, when she'd said she had a free period, and she seemed to be expecting me. She said she was pleased to see me, and I didn't think she was only being polite.

She started about the man. Sitting in the room where the teachers did their correcting in the day, with the sunshine coming through the window on to the yellow tables, it did seem stupid. Dozey Joan Ferguson, stupid Joan, can't even read. Looks like him, dresses like him, what do you mean, dear? What does he wear? I see, but don't a lot of men wear grey trousers and a jacket? And when you fell over, naturally you'd had a shock. Anybody would, not just you, thinking that dreadful man was back. I think I'd have fainted, if it had happened to me. But Joan, don't you think it's just possible you misheard? After such a shock, it would only be natural, wouldn't it? Such a dreadful experience, there's bound to be a nervous reaction. I don't mean falling over, I mean being held prisoner, those awful days. Of course you're nervous. And a man of similar appearance, so unfortunately sitting in the same seat on the bus, it's bound to frighten you. But let's look at it again.

How many times have you seen him? Just for the moment, let's assume he has to go on the bus to get to work. Now, apart from that?

If he threatens you, of *course* you must go back to the police, and if you like I'll come with you. But as it is, my dear, I don't see what they can do. The man, Nicholas Parry I mean, he isn't even to be put on trial, is he? I understood he's unfit to plead. So you see, it isn't even a case of intimidating a witness. If there's no trial there are no witnesses, are there?

'But *now*,' she said, and she had a pile of papers in her drawer, 'the really important thing, my dear. You learning to read and write properly. Better late than never, and it's certainly not *too* late.'

Papers to take away with me, Sheila could read them to me. Special classes to help adults. One-to-one teaching, with volunteers.

Thank you, Miss Clarkson.

It's been so nice seeing you, dear. And the very best of luck with your literacy programme. Do please come again and let me know how you're getting on.

I'm not going to cry. Even though I thought she'd help me, and she doesn't believe me, I'm not going to cry. She was trying to be nice.

But I did want to cry. It had seemed like such a good idea, going back and asking a teacher.

When there'd been all the trouble with Dad, just after my operation, with the police and the social workers, they'd tried to be nice. Come and talk any time you like, Joan. We're here to help. Yes, Miss. Thank you, Miss.

I'd never known what to say, when they said that. So, yes, Miss. Thank you, Miss.

I don't want to talk to you. I just want to know what to do. I don't know how to ask. Mum's crying, and Dad's not there, people telling me not to worry. What's happening?

Him and Sheila. And that woman, with the others, sitting down on the sofa. How did Daddy play with you? What did he say? Did he come in when you were in the bath?

No good asking Joan. She won't know, she never listens, she's had an operation on her ears. She couldn't have heard.

Having that trouble with her ears set her back a bit. Not too bright, our Joanie. Sheila, now, she's different. There's a sparky little madam for you. And let's not forget, it wasn't Sheila who complained.

When you were in the bath, Joanie, did Daddy come in?

No, because I locked the door.

But don't say. Just look at them, and don't say anything. It's better not to say anything.

You won't get anything out of her. We've tried. She was stone deaf, or near as makes no difference. Hard of hearing, anyway. None so deaf as those that won't hear.

There's something in that old saying, and *stone* deaf she certainly wasn't. So I'd like just *one* more chance to talk to Joan, if you don't mind. I'm absolutely certain she knows something.

Come and talk to us, dear. We're here to help.

Well, I do have to admit she's probably not very bright. Not much point, a barrister could tear her evidence to shreds. You can get a child like that to say anything you like.

Oh, yes? I can't get her to say anything at all, unless you count 'Um'. But I still think she knows something. Did she have trouble talking? As well as hearing?

Never listens, always been a bit on the quiet side. Sheila's the bright one in *this* family.

If she's shy about talking, she might write it down.

She can't read or write.

Oh. If it's not one damned thing it's another. Well, let's

get back and see what we've got for the case conference. We can always come back later if we get any ideas.

I *can* hear. I could always hear a bit, only everything was quiet, with a sort of buzzing on the top. I can hear what you say. I heard Dad and Sheila too, and I heard the telephone call, the one that started all the trouble. Even though the voice wasn't the same, talking through a hankie.

Number twenty-three Goldstone Road. Their name's Ferguson. He's fucking his own daughter, and she's only a child.

That you, Joan? That you on the stairs? Say a word about this and I'll cut your tongue out.

Do you want to talk about it, Joan? We'll help you if we can. There's nothing we can do if you won't tell us.

Everybody was telling, and talking, and it was like little boys playing cowboys and Indians. Bang, bang, you're dead. Talk, talk, that's him fixed. It was all so stupid. If they hadn't said anything nothing would have happened. They told you all the time, if you don't say anything, they said, we can't do anything. They said. So why was everybody talking? Why were they saying everything?

I didn't say anything. It wasn't me. I won't tell.

She's not very bright. It's Sheila who's the clever one in this family, and she told you to mind your own business, the cheeky little nympho.

Hey, just a minute!

Oh, *she* isn't listening. She never listens.

Now, years later, it's all different. I wish I knew how to say it. I'd thought, if I say, they'll do something. They'd said they would. Come and talk to us, and this time I had, and they still didn't listen. Not to what I wanted to say. They only listen to what they think I'm saying. Because I can't put it in all the right words.

I can't even *think* in the right words. I'm getting worse.

I still had a bit of time before I had to walk to work. I'd thought Miss Clarkson would talk to me for a while, might have some ideas, so I'd gone early.

I went to the park and I sat on a bench and took out the papers she'd given me. There were a lot of drawings, like in the baby books, but there was writing too.

Adult Literacy Programme.

It took me a long time even to read that, because when I looked at it I just thought, can't, and then I had to work through it, a few letters at a time, remembering. It was hard, but I did it in the end. I did remember.

Adult Literacy Programme.

All right, Theresa, but I've got to get rid of that man first. I've got to clear this up.

I went on for a bit, working at the reading. Reading is fun, it said, and I thought, that's a laugh. It said, think of all the things you could do if you could read. Then there were pictures, with writing underneath them, of all the things you're supposed to be able to do if you can read, and can't do if you can't read. There wasn't one for stopping people treating you like dirt, thinking you're stupid. Even people who want to help, and who try to be friendly.

Miss Clarkson had meant to help me. I knew that. She'd probably said in the staff room, guess who came to see me today? Joan Ferguson. She wants to learn to read.

There were little splashes on the papers, and I couldn't see properly. Cry-baby.

Reading is fun. You can do it. It's like walking down a road, one step at a time.

All right, but there's this big brick wall right across the road.

Never mind the big brick wall, just walk down the road. You can do it.

More splashes on the paper.

Time to walk to work. There were clouds coming up over the town; it was going to rain later. Maybe I could get the bus. If I went just one stop further along, I'd be able to see. Is he on it? I wouldn't even have to go past the stop at the end of the alley. I could just look, it wouldn't take a moment, and if he's not on the bus I could go. Save getting wet. Save getting tired.

How long can I keep trying to stay out of his way?

I'd really thought, this time somebody will tell me what to do. Miss Clarkson will know what I should do, and she'll tell me. How to stop him. What it all means, him looking like Nicholas Parry and going on the bus and having a knife and saying, told you you'd be sorry.

Cry-baby. People will start looking at you. Stop it. Wipe your nose.

There's nobody left to ask, so work it out for yourself. Think about it. You don't need to be able to read to use your brain.

I was thinking about it all the time I was loading up the shelves. Mr Bradwell said I could check for myself, couldn't I, what was running low on the shelves? I didn't need him to do it for me?

'Yes,' I said, and it seemed funny, him asking. He knew I could.

'I wish I could leave it to the others, too,' he said. 'I've got to take my wife to hospital for her appointment.'

I went on working that day, and it wasn't hard. Load up one lot, walk down the shelves looking, go down to the stores and get what was needed, load it up, and do it all again. Anybody could do that.

Sue and Donna put the stuff that was on their cages on to the shelves, and then they sat around in the storeroom. Nobody to tell them what to do, so they didn't do anything. Mr Bradwell used to give them lists, all written down of what they had to take upstairs. He just told me. Finished, Joan? Full-cream milk, Flora margarine, quarter pound, the Anchor butter, the half-pound packs. And when he'd finished saying it, I'd get it. Sometimes I'd say something like, we need more single cream, and he'd nod, and make a note, and I'd put that on the cage too.

I'd never done that for Davie Evans. I never wanted to help him do his job. I never minded when Mr Kennedy came down shouting for him, how much longer do you expect the customers to wait for frozen peas? That section's been empty half the morning, will you *please* do something about it. Davie Evans used to lie. He used to say, I've told that girl twice. Liar.

My job was so easy I could think about anything while I was doing it. I remembered how hard it had been when I first started, not knowing where the things went, and if they changed the layout, it could still muddle me. But I didn't mind asking now.

'Carol?'

'Oh, them. Top shelf over the tinned sweetcorn, I think.'

Carol was a trainee manager now. I could still ask her where things went, and she used to come and look for me if she didn't know. But she got to wear a badge and she didn't have to push a cage around, and some of the time she was in the office. She had a key.

She never asked me to go to the pictures with her any

more. I'd always said no, I didn't want to, so she'd given up. She was still all right, but not as friendly as before. Before, when I'd asked where something went, she always used to come right away. Now, she'd stop for a bit, like she was thinking of something else. Be with you in a mo. Hang on, I've just got to finish this. Can you come back in a couple of minutes? I'm ever so busy.

I knew what she was saying. I'm important now. You'll have to wait. What I do is more important than what you do.

I didn't mind, if she wanted to be a manager. I suppose she would be more important than me. It didn't matter.

I'd done the second load of the morning, and I'd put my cage by the lifts, ready to go down. I knew most of the stuff I needed to load up, but I wanted to check a couple of the shelves, so I went back.

I was looking down, on to the bottom shelf, so I didn't see him until it was too late. He was standing at the end of the row.

He was wearing jeans this time, and a sort of sports shirt with something written on the front, but he was looking at me in just the same way; looking, as if he was waiting for me to talk, but there was a smile.

Found you. Got you now. I know where you work now. Got you.

He wasn't moving, just standing there, looking at me, so I walked backwards, to try and get away from him. A woman came round the corner with a trolley, and he stopped and he turned his head as if he was looking at the biscuits, going to choose a packet of biscuits. I went on walking backwards, not wanting to turn round. I didn't want him behind me, where I couldn't see him.

The woman went past, not even looking at us, in a

hurry. Why couldn't it be a busy time, with all the shop crowded? Hardly anybody here, and he didn't bother looking at the biscuits any more, just walked towards me.

'Hello, Your Majesty.'

Oh, no. You're not Nicholas Parry. But maybe they've sent somebody else.

Please, go away. I don't want to go back. Please leave me alone.

The knife was in his hand, I didn't even see him take it out of his pocket, but it was in his hand and he was opening it.

There was the little glitter along the edge of the blade. Sharp, that meant it was sharp. Theresa had told me, when she was telling me about cut glass, just brush your thumb across it, don't press against it. That little glitter means it's sharp.

'I knew I'd find you. I only had to keep looking. Destiny.'

I could turn around and run away. He wouldn't dare do anything, not with everybody here.

Nobody helped me before. Why would they help me now?

'Please go away,' I said, but my voice was so quiet I could hardly hear myself, and he only laughed.

Somebody walked across the end of the row, a woman with two kids, but she was talking to the kids. It was your turn to choose yesterday, today Sam says what we have.

He didn't even look round. He went on coming towards me, and he had the knife out in front of him, moving it, twisting it around in the air.

'Told you you'd be sorry.'

I did hear it, I did hear it, no mistake, that was what he said. It was what was written in the card, and I did hear it. And that knife is real, and he is threatening me. If he threatens you, of course you must go to the police.

'Please leave me alone.'

I was at the end of the row now, and still walking backwards. He stopped and he looked, both ways, almost as if he was crossing a road. There was nobody there, except right at the end by the frozen meat section. Nobody was watching, but Nicholas Parry wouldn't even have looked.

If they've sent somebody else he might kill me right now. He might not wait until I say, all right, let's go, let's go back to the Dark Universe, to that place with the dark and cloudy skies.

Because I'm tired now, tired of this place, where the skies are blue, and I'm only Joan Ferguson, nobody special. I'm tired of being hunted, by Nicholas Parry and now you.

I think I want to give up. You've found me, haven't you? You know where I work. You can come here any time, and I can't get away.

Nobody wants to help me. Nobody believes Joan Ferguson, not Dozey Joan Ferguson, can't even read, no point listening to Joanie. He looks like him, looks at me the same way, sits in the same place on the bus, and the only one who ever did believe me, she's dead.

Did they kill her? Not with a knife, not like that. But maybe they can do that, make somebody die.

Standing there, looking at me, holding that knife. I can't back away any more. I'm standing here, pressed up against a dump bin with French bread in it, and I can't go any further. It's stupid. But maybe it's for the best.

So, stand here, and wait. See what he does. Let him do it. If there is a Dark Universe, it might be nice to be somebody important. Have people listen to me, and hear what I'm saying. What I'm really saying, not just what they think they hear. Wear linen and cotton, nice things, not this horrible overall that makes me sweat even when I'm cold. Maybe have some proper friends.

He's still standing there, just looking.

'Go on, then,' I said, and it sounded as if I was dead tired.

Then I saw Mr Bradwell going towards the lift, and it was as if there was a door opening, just a crack, but I might get through.

'Mr Bradwell! Help me!'

The man was walking away, fast as he could, and Mr Bradwell was looking at me.

The knife. He turned back quickly, and the knife, he was closing it, the back of the blade against his hand, snap, gone.

That's not how they close knives in the Dark Universe.

Stupid. Nicholas Parry closed the knife by pressing it against something else, like a door-frame, not against his hand.

But I know that's not Nicholas Parry.

'Miss Ferguson? What's the matter?'

'That man.'

He'd gone. Down to the end of the row, he'd gone, round the corner and he might even be out of the store by now, if he'd run. Trainers, he'd been wearing. Could have run.

'What man? Has somebody harmed you? Shall I call Security?'

Too late, and what could they do? I could say, he

194

threatened me with a knife, and he's say he never did. I never did, what would I do that for?

Nobody would believe me.

'He's gone now,' I said.

'You don't look very well, Miss Ferguson. I think you'd better come downstairs and sit in my office for a little while.'

It won't make any difference, sitting in an office until I feel better. He's found me again, and now he knows where I work. He can come back any time.

He *has* threatened me, like they said. He has, and nobody's going to believe me. I never, he'd say. Why would I do that?

Did anybody see? Did anybody hear? In the middle of one of the biggest supermarkets in the town, broad daylight, and nobody saw or heard a man with a knife, threatening you?

Dozey Joan Ferguson, started saying the customers are threatening her. That thing what happened to her, you know. Must have turned her a bit funny.

He'd run away, but I started feeling as if I wished he hadn't. It was like playing hide-and-seek, when I was little. I always gave up. When whoever it was who was looking got close I'd stand up.

Here I am.

I hated it, them being that close, and not finding me. I wanted it to be all over. I knew, when they got closer and closer, they were going to find me, any minute now, going to find me. Couldn't stand it.

Here I am.

'Come and sit down, Miss Ferguson. You look as if you've had a shock. Do you want to tell me about it?'

He's got a nice face, Mr Bradwell. Never touches us,

ever so careful about that. I expect they told him about Davie Evans. Holds the door open, but stands right back, so we don't brush against him. Sometimes I had that feeling, that he wanted to pat me on the shoulder. When I broke the mayonnaise, I thought he was going to do that. But he never did.

'Was it somebody you knew?'

Not much point telling him. But he was being kind, and I still hadn't said anything. It's rude, not to answer when somebody speaks to you.

'I was ever so pleased to see you,' I said, and he smiled at me.

13

Nobody was home when I got back. Sheila had said she'd be working late, and you never knew with Mum. I'd really wanted to sit down and talk about it. Now they'd have to believe me.

When Mum came in she'd been shopping. She'd bought a new pair of shoes, wanted me to look at them and say they were nice. They're great, Mum, really good. Go with your summer dress.

She laughed at that, and said she'd get a new summer dress next week to go with the shoes, never mind last year's old rag. What did I fancy for tea tonight? What about a nice salad?

'That man came into the shop,' I said, but she was putting a packet of sugar on to the shelf so she had her back to me.

'What man's that?' she asked, and then, before I could answer, 'Funny, the way you call it the shop. Sounds like Mrs Brett's on the corner.'

'The man who looks like Nicholas Parry.' I was going to make her listen to me this time. 'Mum, listen to me. Please, listen.'

'Oh, Joanie!'

'Mum, he had the knife. He said he knew he'd find me. Mum, please.'

I thought I was going to cry, and Mum turned round and looked at me. She was surprised. Hadn't she heard what I'd said? Even Mum, couldn't she hear what I said?

'Joan? Oh, lovey, what's up? What did he do, then? Come on, tell Mum.'

She sat down beside me, and put her arm round my shoulder, gave me a little hug. 'Joanie, love. What's upset you, then? Tell me about it.'

'He had the knife. Called me "Your Majesty". Said he knew he'd find me.'

'Right in the middle of Fletchers?'

'*Listen to me!*'

If I let her argue with me, I'd give up. I can't argue. Even when I know what I'm saying is right, and I know they're wrong, they've got all the words. They can make it sound right.

'I'm listening, lovey. Tell me all about it.'

I'd already told her he had the knife, I'd told her what he'd said. Wasn't that enough? What am I supposed to say now?

'I was looking at the shelves,' I said. 'To see what was running out, what to bring up on the cage. On the biscuits. See?'

'Yes?'

'He was there. Mum, he had the knife. Like Nicholas Parry.'

'Did he hurt you? Joanie, what did he do?'

She was listening now. She was looking at me, her eyes all wide. 'What did he do?'

'He said. Said he knew he'd find me. Mum, he knows where I work now. What am I going to do?'

'What did he do with the knife?' She shook my shoulder, almost like she was getting angry with me. 'What did he do with the knife, Joanie?'

'Held it.'

I held out my hand in front of me, pointing it as if there was a knife in it. I tried to remember. He'd moved it, as if he was making little circles in the air. I moved my hand the way he had, when I'd been watching the knife, and watching his face, not knowing what he was going to do.

'"Destiny", he said.'

There was a girl at school called Destiny. Why had he said that? I didn't know. Did he think that was my name? No, he knew my name.

'What's destiny?' I asked Mum.

'Something that's going to happen. Joanie, go on. What happened?'

'Mr Bradwell came back, so he ran away.'

'He didn't hurt you, then?'

I looked at her. Hadn't I said it right? I thought I'd said it right. He'd had the knife, the way he held it, what he'd said about finding me, wasn't that right? What were the words, then, if she still didn't understand?

'I thought he was going to kill me.'

She still had her arm around me, and she was looking into my face. It wasn't that she didn't care. She could see I was upset, and it did matter. He hadn't touched me with the knife, but he'd upset me.

'Oh, Joanie. Poor old Joanie.'

She hugged me again, and then she looked away, out of the window. 'Oh, Joanie, I don't know. Maybe they could stop him coming into Fletchers. They can, can't they? Didn't they have that thing, where they said shoplifters got banned? Maybe they could stop him coming in? You could ask.'

Fletchers did that. If they caught somebody shoplifting they called the police, and they said, you're banned for six months so don't come back. They gave the name to Security, and sometimes there were photographs. I don't think Security did anything about it. How could they go round the shop with the list of names and photographs, looking at all the customers? Do you look like this one? Right, get out, you're banned.

Mrs Lovell was in charge of all that, personnel and security, and she said it was just so they could watch out for the gangs. So they didn't even have to let them in when they knew they were on a raid. We've only got two security guards at Fletchers, with extras brought in at Christmas, how could they know all the names and the faces in the files?

But they knew the gangs, because the police used to send round the lists. One of the guards said they were mostly nignogs and Pakis, but don't tell anybody he'd said so, the way things were now he'd end up in the nick, banged up with them, now they'd done away with free speech.

I didn't even know the man's name. How could I go to Mrs Lovell and tell her? Even if she listened, even if she said, okay, we'll ban him, what could she do? No name, no photo, just this man bothering Dozey Joan.

'Joanie? They'd stop him, wouldn't they? Stop him coming in?'

Oh, Mum. I wish you'd understand.

I tried to smile at her, but the tears started rolling

down my cheeks, and Mum got really upset then. She put the kettle on, and I thought, I wish that was a real cure. Put the kettle on, make it all better. Make all the bad things go away. A nice cup of tea.

Sheila came in, and Mum told her. Bloody man, that one that looks like that pervert, been bothering our Joan again. Would you believe it? Threatening her with a knife in the middle of the supermarket, up by the biscuits, broad daylight.

'He never!'

'Did then, didn't he, Joan?'

'Yes.'

'Waving a knife about in her face, just as well that Mr Wotsit came back, God knows what might have happened.'

Mum was putting on an act, like she was saying, this is me being angry. But it was good. When she gets like that she can stir things up, make things happen. It's like there are sparks all around her. Sometimes something catches fire, it's a bit like that.

And Sheila too. They like it, being angry, it gets them going. Sheila's like that when she's been dancing, all excited and happy, and it's the same when she's angry.

'Bastard! What's he think he's playing at? He can't do that, knives and things. Wants bloody locking up.'

'What we going to do, then?'

'Tell the bloody cops, that's what. Get him taken care of. Threatening our Joan with a knife in broad daylight. Bastard.'

They went on about it, and it got more and more like a dance. I say this, and you say that, and then comes this bit where I turn round and shake my finger at you, and you say you'd like to kill him, and I say they should bring back hanging. Then it goes slow again, what are we going to do about it? Look at each other, angry faces, but all happy, too. This is exciting, like in the films. Call the bloody cops. Tell Steve and Dave, get the lads together, give him a kicking, sort him out.

Got to find him first.

Mum had poured out the tea, so I drank mine, and I watched and I listened, because I thought maybe they'd know what to do. Once they'd done the dance about it, there might be some ideas. They know quite a lot, Mum and Sheila, much more than I do.

'What did he do with this knife, then?' asked Sheila, and I showed her, the way I'd showed Mum. He held it out in front of him, pointing it at me, then he moved it in little circles.

'How close was he?'

Did that matter? Just a little jab and it goes into my face, or two big, running steps, does it matter?

Close enough to see it wasn't Nicholas Parry, but so like him. If he hadn't talked I might still think it was him. It's mostly the voice that's different, and what he says.

Nicholas Parry had been to university, and had a nervous breakdown, that was what the police had told Sheila. Too much work, too much strain. That's clever people for you, Sheila had said. But the way he talked, it was like every word was in the right place, and he knew what it all meant, and how to say it. He never had to stop and think about how to say it. He wouldn't have said, 'Morning'. It would have been '*Good* morning.' Nothing sloppy. All the words mattered, or they didn't get said.

'I thought he was going to kill me,' I said.

'Right,' said Mum. 'Call the police. Sheila, call the police. They've got to do something.'

Police, she was saying now. Not cops. That meant she was serious, so Sheila went to the phone. Mum poured another cup of tea, and then we both listened to Sheila. Threatening my sister with a knife, she said. When are you going to do something about it? You going to wait till he kills her? Broad daylight in the middle of the supermarket. When are you lot going to start doing what we pay you for?

Mum was nodding, pleased with Sheila. You tell them, girl.

'They're sending somebody round,' said Sheila, and Mum said, I should hope so too. Better put the kettle on again, though God knows when they'll turn up, middle of the night wouldn't surprise me.

Two men in uniform came, about an hour later. They asked all the same questions. Would I know him again? Were there any witnesses? I tried to tell them about the woman with the two children, but he'd hidden the knife then, so she couldn't have seen it. What did he look like, then?

'Like Nicholas Parry,' I said. 'Just different clothes.'

'We'll go and have a word with him,' the younger one said, and Mum seemed like she was jumping at him.

'Who is he, then? You know, don't you? Who is he?'

'You just leave it to us, Mrs Ferguson,' said the older one. 'No good taking the law into your own hands.'

'It's no bloody use leaving it in yours,' said Sheila. 'All this crap about prioritising or whatever you call it. How far down your list of sodding priorities does my sister come? Just you tell me that.'

'Just you tell me who he is,' said Mum, but they wouldn't.

Useless buggers, Mum said after they'd gone. Wished

203

she had a car, so she could follow them. Back to the bloody police station, most likely, straight into the canteen, sit there for the rest of the night. Useless buggers.

But they had known who he was.

I just let Mum and Sheila talk about what they'd like to do to him, whoever he was, if they ever caught him, and I was thinking, the police know who it is. So if they know, maybe I could find out.

I didn't have to. Sheila was saying we should get Steve and Dave to sort him out, and I thought, Steve and Dave are brothers. They don't look like each other, but that man, the one who looks like Nicholas Parry, so you couldn't tell them apart unless they spoke – it had to be his brother.

Forget all that about the Dark Universe, that was Nicholas, because he was ill. Nobody was coming to take the Empress home. This was just a man angry because his brother had been locked up. If Nicholas Parry is locked up you'll be sorry. Wearing his brother's clothes, holding his brother's knife, he was trying to scare me; trying to make me sorry.

Mum and Sheila were still going on about it, but it was only talk now. In a little while they'd be bored with it. They'd say, well, we did what we could, it's up to the cops now, useless buggers. Then they'd turn on the telly. But I wanted to think about it, so I went up to my room and I kicked off my shoes and lay on my bed.

I still had the papers about the adult literacy programme in my bag, and I thought, one step at a time, and I'd taken a big one. Now I'd worked it out, who he was, I wondered why I'd never thought of it before. It was easy, when you knew.

I felt quite calm, lying there on my bed. I put one foot on top of the other, and I looked at my feet, and did a

204

little pattern, like I was walking up the air over my bed, heel on toe, and then swap, and do it again and again and again, one step at a time like it said in the papers.

The two policemen would go and see him, Nicholas Parry's brother. He'd say, don't know what she's talking about. He might say, okay I was in Fletchers, so what? Didn't even know she worked there. He'd never say, yes, I had his knife, I scared her, made her think I might kill her.

One foot over the other, heel on toe, heel on toe, one step at a time. Like walking down a road, the first step's the most difficult. It said that, too, in words a bit like that, only I couldn't be bothered to look at the papers again. The first step, find out who he is.

Okay, Theresa, I've done that.

'You all right, Joanie?'

'Yes, thanks, Mum.'

Maybe the two policemen going to see him would be enough. Right, I've scared her. Made her sorry. Leave her alone now. Done what I meant to do. Maybe he'd be scared now, with the cops knowing what he'd done. Couldn't prove it, but I'd told them. Do anything now, Nicholas Parry's brother, and they'll know who to go after, won't they?

I was playing with the ideas as if they didn't matter. I should have been upset and angry, or frightened, but I was happy. Only that afternoon he'd held a knife and pointed it at my face, and said he knew he'd find me, and now I was happy. I was humming a little tune to myself, I couldn't even remember what it was. Heel on toe, heel on toe, one step at a time, and Theresa had said I was a disgrace because I hadn't even had a decent nervous breakdown.

I laughed.

'I've done it,' I said, and I said it out loud, as loudly as I could without shouting. 'I've done it, Theresa. There's no mystery, it's all simple. When you know, it's easy. It's his brother, Theresa. His brother, looks like him. He's got his clothes and his knife. He knows about the Dark Universe. His brother.'

Heel on toe, heel on toe, and then I made a huge swing with my legs, like big scissors, because that wasn't just a little step along the road, that was halfway there, or maybe even more.

Was it because I was stupid, that I hadn't thought of it before?

I sat up on the edge of my bed, and I tried to work it out. All the things that had happened, when I'd seen him, what he'd done. Had it been stupid, not to think of a brother?

Would Theresa have thought of a brother?

Theresa thought the hospital might have let him out, maybe by accident. Then she thought it was natural for me to be nervous. And if you're nervous, you might see things. Like Nicholas Parry. Thought you might, she'd said when I first told her I'd seen him.

But I had worked it out, by myself. As soon as the policeman had said they'd go and have a word with him, and I'd thought of Steve and Dave who were brothers, and this time two and two made four, not forty-eight, or whatever sort of muddle I'd made of it before.

I'd done it. I'd worked it out, by myself, just with what I knew, and if I'd been stupid, I wouldn't have been able to do that.

I'm not stupid after all. I'm not. I'm not brilliant either, but I was good enough for this. Sheila hasn't thought of it, neither has Mum. But then they didn't mind so much. They'd just thought I was making a fuss. Time I got over it, after all he didn't *do* anything.

Learn to read now. One step at a time, like it says in those papers. Maybe I'll never get so good at it I can do it without thinking, but I'll get good enough so I can find out things I want to know. I'll get good enough so I can write a letter to a solicitor, telling him about a bank account. And I won't have to ask Carol where a new sort of washing powder goes on the shelves.

Theresa would have worked it out, maybe a bit faster than me.

In a way I was pleased she hadn't, because now I'd done it by myself. If I could do that, I was all right.

If he'd just leave me alone now.

14

Late that night I went downstairs, and I sat in the living room with Mum and Sheila, in the easy chair in the corner. They were watching a love story on the telly, and Mum had her hankie out, sniffing into it. She's always like that with love stories.

'All right, Joanie?' asked Sheila, but she didn't want me to answer. She wanted to watch the story.

I'd brought the papers down. There was a form at the back that had to be filled in. Stupid, I thought. Supposed to be about teaching you to read, and they put a form on the back. If you could read that you wouldn't need the course.

But I turned on the little lamp on the dresser, and I looked at the form. First thing I thought was 'can't', so I looked at the telly for a minute or two. Can't do this. Oh, I can't, I can't do it.

Looked again. All boxes, with printing and spaces.

One at a time, maybe I can do it.

The first one wasn't so bad. 'Name', and I could write that, or I thought I could. I tried to hold the pencil and press it down on the paper, and it slipped. I couldn't make my fingers curl up enough to hold it, not properly.

I looked at the pencil, and I thought, at least he didn't *do* anything.

I tried again, and this time I dropped the pencil, Sheila looked across at me when it fell on the floor, but she wasn't noticing.

Pick it up, and do it. Just do it. Like it said in that stupid bit of paper with the baby pictures. Like walking down a road. First step and I've fallen down and hurt my knee.

That seemed a bit funny, that idea, so then I felt better.

Got to do this. Got to.

I held the pencil in my fist, like a baby, and I could hold it like that, it didn't slip, or not much.

Name, it said in that first box, and I thought okay, and I wrote it in and looked at it.

A bit funny, writing holding the pencil like that, but I could read it. Doing all right, I thought.

But then the next box said 'First Name', and I'd already written that in the first box.

Done it wrong. Can't do this. I can't.

Cross out 'Joan' in the first box, and put it in the next one. Looks a mess, and I haven't even done the first line yet, but I can't help it. Maybe best to read it all through before I start trying the writing bit.

I did all right at first. It wasn't too bad. But then I got to 'Education', and I'd just worked that out, and was feeling really pleased because it was a long word, and then it said 'Schools Attended', and I couldn't read 'Schools'.

I put it down and watched the film for a bit, but I didn't like it. I don't like love stories, and Mum was sniffing into her hankie and Sheila was looking like she wasn't thinking anything at all, only all empty, and I hate it when she looks like that. So I picked up the form again, and I looked at that word, and I couldn't do it. I started to get angry. I couldn't even say the first bit. Ssss-Cha! S-cha. S-cha. There weren't any words I knew that began like that.

I got up and I went over to Sheila and I held the form in front of her face, my finger on that word.

'What's that say?'

'"Schools Attended",' she said.

Schools. Why do they write it like that? Stupid, writing it like that. Doesn't make sense. Can't do it if they're going to write it all stupid. But I should have known. I know what Education is, and that word comes right after the bit where it says Education. I should have known.

I can't do this. I can't.

Look at the film instead, but that's stupid too. I don't know anybody who looks like that, everybody on that film looks all perfect. Nobody's got spots, and nobody's fat or skinny or bald. Or has anything wrong with them. It's not real.

School. Schools. I'll know next time, but I hope there isn't too much more that's stupid on this form.

'Joan?'

Oh, shut up. I only needed that word, leave me alone. You'll only laugh.

'Joanie? What you doing?'

'Got to do this form.'

She looked at the telly again, and said she'd give me a hand when the film was over.

Don't want a hand. Want to do this myself. *By myself*, thank you very much, Miss Sheila Ferguson think you're so clever.

I was beginning to get angry with Sheila too, so I went into the kitchen and sat at the table and looked down at the form. Boxes and writing, and the bit where I'd written my name and crossed it out and written it again, was all crooked and smudged. Send that in, and they'd laugh at me.

It was the only form I'd got, so it would have to do. I suppose they thought you could get somebody to fill it in for you, but if I asked Mum or Sheila they'd go on about it. And they'd tell people. Our Joanie's starting to learn to read. They never taught her properly in school.

I can read. It's just it takes a long time, and there are words I don't know, because they write them all stupid, like 'school'.

I sat back in the chair and I looked up at the ceiling, and I thought, no, I can't. I can't read. Might as well face it. Reading age of six, they'd said last time Mum came to school about me and my work, but Mum had given up by then. Never mind, our Joanie, we can't all be clever, can we?

I didn't want to be at school anyway. It was all loud since the operations on my ears, all the time I was frightened. Things made me jump, and I couldn't breathe properly when I was frightened. My heart going fast so I could feel it, just start to get quiet again and there'd be something else loud and sudden, jump, can't breathe, heart going bump bump bump. Hands over my ears, just to make the noise quieter. Is there some sort of psychological problem, do you think? That's a classic symptom.

Then there were the social workers again.

Be surprising if there wasn't a psychological problem, frankly. I suppose you have seen the report? Frankly, we don't write them for fun, although for all the notice people take, we might as well write them in Chinese. No, Mrs Gerhard, I do *not* speak Mandarin, let's not be facetious, this is a serious matter. We *are* being as supportive as we can, but we can't do everything, and there *are* such things as sows' ears and silk purses, if you understand what I mean. *Pas devant les enfants*, and all that.

Quite the linguist this morning. Joan, dear, would you wait outside? Take your reading book with you.

Dad had gone. He'll be away for a while, dear, they said. Never mind. He does love you, he said we should tell you so. He didn't go away because of anything you did wrong.

Then it was just me and Mum and Sheila, and sometimes a social worker. When they came Mum was either happy, because they'd given her some extra money, or angry because they'd said she didn't need it, she should be able to manage without it. Once the police came, because a social worker said Mum had tried to suffocate her. Mum wanted money for new blankets for the winter, and the social worker said she could mend the ones she had. But Mum said they were thin as paper, no point in mending them. What's the use of a blanket when there's no warmth left in it?

Mum said she was trying to show the social worker you could see through it, and the social worker said she had tried to suffocate her with it. A few days later there was a letter from the Social. Verbal or physical abuse of our representatives will not be tolerated. But nothing happened.

There was never enough money for what we wanted.

I didn't want to go to school. Some of the girls said my dad was a pervert, that was why I was a retard. They said it like it was American, *re*tard. Learned it from a film. Mrs Gerhard heard them, and told them they were not only spiteful and unpleasant, but quite remarkably misinformed as well. Also, if they were to spend a little less of their pocket money on cosmetics and a little more on simple soap, they might not have quite so many problems with their complexions. Nasty, ignorant, spotty adolescents.

'What's "psychological"?' I'd asked Mum.

'Mental. Nutcase,' she'd said.

Social workers thought I was mental, then. Never listens, blocks it all out, hands over her ears, classic symptom. But if you hear a sudden noise and it's loud enough to make you jump, you put your hands over your ears because they hurt. If you burn yourself, you put your hand over the bit you've burned. Everybody does, not just nutcases.

Sitting at the kitchen table, staring down at the form, I was thinking about being at school, when I'd been trying to learn to read, when people had been talking about me all the time. They'd all been so stupid. It wasn't me. Thinking about it, I began to understand. Nobody seemed to take the time to stop and think what it must be like. All your life your ears are blocked, then suddenly they're not. What you thought were normal sounds were too quiet for everybody else. Suddenly, everything's loud, and it's horrible, it's frightening. Normal noises, what other people think are normal they make you jump, and you don't like it. So you put your hands over your ears to stop it.

I wasn't mental. I wasn't even stupid. I was only trying not to be frightened all the time. Anybody would do that.

At school, if I asked a question, everybody looked at me. Even some of the teachers. Stupid question, stupid Joan Ferguson. Doesn't even know *that*. *Re*tard, *re*tard, *re*tard. Better not to ask. Just keep quiet if you don't understand. Wait, sometimes somebody else asks. If not, too bad.

'Joanie? What's this form, then?'

I jumped. I hadn't heard Sheila coming in. I'd been thinking. That horrible feeling again, thump thump thump in my chest, just like school, just like I remembered, and I hated it.

'Nothing.'

I turned it over, but she was leaning across the table, and she read the front, where it said Adult Literacy Programme.

'What's this then, Joanie?'

'Nothing. It's private.'

Why was I being like this with Sheila? Bad-tempered, remembering school, how everybody thought I was stupid when it was only my ears. Nobody ever asked me, Why do you do that, Joan? I could have told them. But they didn't ask, they just said, classic symptom.

'You made me jump,' I said, and Sheila said, 'Sorry.'

She was looking at me in a funny way, as if she hadn't seen me for a long time and there was something different.

I put my hands over the papers so she wouldn't see them, but it was too late. She'd read it. Even upside down, she'd read it.

'Go on, then. Have a laugh.'

'I'm not laughing, Joanie.'

She sounded worried, as if I'd told her I was ill or something. Whatever it was, she wasn't laughing at me, so I looked at her, and I told her, I want to learn to read. I'm sick of being like this. Oh, and another thing, that man, he's got to be Nicholas Parry's brother.

'How do you know?'

She sounded really surprised, she was staring at me, but I just shrugged.

'Got to be. What else?'

She's still staring at me, so I thought, better try to explain.

'Looks like him. Knows a bit about me. Got his clothes, hasn't he? Got his knife. Called me "Your Majesty", knows about the Dark Universe and all that. And those cops, they knew who he was, didn't they? When I said, looks like Nicholas Parry, they said they'd go and have a word with him.'

'Joanie, are you sure?'

Not much point in answering that.

'Who told you?'

It wasn't Sheila's fault, but I got angry then. Nobody told me, she knew that. Who could have told me?

'I *worked* it *out*. Dozey Joan worked it out all by her stupid self.'

Then I started to cry. I couldn't read the word 'school', reading age of six, everybody was going to know, because Sheila and Mum would tell them. Our Joan's trying to learn to read, bless her. Nobody knew before, nobody knew I wasn't very quick at reading. But I didn't think I could manage the form. What was I supposed to write, where it said 'Schools Attended'? I'd been to three schools, did I have to write them all in? And why did it matter, all these questions?

It was late, and I was tired.

And there wasn't any Dark Universe; I wasn't the Empress of anything.

I'd never believed it, but there'd seemed to be just this little chance that maybe it was true. Maybe there was this place where I was somebody important, where they needed me. I had a picture in my mind of what he'd said about the dark and cloudy skies, and it was beautiful. I so wanted to see that, not just in daydreams. I never

215

believed it, but I wanted it to be true, and now it wasn't. They hadn't sent anybody else to bring the Empress home, it was just his brother, trying to frighten me.

I didn't want to die, but I wanted the Dark Universe to be true.

Sheila came round the table and sat beside me. She started stroking my hair, and I was sorry I'd been angry with her.

'What a day,' she said. 'Poor old Joanie. Don't you worry, they'll sort it out. They won't let him get you. Fancy that, then, you working out who it was.'

We sat quietly for a bit. Mum called out she was going to bed, don't stay up too late wasting the electric. We heard her going upstairs, then I turned the paper over, and I asked Sheila to help me fill in the form and not tell anybody.

'I'll help you with the reading, if you want to learn,' she said. 'No need for this.'

But I knew what would happen. After a couple of weeks, she'd be fed up with it. She'd have something else to do. Oh, Joanie, not tonight, I'm tired. We'll do it tomorrow.

'Don't have to pay for it,' I told her. 'Might as well get proper teachers. You got enough to do.'

She filled in the form for me, and I watched her, and I thought, I wanted to do that myself. You could have just helped a bit, couldn't you? Anything like that, people take over. I only wanted a bit of help. Anybody could need help.

Mr Bradwell wanted me to help him the next morning. I'd gone in early because I'd forgotten not to. I sat down in the bus, and then I thought, I don't have to do this. I know who he is now, I don't have to come in early.

It was a funny feeling. It seemed like ages since I'd started worrying. Now everything had changed, and it was like trying to look at it all through mirrors. I had to think about how it really was now, not just how it looked. The man was still around, still might try to frighten me, but knowing who he was made it different.

There's no Dark Universe, and that made it different, too. Sometimes I'd thought about it. Sitting over my coffee in the break, when the other girls had been talking and I couldn't be bothered, I'd looked down into my mug, seeing the way the brown coffee and the sort of yellow-white of the creamer powder made a pattern, and I'd think about dark skies and bright green grass. I'm drinking something nice, I'd think. My friends are talking, but I'm not listening. If I say something, they'll stop talking, and they'll listen to me, because I'm the Empress. But if we're laughing, having a bit of a joke, then they won't stop. So when one of the girls said something that made the others laugh, I'd think, that was me, making a joke, everybody laughed. And one of my friends made some sort of crack back at me, and I can laugh, too, because it wasn't nasty. The green grass is beautiful, and so are the star flowers. If I look up, I'll see the moons.

When I die, I'll go there.

I'd thought that. When we had to go back to work after the break, I'd finished my coffee, and I'd thought, when I die, I'll go there.

That had changed too, like somebody switching off a light. They hadn't sent somebody else to bring the Empress home, somebody who looked like Nicholas Parry so I'd recognise him. There wasn't anybody, nobody to send, nobody to be sent. No need for the Empress. No Empress.

'You look sad,' said Mr Bradwell, and I tried to smile at him.

I was trying to remember how many times we'd run out of cooking oil. There'd been last week, and a month before, and just after Christmas. Mr Bradwell said those suppliers wanted a rocket under their chairs. Telling the customers the suppliers had let us down wasn't good enough, not with Sainsbury's only five minutes away, with television advertising behind them. So, Miss Ferguson, if you'd be kind enough to use that remarkable memory of yours, let's see if we can put in our orders early enough to solve the problem.

'Just the oil?' I'd asked, and he'd said that would do to begin with. The whole concept of logistics needed updating in this storeroom, and we had to start somewhere.

Don't ask, it'll look stupid. Just remember the word. Logistics.

We were having a cup of tea, and he'd made mine in my mug. He never forgot I found the little plastic holders hard to handle.

'You look sad.'

'Thinking,' I said, and then I asked, 'What do you think Heaven's like?'

He was a bit surprised. It's a funny sort of thing to ask, when you're working on the stocktaking, but he thought about it, and then he said he supposed it would be different for different people. Depends on what you like. Maybe you can choose. He thought it was a strange thing that he'd wondered about Hell, and knew exactly what that would be like for him, but never Heaven. Hell was frozen fish fingers and canned music and nothing to talk about except football, but now I came to mention it, he did rather hope he'd find his tomato greenhouse somewhere in Heaven. If he ever got there.

Sunflower oil and margarine, and that other oil, the one they put on television. We kept running out of those. And the pickles.

'We never used to have trouble with the pickles,' I said, 'but they changed the supplier.'

'Suppliers can be changed back. Have you quite recovered from what happened yesterday?'

Only yesterday he'd been there with the knife. Something that makes everything so different shouldn't happen all at once. All my ideas had changed and it had only been yesterday.

'Yes,' I said, and then, 'Thank you for asking.'

It wasn't the right thing to say.

'Thank you for helping me, Miss Ferguson.'

If he was right, my heaven could be the Dark Universe. I might go there when I was dead. I might still be the Empress, but it would be a funny sort of God who'd let somebody else be in charge, wouldn't it?

Mince pies, we'd run out of them two days before Christmas, I told Mr Bradwell. Mr Kennedy had gone wild, shouting at Mr Evans. Even in his office, with the door shut, we'd all heard. Idle cretin, do this one more time and you're out. Customers like to buy their mince pies at the last moment, he'd shouted at Mr Evans, because they think they're fresher then, they don't know we've had them in stock for the past six weeks. Any fool knows that, and any fool knows to look at last year's sales graph and be ready for the peak.

'I'll be ready,' said Mr Bradwell. 'But thank you for the warning. Perhaps Mr Kennedy should have a thicker office door. Does he know you can hear through it?'

In the Dark Universe teachers would have to ask

children, not just tell them. Maybe you've got it all wrong, I'd say. You've got to ask. Why do you put your hands over your ears? Not just, classic symptom, that's stupid. Spots are a classic symptom too, of chicken pox and some really horrible things, but it might just be a pimple. Don't say it's psychological problems until you've asked. There're other things besides psychological problems.

'Miss Ferguson, if you could brush up on your reading skills I think there might be a career for you in Fletchers.'

That was daft. He was being nice to me because I was helping him, but he didn't have to be daft.

I'd sent off the form on my way to work. There'd been an envelope with the address already printed, it didn't even need a stamp, so I'd put it in the letter-box, trying not to think too much, or perhaps I wouldn't have done it. Perhaps, if I'd thought about it, I'd have torn it up and put it in the litter bin instead. That first line, where I'd had to cross out my name, that looked messy.

'What are you thinking?' asked Mr Bradwell.

'About reading.'

I could say it to him because I knew he wouldn't go on at me. Why can't you read? What went wrong at school? Why didn't you go to the extra lessons they put on?

But this time there was a long silence, so I thought a bit faster, and I told him we ran out of greengrocery sometimes, but that was Trevor, so I didn't know so much about it. Cauliflowers had been a problem, people had been asking.

He wrote something down. But then there was another silence, and I thought, he's going to go on at me. He's going to ask all those questions.

I wanted to put my hands over my ears. I don't want to hear things that frighten me.

220

'I think it's time to start work, Miss Ferguson.'

I told Sheila that evening, I've been helping Mr Bradwell again. What's logistics?

'Don't know.'

I hate that answer. I hate it, when the question's something easy. I don't know what logistics is, and you don't know, but *you* could find out. There's an old dictionary in the dresser downstairs, left over from school. You could look it up for me.

'I want to *know*,' I said.

'Why are you being so snappy these days?' she asked. She sounded fed up. 'Bad enough people at work carrying on. Come home, have to put up with it from you. Sod off. I don't care what you want.'

I asked Mum later, and she said it was something to do with the army.

'It's *not*,' I said, and I was getting angry. 'Mr Bradwell said it today, and he was talking about work. Mum, I ought to know. Please.'

'Oh, *Joanie*!'

But she went and looked it up, and came back and said, it *is* army, moving things about. I don't know what Mr Bradwell's on about in the storerooms.

'Moving things about,' I answered, and she said if I got any sharper I'd cut myself.

'I hope you're getting paid for all this overtime,' she added.

'I don't have to go in early tomorrow.'

I don't. I won't. I'll see Sarah and Diane again. I'll go in on that bus, and if he's there, I won't take any notice. He's nothing special, he's just trying to frighten me. Even if he's got the knife, I won't be frightened.

But I was. I was frightened. I stood at the bus stop, and

221

I thought, he might have the knife, and he might be angry. The cops have been to see him.

He wasn't on the bus, but Sarah and Diane were, and I could see them waving at me as it came in to the bus stop. They were excited, and happy to see me, so I sat down in the front of the bus, opposite them, and they were chatting to me, and Diane was still waving, even though I was only a couple of feet away from her, across the passage.

'Where you *been*? We was worried.'

'Different work times,' I said. 'Had to go in early. It's all right now, just something needed sorting.'

'We worried. Didn't we, Sarah? We worried about you. We said, where's Joan, then? We said. We worried.'

'Nice to see you.'

'Nice weather we've been having,' I said, and they both smiled and said, yes, it was, wasn't it? Nice weather.

I thought, they're my friends. When I fell over, they got off the bus and came to help me. They worried about me when I didn't come. It had been three weeks, and they'd been worried.

'You been all right?' I asked, and they said they had. They were going on holiday soon, down to Brighton. Was I going on holiday?

Mum had been dropping hints about the money. Enough for a nice holiday, she kept saying. I told her, I'm not using it for a holiday, and she wanted to know why not.

Because Theresa had other ideas, I thought, but I didn't say it. I love my Mum, but it's hard to make her understand.

'Save a bit to put with it, there'd be enough for two people,' she said. 'Enough for a week in Spain.'

She'd sounded sad. She'd never been abroad. Sheila went to France once on a shopping trip, just over the Channel, and said she didn't think much of it. France was supposed to be beautiful, but it was just all flat, with little villages. Two houses and a cow. And oil refineries and things. Bloody ugly, she thought. But there was this big, big place for shopping. It had everything.

'Wouldn't you like to go to Spain?' asked Mum. 'Or maybe somewhere else? It's your money.'

Sometimes Mum gets ideas that start off as dreams, then she thinks they're real. If we ever win the Lottery, she used to say, we'll buy a house. We'll have a holiday. We'll all have nice things. See something on the telly, she'd say, when we win the Lottery, we'll have one of those. She'd start off saying if, but it wouldn't be long before it was when. Then she'd start to get cross about it. Hope the Lottery comes up before Christmas, God knows we could do with the money. Wish the bloody Lottery would come up. If the Lottery doesn't come up in time for our summer holiday, I swear I'll murder somebody.

She'd forget it after a while, and then it would be, you don't still bother with the Lottery, do you? Waste of time, I say.

She's still got a few Premium Bonds, she won them in a sort of raffle at the restaurant. You put in a quid a week, and if you win a number in the draw, you get a Premium Bond. Same thing happened when she got her first one. She was down the Post Office nearly every week, even though they told her, Mrs Ferguson, if the number comes up in the draw, they write and tell you.

Letters can get lost in the post, as you lot ought to know, she'd say. You just give me the list, I'll worry about whether my number's come up in the draw.

They gave her the book of unclaimed prizes, the same book every week. They only get a new one every three months, or maybe it's six. It was weeks before she realised.

Now she'd got the idea that Theresa's money would be nice for a holiday, and it would be a while before she gave it up. I hoped she wouldn't get angry with me.

Maybe I'd have to buy reading books. I didn't know how much books cost. Perhaps they were a lot of money. Mrs Gerhard used to get very upset if books got lost or spoiled at school.

I asked Mr Bradwell that day, without even thinking about it. How much do books cost? I asked, and he said, anything from about two pounds to thousands. Antique books, they could be very valuable. First editions, if they were in good condition, particularly if they were early books by famous authors. Old manuscripts cost almost as much as paintings. There were auctions. Even letters written by famous people.

He went on talking about it for quite a long time while I was putting cases of washing-up liquid on my cage, and I wondered how he knew so much.

'My father used to collect old books,' he said. 'His house was bombed in the war. They were all burned.'

He looked at his watch, and said he'd better get back to work and stop wasting my time. Oh, but ordinary books, they usually cost somewhere between ten and twenty pounds. Paperbacks were cheaper, and you could pick up second-hand books at jumble sales or charity shops for a few pennies.

He didn't ask why I wanted to know. He wasn't the sort of man to make a fuss.

15

The letter from the council came a week later, and Sheila read it to me. It said they were pleased to welcome me to the Adult Literacy Programme, and then there was a telephone number I had to ring to make an appointment.

I rang on my way home from work, and a woman said the office was closed. Could I ring again the next morning?

'I'll be at work,' I said.

'I haven't got any management here now. You have to make an appointment with a supervisor.'

I couldn't telephone in the mornings. There wasn't a telephone I could use.

'Can you phone for me?' I asked Sheila, and she said she'd try.

'He was in a meeting,' she said that evening. 'I tried twice.'

Now I'd sent off the form and they'd answered, I wanted to start. In the mornings while I waited for the bus I'd look at the numbers, and I could remember them. I didn't have to think, that's two lines joined at the top, so it's a seven. I'd never had that much trouble with numbers at school, but I'd got nervous about them since I'd left. I knew what a seventeen looked like without thinking, flagpole, and the lines joined at the top. Just, a one and a seven, that's what it looked like.

That was good.

I looked at the other numbers. Twenty-two, and twenty-two A. Got it. Eight, forty-three, and two hundred and eighteen, that one went to London.

'I can do numbers,' I told Sheila.

'Great. What numbers?'

'Bus numbers. I know them. I can read them.'

But Sheila hadn't known I'd stopped being able to, so she just gave me a funny look. I went up to my room, and I thought, she's right to give me a funny look. I could always do numbers, I'd just forgotten I could do them. That's stupid.

What else can I do that I'd forgotten?

I sat on my bed for about an hour, trying to think. I can't read, but it doesn't mean I can't do anything else. I don't have to believe it, when people say I'm stupid. And if I am, maybe I can stop. Maybe I can get cleverer. If somebody can tell me how.

'Can you try to ring the council again?' I asked Sheila, and then Mum came in and asked what we wanted with the council.

'Night school,' said Sheila. 'I might have to do book-keeping.'

It was nice of her to lie for me. She doesn't often tell lies, our Sheila, she says she always forgets what she's said, then there's a right muddle. It's easier to tell the truth, if you can; you never have to try to remember what you've said.

Mum wasn't very interested, except she hoped nobody expected her to pay for it.

Sheila tried for three days, and then her boss said something nasty about personal calls in working hours, so she had to stop. She was getting close to her exam for her diploma, and her boss's reference was important. She didn't want to go on working there, after she'd got her diploma.

'Sorry, Joanie.'

'That's all right. Thanks for trying.'

'He's a miserable git, and I hate him. I hope he goes bald.'

What was I supposed to do?

I went to the offices in my lunch hour, went on the bus. At least I could read the numbers now. Carol told me which bus to take, and I thought I might just have time.

'It's the lunch-hour,' said the woman at reception. 'Can you come back in an hour? There might be somebody here then.'

'Can I make an appointment? It said to in my letter.'

'You'll have to telephone to do that. There's nobody here right now.'

'There's never anybody here,' I said, and I was getting really angry. 'My sister tried all week. What am I supposed to do?'

'It's not my fault. There's no need to shout at me.'

I went back to work, and I was so angry I could have cried. She hadn't been sorry she couldn't make the appointment. She'd been glad. All week, telephoning, like they'd said, and never anybody there, or in meetings, or on the other line, or got a client with them. Now

I'd used up my money on the bus, and still I hadn't got my appointment, not even just to see somebody to find out about reading.

I hated them. Horrible people, all safe in their jobs, don't have to worry. If we treated customers like that at Fletchers we'd get the sack.

I hate you, I thought. Sitting in your office with bars on the window, now I know why you need them. You make people angry, so you've got to be careful. Make people angry enough, they might try to hurt you. I hate you, woman behind the bars. I wish *I* could hurt you.

If I could read and write, I'd write a letter and complain. But I can't.

'What's up with you, then?' asked Sue that afternoon, and I said, nothing, what do you mean?

'All snappy. I only asked.'

I couldn't even remember what she'd asked, just that she annoyed me. She was standing in the way and I wanted to get on. Stupid cow.

I wish I could hold things properly. Slows me up, having to hold them the wrong way. My hands are never going to be right again, and I'm never going to get used to it.

It's not fair.

'Joan?'

'What?'

'Come on, Joanie. You know me. Only old Rita, poking her nose again. Here, have a hankie. We can skank off five minutes, they owe us that. Park your bum on that box and blow your nose, you look a right sight. Tell me what it's all about. Or tell me to bugger off.'

Old Rita poking her nose was what I needed. She wouldn't laugh at me, or go round telling everybody. I started. I said I want to learn to read, and I tried to tell her about Theresa, and the man who was Nicholas Parry's brother, and then I started to cry again, because when it came to talking about the woman at the council offices I got so angry I couldn't remember what I wanted to say.

'Bitch,' said Rita. 'Give them a little bit of authority and they think they're God. And the women are worse than the men.'

'Mr Bradwell said if I could read there might be a career for me,' I said when I could talk again, and even Rita stared at me when I said that.

'Was he joking, then?' I asked, and she chewed at her lip and looked away over the racks.

'Wouldn't think so,' she said. 'Been helping him, haven't you? He might have meant it.'

'I don't know what to do.' I wasn't crying any more, but the angry feeling was still there. Why did they say they wanted people to learn to read if they wouldn't help them? Why did they write those forms and those letters if it was all going to be like that? Can you call back later, in a meeting, nobody here at the moment, its the lunch-hour, got to make an appointment.

I wanted to start, and I couldn't get an appointment to see somebody to fix it.

'Joanie?'

'Yes?'

'Look, I'm not trying to be funny, but maybe I can help a bit. I helped my two learn to read. Maybe I can help you.'

I looked at her, and she went red, and then she said she'd done quite well at school. Might not think it now, working here, but she had. Passed exams and all.

229

'Why you working here, then?' I asked, and she tried to make a joke. It's not 'why you working here', it's 'why *are* you working here'. If she was going to be a teacher she was going to be a proper teacher, and I'd better not forget it.

I was feeling a bit better by then, so I smiled at her, and went back to my work, but I thought a lot about what she'd said. I couldn't keep on and on going to the council, and telephoning them, and Rita isn't the sort to say something and not mean it. Sheila had offered to help, and she'd meant it too, but it wouldn't last with Sheila. It might with Rita.

Maybe she'd said it without thinking about it. Right now she might be wishing she'd kept her mouth shut. Try and teach Dozey Joan to read? Must be joking. Like that social worker had said, thinking I was too stupid to understand, sows' ears and silk purses. I know that saying, can't make a silk purse out of a sow's ear. She meant I was too stupid, they'd never make anything of me.

I'd thought she was right. I'd accepted that. Not everybody had been nasty about it. Can't all be clever, can we? they'd said. You'll manage. Get yourself a nice, steady job, Joan. You'll get by.

Theresa hadn't thought I was stupid, and neither had Nicholas Parry, and they'd both been clever people. Even if Nicholas Parry was mad, he wasn't stupid. He'd gone mad at university. That's clever people for you, Sheila had said, and that worried me. I wanted to think about that.

If you try to lift something that's too heavy, if you're not strong enough, you can hurt yourself. Maybe, if you try to do something that's too difficult, if you're not

230

clever enough, you can hurt yourself too. If I'm not clever enough to learn to read, I might go mad.

I was feeling cold. It was a hot day, and I seemed to be doing nothing but putting ice-cream in the freezers, it was making me shiver. I wanted to go out in the sun for a bit. All the customers were coming in wearing summer dresses or shorts, saying, lovely day. I wanted a bit of sunshine, not more ice-cream, frozen chocolate gateau, cold drinks. Lovely day, and I was feeling cold, making me shiver.

Might walk home through the park. Might sit on a bench and get a bit of sun.

If you hurt yourself when you lift something, you feel it. Would you know if you hurt your brain? Would it be the same?

Was it a stupid question?

I'd always wondered that at school, if there was something I wanted to know. I'd have to think about it. Was it stupid, to ask that? By the time I'd worked it out, it was too late. Never will know, now.

Still, better that than everybody looking, thinking, stupid Joan Ferguson, *re*tard.

Might be able to ask Rita.

'Enough to drive anybody mad, just sitting there looking at books,' she said. 'I heard some of them work all night, don't get any sleep for days. Take drugs to stay awake. Stupid. Not surprising they get ill.'

Later on she said she thought people put too much pressure on their kids. Made them feel everything depended on them. Everybody works hard for their kids, she said, everybody worth anything. But you don't tell them. How would you like it if you thought your whole family was going to be really disappointed if you didn't get that shelf filled just exactly right? And it was all new, and you didn't know how to do it? Rotten, the way some people treated youngsters like that. Her two worked in offices, made enough money and had time for some fun. That was good enough for her, and for them too.

We were stuffing yesterday's bread into the dump bin with the big sign saying it was half price, and Rita was a bit cross because there was so much of it. No bleeding sense at all, they knew there was hot weather coming, knew it meant people didn't buy so much bread, and did they cut down the order? Did they hell. Be offering jam roly-poly and suet dumplings in the canteen next.

Rita seemed to be everywhere that afternoon, on the checkouts, down in the stores, up in the office, and I wondered about that. She didn't seem to have just one job, like the rest of us. She could do anything.

I was quite glad to get out of the shop that day. I wanted to think, and I was going to have to walk home because of using up my money in the lunch-hour, going to the council. It didn't matter because I'd wanted to anyway. I thought about it while I was putting the ice-cream in the freezers, all the times I wasn't wondering if you could hurt yourself by doing things that were too hard for you.

I went through the park. It was longer, but it was nice. Still in the town, you could hear the cars, even smell them a bit, but I liked the green leaves, and I liked walking on the grass.

There was warm sunshine, and I'd thought I'd sit on the bench by the trees for a little while. Just thinking, how nice it would be to be able to talk like Theresa without thinking about the words, and I found I was crying again. It wasn't the way you cry when you're really upset or angry, but there were tears, and I was crying for Theresa. I'd liked her so much, and she'd liked me enough to leave me the money, and I wished I could have known her better.

Every day I'd thought about the things she'd taught me. The shape of silver under the decorations, how you tell the difference between cut glass and moulded glass, all the things she'd taught me. It had been a bit like talking to her at first, and then I thought, it's the only way I can say thank you. That seemed very important, now I knew what she wanted me to do. Don't lose what she gave you, I thought. Keep it safe, and never forget it.

I wondered where she was, now she was dead. Mr Bradwell wanted his tomato greenhouse, and I wanted the dark and cloudy skies and my friends sitting on the green grass with me. I wondered what Theresa wanted, and whether she was there now.

Or maybe not so far away.

She'd wanted me to learn to read, and Rita had said she'd helped her two daughters. Maybe Theresa had got Rita to say she'd help me. Go on, Rita, you can do it. Tell Joan you'll help her.

I got up, and I began to walk back towards the High Street.

She'd offered. I hadn't asked, she'd offered. So I could say, did you mean it? And if she said, yes, I wouldn't have to try and make an appointment, waste all that time. If she really meant it, she could teach me.

'Rita?'

'Yes?'

'Did you mean it?'

She had a lovely smile, all crinkly round her eyes,

made me want to give her a hug. So I did, and she told me I was daft and soppy, but she liked it, I could tell.

We went down the High Street to Smith's to buy a reading book. I told her I hadn't got any money with me, and she said that was all right, she was going to win the Lottery on Saturday. But I tried to tell her I wanted to buy my own books. That was what the money was for. That was what Theresa meant. Only, I had to get it out of the building society, and I didn't know how.

Rita just wanted a laugh that afternoon. She said a man down her road had got money out of the building society dead easy. Gone in with a gun and said, hand it over, and they had.

When she saw I was serious she said I could pay her back next week, after I'd got my money out. Otherwise it would have to be down to the library, and we hadn't got time.

The girl in Smith's asked what level reading book we wanted, and Rita didn't know. I could see her thinking, should have asked before we came in.

'Six,' I said, and I wanted to cry again. Cry-baby that day, stop being so stupid. I bit my lip so hard it started to bleed, and then the girl came back, and I looked at the book and it was much too difficult. I knew I couldn't do it. I'd meant the reading age, and she'd brought something else.

'Can you pay at the desk?' she said, and Rita took the book and didn't even ask me if I thought it was all right.

I wanted to say, I can't do that one. I can't read that. But she was already going away with the book.

I couldn't say, not there in the shop where everybody could hear. I couldn't say, I read like a six-year-old, that's too hard, I can't read that book.

Four pounds fifty, and Rita handed over a fiver and waited for her change, and she smiled at me and didn't even notice. I was trying to smile, but I couldn't.

I can't do that. I can't do that book. Now you're going to think I'm stupid, too. How can I tell you?

She had to pay my bus fare to her house, because I'd used up all my money. Pay you back tomorrow, I said, and she nodded. I'd have to borrow the money from Mum, but that would be all right. Think of some excuse, how I'd lost my money. Dropped my purse, some of the money fell down a drain.

Nearly five miles, I'd have to walk home and I'd only got my thin shoes on. Can't ask Rita for my bus fare home. Don't even know the number of the bus. Going to be late, Mum might worry.

I'd been so happy when I'd asked her, back at the shop. I'd even given her a hug, she'd called me daft and soppy, but she'd been laughing. Now it was all going wrong. We'd got the wrong book, and I'd never manage that. I'd never be able to read that one.

Rita's council flat was up the stairs, and there were thirteen stairs. I thought, that's unlucky. Rita said they'd have to move soon, once the council found out it was only her and Charlie now Kathleen had moved out. They didn't need two bedrooms any more. There were waiting lists. Fair enough, but she wasn't going to tell them. Let them find out for themselves.

'Cup of tea before we start,' she said, and I couldn't even speak by then, I could only nod, and try to smile at her. She seemed sort of excited, as if it was all going to be a treat, teaching me to read.

But I'd spoilt it all, by not getting the right book.

She came in with the tea on a plastic tray, a mug with

a nice big handle for me because she hadn't forgotten, and a cup and saucer for her. She put them down on the coffee table in front of the gas fire. The cup was lovely, and I looked at it again, and I said, 'That's Rockingham.'

'What's Rockingham?' she asked.

'That cup,' I said. 'Could be wrong, but I think that's Rockingham. It looks like the ones in Theresa's book.'

She said she had a whole set, it had been her mother's. They were only for best, but she'd got one out for a treat. Were they really good then?

'I could be wrong,' I said again, but I didn't think I was. It looked the right shape.

We drank some of our tea, and then she asked if I thought they might be worth a bit.

'If I'm right,' I said. And then again, 'I could be wrong.'

'Don't keep on about being wrong.' Rita was looking at her cup as if she'd never seen it before. 'I've always thought they were nice.'

I wished we could go on drinking tea for ever, and never have to start with the reading, but then Rita said we'd best get on because Charlie would be home soon and she'd have to get him something to eat. So we went and sat at the table, and she got out the book, and opened it, and stuck her finger under the first word.

'What's that say, then?'

'It's the wrong book,' I said. I didn't even want to look at it.

'What do you mean?'

'I can't do it. It's the wrong book.'

She was staring at me, so I tried to explain, but I felt so stupid, and I was sure she'd be angry. We'd gone to all that trouble, going down to Smith's, coming back on the bus and she'd had to lend me the fare, and it was all for nothing, because I hadn't said.

'It's too difficult.'

'You haven't even looked at the bleeding thing. What's that word say? Go on, look at it.'

I looked down to where her finger was pointing, pressed down hard on the page so the fingernail was white. All I could think was, that's a long, big paragraph. There's lots of writing, and some of those words look really long. I can't do this.

'The first word,' Rita said. 'What does the bleeding thing say? Just the first word.'

'"The",' I said.

'At last,' she said. 'We've made a start. We've done the first word. What do you want now, another tea break?'

She was grinning at me, so I smiled back, and I looked down at her finger again. It was still under the first word, 'the', but the next word was long. It was too long.

'I can't do the next one,' I said. 'I can't, Rita. Honest.'

I can't, I thought. Can't do it.

My chest felt tight, and I couldn't breathe very well. Can't do it. Now she'll think I'm stupid. Dozey Joan, can't even read a little kid's book.

But she closed it, and didn't ask me to do the second word.

'Just as well she left you that money, if we're going to buy all the wrong books,' she said. 'We're going to need it.'

I started to breathe properly again. I still thought, if I have to talk I might start to cry again, but that feeling like a dry lump in my throat wasn't so bad, and my chest didn't hurt any more.

I don't want to talk, I thought, but she asked me, how come I didn't say in Smiths, that's the wrong book? Hadn't I noticed, or what?

Wasted her time, I thought. Can't talk. Can't tell her.

'It's level six,' she said. 'Isn't that what you said?'

Reading age of six. That's what Dozey Joan's got, Rita. Not level six. That's quite hard, level six. That's more like nine, isn't it? Reading age of nine, or something?

'I forgot.'

'What did you say?'

'I forgot.'

She didn't believe me. She had her eyes screwed up when she looked at me, and her head was a bit on one side.

I didn't know what to say. I sat at her table, looking down, wishing I hadn't come. Wishing I'd never told her about the woman at the council offices, or wanting to learn to read.

'Never mind,' she said, but it had been a long time since I'd spoken. 'We'll get the right one tomorrow. We can keep this one for later. Do you know what level you are?'

I shook my head. I couldn't tell her. Even though she'd been kind, I couldn't say, because Rita was one of the few people who'd been nice to me. She'd never treated me like an idiot. She'd helped me. But if I said I had a reading age of six when I left school, that would all change.

'How do I find out if my teaset's what you said?' she asked.

'Rockingham. Take it to a shop. But don't sell it.'

'What do I say, then?'

'Say it's for the insurance.'

She didn't think they'd help her. Why would they tell her what it was worth if there wasn't something in it for them?

'Go to Bellinghams,' I said. 'That's where Theresa used to go, when she didn't know. They were okay.'

'Come with me, Joan? I'd feel an idiot. I don't know anything about it.'

'All right.'

'What book do we ask for tomorrow?'

'Six,' I said, and I could feel the tears in my eyes, but I wasn't going to cry. 'Like, for age six. Not level six.'

'Right. Do you know your numbers?'

She wrote down some words. Ten a day, she said, and I had to learn them. Words we used all the time. 'And', 'but', 'the', words like that, so that when I saw them I didn't have to stop and think. Just, see them, and say them.

'How will I know?'

'You use your memory,' she said, and she looked up at me and smiled, that nice smile with the crinkle around her eyes. 'Mr Bradwell said your memory is quite extraordinary. That's what he said. So I'm going to read them to you, and you're going to remember. Just ten words. Can you do that?'

'Oh, yes,' I said. 'I can do ten words. I can do that, no trouble.'

16

I went home with Rita the next night too, but then it was the weekend, and she said Rosalie and Kathleen were coming down, so the reading lessons would have to wait till Monday.

I wondered if it was true, or just an excuse.

I learned the words she wrote down, but I knew them anyway. They were the easy ones you find in every sentence. But I couldn't say, that's too easy. I'd said often enough, that's too hard, I can't do that. I'd better be glad I could do what she wanted.

She'd bought another book for me. She'd gone out in her lunch hour, down to Smith's, and bought a book I could manage. It was a book for little kids. That was all there was. Reading age of six, you'd be reading books written for six-year-old children. Too easy. But I read it three times over that weekend, and I thought, learn it. Learn the words, so you don't have to think when you see them again.

'Read fast,' Rita said. 'Fast as you can.'

You should be able to read without stopping at every word, she said. Keep your eyes moving. Don't stop.

How can you do that? If you don't look at the words, how can you tell what they say? You have to look.

Faster. Read it faster. I want all those five words on that page, one after the other, before you take in another breath. Go on, Joanie. You can do it.

It got pointless after that, because I knew the book off by heart.

'Your bloody memory,' said Rita, but she was laughing.

'Write these words,' she said, and I was surprised.

'Write them?'

'Got to learn to write,' she said, and she repeated it. '*Got* to learn to write, Joanie. Can't manage without writing, not properly. Got to learn.'

But I couldn't do it, I couldn't hold the pencil properly. It kept slipping out of my fingers, I couldn't grip it.

'Can't,' I said, and I thought, I really can't.

'How did you sign your name then?' Rita asked, and I showed her, with the pencil held tight in my fist.

'That's no good for proper writing,' she said. 'Let's have a little think, then.'

She was fiddling around with the pencil, trying different ways of holding it, and then she thought she'd got it right. This might work.

'Clench your fist. Right, now, can you hold that between your fingers? Keep your fist clenched, with the pencil between the knuckles. Try that, then.'

It was awkward, but it wasn't too bad.

'I can do that,' I said, and I felt like laughing.

I can do that. You didn't win *that* one, you bugger.

I wondered why I thought like that, but then I forgot, because I was trying to write. Me, Dozey Joan Ferguson, trying to write. And I can do it, too.

241

I'd taken thirty pounds out of the building society. I'd taken my passbook and gone in, and the woman behind the counter had helped me. I'd have to get some more money out soon. I'd bought two books, and now a writing book and pencils, and I thought, I should be paying Rita.

'What do I say to her?' I asked Sheila, but she didn't know.

She'd promised to keep it a secret from Mum, and sometimes, if I couldn't remember a word, she'd help me. At first she was a bit miffed, that Rita was teaching me when she'd offered, but I said, Rita would have been hurt. Rita had wanted to be a teacher once, I said.

'How do I offer to pay her?' I asked again, and she shrugged. I don't know. She's your friend.

All that weekend I wondered about it, and I thought I'd got it right. On the Monday, when I saw Rita, I said what I'd practised. I'd learned it, and practised it. 'Theresa left me the money to pay for lessons. That's what Theresa wanted. So Theresa wants me to pay for my lessons. That means paying you.'

'Don't be so daft,' said Rita.

'It's what she wanted.'

'It's not what *I* want. What you going to do about *that*?'

She's only little, but she can stick her chin out and make you think she's big as a house.

Mum was working late the next week, so I sat at the kitchen table to do my writing when I got back. I could almost see myself, like a little kid doing homework, sitting there with my feet wrapped round the legs of the chair, and if I was trying really hard I'd notice my tongue sticking out of the side of my mouth. I even chewed the end of my pencil when I looked at what I'd written.

'Write it slowly,' said Rita. 'There's no hurry.'

Write slow, read fast. Two more books, and I learned them, so it was easy.

'Too easy,' said Rita.

I was learning the words off by heart, so I could just say them; turn the page and say them.

'Your bloody memory,' said Rita again.

She wrote something down while I made the tea and then she showed it to me.

'Read that.'

They were all the same words that were in the book, but making different sentences. I could read them, but it took me a long time.

'Read, don't recite,' said Rita.

We took one of her cups along to Bellinghams, and Samantha Bellingham looked at it and said, it's Rockingham. How much of this have you got?

I wandered off and looked at some things at the back of the shop. If Rita wanted to know what it was worth, it seemed nosey to stand there and listen.

There was a cameo pendant on a black velvet ribbon, and there was a little note on it. I tried to read it. One of the words was 'Gift'.

I thought, I could buy a present for Rita. Not the cameo, that's not her style. But something she'd like.

I'd first met Theresa when I'd bought a cup and saucer, then I'd got to know her better when I'd bought a spoon. I could buy Rita spoons to go with her cups and saucers. I didn't think she had any nice ones.

Samantha remembered me, asked me how it was going. Fine, I said. She missed Theresa. Couldn't believe she'd never see her again. Always had liked her, even if she had been little better than a pirate at auctions.

Rita wouldn't even let me talk about paying her. I tried a few times. I'd go home in the evening and think about what she'd said, and then I'd try to work out an answer. I'd think to myself, Theresa could have done this, right there. Right away, she'd have thought of an answer. Wouldn't have to go home and think about it.

'That's what the money was *for*,' I said, and I said that almost every time.

'I'm pissed off with this subject,' said Rita. 'Read your damned book.'

I wrote her a letter:

> Dear Rita,
>   Thank you for helping me reading. Theresa
> wanted me to read. She gave me the money for
> that. You are dennying a dead womans will.
> Love from Joan.

I read it through, and I thought, only a couple of months ago I couldn't have read that, let alone written it.

'Write out "denying" three times,' said Rita. 'I don't reckon it's like learning for you; it's more like remembering. That's why it's going so fast. Shall we look at that level six book again?'

Long words, big paragraphs, and I thought, I can't. But Rita said I should read the words I knew, and she'd underline the ones I missed, and in that whole big first paragraph there were only five words I couldn't do.

'Guess them, then,' she said.

She wrote them down for me for my list that evening,

and I learned them. The next day I read the paragraph again.

I remembered when I'd first looked at that book. I'd nearly cried. Now I was reading it.

'Listen to the radio,' Rita said. 'There's some good stuff. You can learn some new words from listening to the radio.'

I went back to Bellinghams, and I saw Samantha. I asked her about a set of silver spoons to go with the Rockingham, about a hundred and fifty pounds?

'I know where I can get them,' she said. 'Come back on Thursday.'

Rita brought a stock list home for me to read. It's not so easy, she said, reading words from a list. Can't guess the words. But I'd have to do it. Give it a go.

It took a long time. Some of the names were hard.

The next day Mr Bradwell wanted me to help him with a stock check. He had a clipboard with a list on it, the same one Rita had shown me.

She was in the stockroom, telling Sue to bring something up. She looked across at me, and she raised her eyebrows, as if she was asking a question.

I asked if I could try to do it on my own, noting the things we needed, and Mr Bradwell stared at me over the top of his glasses, but he handed me the clipboard and the pen.

I wished I hadn't said anything. I looked down at the list, and I thought, I can't do it.

Then I thought, that's stupid. I've already read this one. I do know it. 'Might take a bit longer,' I said, and he just nodded.

It did take longer, but we had enough time. When we'd finished he checked off the list, and he said it would be a great help to him, when I could do this by myself.

I thought, I can read. Nearly. I can nearly read now.

One day I'll buy myself a book. I won't think, can I read this? I'll think, is it interesting?

'"Once upon a time there was a king who had a . . ."'

'What does it start with, then?'

'B. Buh . . . eh . . . a . . .'

'Look at the picture. How's she meant to look?'

'Pretty? I suppose.'

'Beginning with B.'

'Beautiful?'

She wrote it down on the list for me to learn that night. Why's it written like that, then? Stupid. And 'daughter'. Beautiful daughter. Long blonde hair and blue eyes. Princess. I managed that one, but Rita wrote it down anyway. I'd had to stop and think about it.

I went back to Bellinghams, but I didn't like the spoons. They were too heavy. I didn't think fiddle pattern was right, it didn't look as if it would go with the Rockingham.

'That's okay,' said Samantha when I said I was sorry. 'I'll keep looking.'

Mum came home early and found me doing my writing at the kitchen table. She went on and on about it until Sheila told her to shut up, and there was a row.

'You make it sound like the bloody goldfish started talking,' said Sheila. 'If you'd taken a bit more notice when she was at school she wouldn't need to learn now.'

Mum threw a pie dish at her. She was really angry.

I wanted to do my writing, so I picked up my books and went out. I could hear them shouting at each other, about me, but I didn't want to listen. I'd heard it all before, and I didn't want to believe it any more.

Leave me alone, I thought.

Sheila came in a little while later and sat down on the bed, hard, so it bounced. My pencil slipped on the paper.

'Sorry,' she said, but she wasn't. She didn't think it mattered. Only Joan, doing her little bit of writing.

When I'd had to do homework they'd always said 'little': Joan's little bit of work, Joan's little bit of reading, Joan's little sums. It couldn't be anything important, if Joan was doing it.

I didn't say anything to Sheila, but I found my rubber and I rubbed out the word I'd spoilt.

'She drives me mad,' said Sheila.

There was quite a lot I had to copy that night. I didn't want to talk to Sheila, I wanted to do my work.

'She can be that nasty.'

Sheila wanted me to talk to her. She wanted me to agree with her, Mum can be nasty. Oh, yes. Do you remember that time. And then when you. All that talk, so Sheila could feel all right. Shouting at Mum, and Mum shouting back, and now Sheila wants me on her side, to make her feel all right. So she comes into my room, and bounces down on my bed and spoils my work. My *little bit* of writing.

'What's the matter with you, then?'

'Nothing.'

There's nothing the matter with me. I didn't want this. If I'd known Mum was going to come back early I'd have come up here to do my writing. Mum never comes into my room without knocking. Gives me time, that does. Shove my books under the pillow before I say come in. When that door opens I'm just sitting on my bed, and I'm smiling at her. Hello, Mum, had a good day? No, I'm not doing anything. You want me to do something?

Not Sheila, she's in and out like she owns the place. Never mind what I'm doing, if Sheila wants to talk I've got to stop. Talk to Sheila. Agree with her. Yes, you were in the right.

'You're getting that bloody miserable since you started this reading lark. You never used to be like this.'

I wonder if that's true. I wonder if it matters. I always used to be scared of upsetting Sheila. She could make life horrible. I had to be really angry before I'd give Sheila a back answer, even more than with Mum.

Now, I think I'd be more scared of upsetting Rita. Sheila can't do much, but I need Rita.

I can nearly read. I can. Writing's a bit hard, but I can nearly *read*. And when I can read, I can do anything. Anything. I can find out, when I can read. I can go to the library, and ask for the book that'll tell me, and I can *read* it, and then I'll know.

I'll find out why Vicky died of bronchitis in just one day. And that history lesson at school, when I'd thought it might be a stupid question, and then it was too late. William Rufus, they said he was murdered, shot by an arrow in the New Forest, and I wanted to ask, how did they know? Out hunting, weren't they? Could have been an accident, couldn't it? How did they know?

'Are you going to *talk* to me, or what?'

Now she's getting really angry. Why have I got to talk? I didn't ask her to come in.

'I want to do my writing.'

'You miserable little bitch. I've had a hell of a row with Mum about you. And *you* want to do your *writing*. Well, go on, then. Go right ahead and *do* your *writing*, much good may it do you. You think it's going to make you different? Think reading and writing can make *you* normal? Take a bloody sight more than that, you dumb thicko.'

I listened to her running down the stairs, and I heard the front door slam. Nobody to talk to, she had a row with Mum, and I wouldn't take her side, so there was nobody she could talk to. So she'd gone out.

Clever, I thought. Managed to work that out all by yourself. Got there in the end.

I looked down at the paper, where Rita had written the words she wanted me to copy. They were so neat, those words, all little straight lines or tidy little curls and circles, the dots right over the top of the letters where they ought to be. Underneath, where I'd tried to copy, it didn't look like that. Hardly any of the lines were straight. The paper was all dented where I'd pressed too hard. It was smudged and dirty where I'd had to rub it out because it wasn't good enough.

What's that word she's written?

I don't know. I don't know that word. She didn't say, and I don't know.

I can't read it.

Take more than reading and writing. You can't make a silk purse out of a sow's ear. Take more than that to make *me* normal. Dumb thicko.

Joanie? Give this letter in at the school, will you, darling? Good girl, Joanie. Don't read it. Don't read, Joanie. Understand? Yes, Dad.

Oh, come on, *she* can't read. Come on.

Joanie? Yes, Dad. Yes, Dad. Yes.

Don't read it, Joanie.

It's safe enough. She can't read. That's safe.

What's the matter with your sister, Joan? Don't know, Miss. This note says she's ill. What's the matter with her? Has she seen the doctor? Don't know, Miss.

Don't know. Don't read. Don't know, Miss. That's safe enough.

All right, Joan. Go to your classroom now.

Can't read, don't know, all right, Joan.

What's this word Rita wrote down here for me to copy? I don't know, I can't read it. Not much point in writing things you don't understand. Not much point, if you can't read it.

I didn't hear Mum knock the first time. Must have been louder the second time, and she called out my name.

'Joanie? You all right?'

'Come in, Mum.'

I didn't put the things under my pillow. No point, she knew now. She'd tell people. Our Joanie's learning to read and write. She wasn't very quick at school, but now she's learning.

'Joanie? Hello, pet.'

'Hello, Mum. Had a good day?'

'Oh, Joanie.'

She sat down on the bed, where it was still all crumpled from where Sheila had been. I smiled at her. She's nice, our Mum. Her hair needed doing again. Down at the roots it was a different colour, a bit grey, a bit dark, where the red from the henna was growing out. I hoped Sheila wouldn't be too angry to do her hair for her. She does it so well, our Sheila. She makes Mum's hair look so beautiful.

Beautiful. I can write that word now. I know that word, I can read and write it.

Rita said we'd do dictation next week. She'd read, I'd write, and then we'd look. How much of it had I got right? How many mistakes?

'Joanie, pet. I do love you.'

'Love you too, Mum.'

Nothing's changed, has it? Just, I'd thought it didn't matter, upsetting Sheila, and I was wrong. She knows, and she can say. Take more than that to make me normal.

How do I get normal, then? Sheila knows me.

'Sheila said I stopped you reading.'

There were tears in Mum's eyes. Oh, Sheila, what have you done? What did you say to her? Sticks and stones will break my bones, but words. Words will never hurt me? Words leave me sitting here looking down at little grey smudges on a dirty bit of paper that was clean and lovely before I started on it, and Mum's got tears in her eyes.

Funny, the things you remember. There's a tribe, somewhere a long way away. When they want to cut down a tree, they go and shout at it. They say, a tree's very strong. You have to break its spirit before you can cut it down. So they shout at it. They use words, they shout cruel words, angry words like they hate the tree, and they break its spirit, and then they can cut it down.

'What's that word say, Mum?'

'It says "trouble", Joanie.'

Why's it written like that, then? I can't do this, if they write things all stupid like that. I can't do this.

'Did I stop you reading?'

'No.'

You didn't help much, but you didn't stop me. I suppose you thought what they all thought, she's not very bright. Not exactly simple, not the sort you have to put in a home, but not very bright. Sheila, now, she was different. She was bright. Like sparks flashing, our Sheila. Dance, could have won a cup, can do just what she likes. Doesn't always like, mind. Doesn't always do so well, but not because she can't. Toss her head in your face and defy you, our Sheila. Don't want to do it, bloody well won't do it, and you know what you can do about it. Don't care who you are, Mum, Dad or teacher, if I don't want to do it I bloody well won't, so stuff you. You can't hit me, Mrs Gerhard, I'll have the police on you.

I can suspend you, you impertinent little madam.

Great. Then we both get what we want. You get rid of me and I get out of this place. So go ahead.

Joan, dear, would you please give this letter to your father? Yes, Miss.

Give me that. You give me that letter, Joan, or I'll push you under that bus. Give it to me. Right. And you say a word, I'll kill you. You hear me?

Yes, Sheila.

Did you read it?

I can't read, Sheila.

Just as well for you. You ever read anything about me, I'll kill you. This is private. You know what happens to snoops? Bad things. Bad things, Joanie, you understand? You listening to me?

Yes, Sheila.

Joan, did you give that letter to your father? Joan? *Joan.* Yes, Miss. Did you understand what I said? Joan, are you listening to me? Yes, Miss. Oh, never mind, dear. Go back to your classroom.

'I never meant to hold you back, Joanie.'

Mum sounded sad, but it was a bit like acting, too.

Never pushed me forward, did you, Mum? Rows, always rows, about Sheila, never about Joan. What did you do with that letter? What letter? I don't know what you're talking about. You've got homework to do. Oh, yes? What about the dancing, then? What are you talking about? Got a project. Got to feed the ducks in the park.

You *bloody* little liar, I rang the school, you *never* had to feed the ducks.

Go on, then. Hit me. I'll show them the marks. Would have thought you'd have had enough of the police and the bloody Social.

Go and do your homework.

Go and get bollocking stuffed.

Don't you *dare* speak to me like that, you cheeky little tart.

Joanie, go down the shop for me. You can do your little bit of work when you get back. There's a love.

This word Rita had put down that I couldn't read. Trouble. I should know that one. I'd better learn that one, if I don't learn any of the others.

But the tears aren't just in Mum's eyes now, they're running down her face. I think it's a bit late for all that, but I do love you, Mum. I just don't understand. Why, when it was Sheila who made the trouble, that word I didn't know how to read, why did you always love her so much more than me?

Why did Dad love Sheila so much more than me?

I never did read the letters. Never once, I never even looked. Don't read, he said, and I didn't.

Then he told me, on the stairs when I overheard. You say a word about this and I'll cut your tongue out.

Yes, Dad.

I never do. I never did, I never said. I know it's bad to talk, bad to read, just keep quiet. If you don't tell them they can't do anything, and it wasn't me who told them, it wasn't me.

'Trouble.'

'That's right, Joanie. That's what that word says. Can you read the others?'

'A bit. I can read a bit.'

I can hear, too.

Don't worry about her, she never listens.

I don't want to go to school today, Dad. I won't go. They might make me tell a secret.

All right, Sheila, love. You stay home, then.

Joanie, give this letter in at the office. Don't read it, Joanie. Never read.

No, Dad.

Dad, I don't want to go to school, I don't feel well.

Joan, you've got some catching up to do. Come on, get your coat.

Dad, I might tell a secret.

Come on, Joan. Get your coat on. Now, Joan. Do as I tell you.

Don't want to. Don't want to.

You don't want a belting either, do you?

Why don't you love me? I do what you say. Why don't you love me?

'Do you want some help with the other words?'

'Don't cry, Mum. I love you.'

'I love you too, Joanie.'

When all the social workers had gone, and Dad had left, and there were just the three of us, she asked, Joan, was it you who told them?

'No, Mum.'

It wasn't Sheila. Oh, no, it wasn't Sheila. She liked it when Dad was there. Could do what she wanted. I'm going out. Where are you going? Wherever I like. Maybe I'll tell you later, if you promise to keep it a secret.

How do you write 'secret'? That's an important word. I should know that one.

Where have you been, Sheila? Don't you shout at me, you'll wake the neighbours. Do you know what the time is? Where have you been?

At least he pays me.

Oh, God. You unspeakable little bitch. You dirty tart.

Go on, then. Hit me. Hit me, and I'll tell. And I'm going tonight, too. I am. Oh, yes, I am.

Sheila. Sheila, don't. Please don't start doing this. I love you.

That's what he says. And he pays me too.

Sweetheart, listen. Listen to me. If you promise not to go, I'll give you money. If that's what you want, I'll give you money. I love you. I can't live without you. That's why we do the secret things, because I love you. It's only for love.

After that the screaming started. Mum, screaming at Dad, what sort of a father are you, letting her go out all hours of the night? Sheila, screaming at both of them, I'll do what I like, you can't stop me. Words, and words, screamed and shouted, words can break your spirit. Shouted words until you don't care any more, do what you like, I don't care any more.

And the whispered words, secret, secret. Oh, I do care, I care too much, and it hurts too much, and I wish I was dead.

17

I went back to the Dark Universe that weekend, or so I think. Mooning about in my room, Mum called it, and she tried to be nice. Sheila didn't mean it. I wasn't a dumb thicko. I'd just been a bit slow at school, that was all. Plenty of people were like that.

Sheila said nothing. She was still angry, as if she knew she'd done wrong but she wasn't going to say sorry. I should have stopped doing my little bit of writing and talked to her after she'd had a row with Mum, especially since it was all about me. It was all my fault. Enough to make anybody lose their temper.

So I closed my eyes. I lay on my back on green grass and I looked up at dark skies, and I listened to my friends talking and laughing. I swam in dark brown pools with silver fish, and the smell of mint in the air. I scrubbed myself with the soapweed, and it foamed. I was clean in the water, and I could swim well, diving down to the shining pebbles with the green water plants growing between them.

There were star flowers growing on the bank.

I had a friend called Tania. I had a lot of friends, but

Tania was my best friend. We'd scrub each other's backs with the soapweed when we swam in the pools, and sometimes I lent her things, bits of jewellery or clothes. I gave her a puppy for her birthday. It used to lie on the grass with us, with its head resting on her foot.

When we were tired we went home, and the rooms were big. Golden floors, all polished wood, and the smell of the polish was nice, a bit like lemon in the wax. They were high rooms. You couldn't reach up and touch the ceilings, they were too high for that. You'd need ladders.

People came to see me. They had problems and they wanted me to tell them what to do. They called me 'Your Majesty', and they bowed to me, but I told them not to bother. I didn't need people to bow to me.

It was nearly time for the summer games, and there were pavilions ready for the teams from all over the universe, and everybody was happy. It was a holiday, the biggest holiday of the year. There were prizes to be won and old friends to meet, evenings to drink together and days to compete. I spent the time with my friends, walking on the running tracks and the playing fields. Tania was in the running team for our world, and we used to watch her, and time her, and tell her she was doing well. She was very fast.

'You going to spend the whole weekend sulking up here?'

'I'm not sulking.'

'Need any help with your reading?'

'No.'

I suppose it was sort of like saying sorry. Maybe she hadn't meant it. But she'd said it, and you don't say things if you don't think them. She'd said I wasn't normal, and Sheila knew me better than anybody else, even Mum.

How do you get normal?

When I can read, I'd thought, I'll be like everybody else. But I hadn't been able to understand everybody else. Sometimes I'd thought about other people, you can read. Why don't you? Why don't you find things out, if you can read? All you talk about is what was on the telly last night, and what you'd do if you won the Lottery, how you'd spend the money. Why don't you find things out if you can read? Interesting things, that you want to know about, why don't you find out? It's all in books, somewhere. You've just got to find them, and read.

But they didn't.

I was on the second shift that week, so I couldn't go home with Rita. Charlie needed his tea cooking, and I didn't want to read and write at the table with him there. He was nice, Rita's husband, but I felt embarrassed. I felt silly, learning to read. Tuesdays and Fridays Charlie works late, Rita said. We could have a short lesson on those days. Just check over what I'd practised, and take a bit more home. Do some more real work the next week.

Samantha Bellingham telephoned and left a message. She'd found a set of spoons for me.

'What you want them for?' asked Mum.

'For Rita.'

'What for?'

Sheila was still being difficult. She hadn't done Mum's hair, said it would bloody well have to wait until she felt like it. Mum was upset. She tried to be nice to me, but most of the time she forgot, and it made her snappy.

'For helping me with my reading. And my writing.'

'I would have done that for nothing.'

I didn't say anything, but I thought, all my life you could have done that, and you never did. You never thought I was worth it before.

The spoons were beautiful. They were just right. Venetian, Samantha said, and sorry, love, but even at trade price they're two hundred. Sorry, Joan.

It's what the money's for, I thought.

'I'll get it out next week. Thank you.'

'You picked up those spoons yet?' Mum asked that night, and I said I'd get them tomorrow.

'How much?'

I could have lied. I could have said, none of your business, but she was upset enough. So I told her, and she burst into tears.

'Two hundred?' She was nearly screaming. It was horrible. 'Two hundred quid for a few spoons? Just for helping you with your reading? Oh, Joanie.'

I didn't say anything. I wanted to go away. I wished she wouldn't be like that.

'You won't have nothing left for your holiday. Nothing. Work all the year round, never had a decent holiday, spend it all on a daft little set of stupid spoons for bloody Rita. You must be bloody mad.'

She wasn't thinking of me. When she said, work all the year round, she meant she did. She'd still hoped we could go on holiday together, with the money. Her and me. I wondered if she even thought about me. When she was thinking about a holiday, was I in her plans at all?

She saw herself on the beach, in the sunshine. Where was I?

I went up to my room again. I seemed to spend most of my time there now. I thought I knew how it had happened. Started off as Joanie couldn't go on holiday by herself, she'd never manage. I'll have to go with her. There's enough money, if we're careful. Might even save a bit to put to it. We could go to Spain. Never been abroad. Like to see Spain. I really would like to see Spain.

Mum came up to my room. She knocked on the door and I said, come in. She'd stopped crying, but her eyes were all red, and her face looked sort of hard and angry.

'You paid for those spoons yet?'

'No.'

'Still time to get out of it, then?'

I didn't want to get out of it. Rita would love those spoons. She'd taken good care of her Rockingham teaset, even more so since she'd found out how much it was worth. She was proud of it. It had its own shelf in the kitchen cupboard, up out of the way so it didn't get knocked, and even when she didn't use it she washed it every week.

'Joanie!'

'Yes.'

'Well, you just tell them, Joanie. You're not having those spoons. You've changed your mind. It's *stupid*, two hundred pounds. Just *stupid*, Joanie. They're taking advantage. Because you're not very bright.'

Now you. Dumb thicko, take more than that to make you normal. That was Sheila. Now you. Because you're not very bright.

But I can nearly read. I can. Nearly.

'Oh, Joanie, I know you mean well. But you can't spend all that money on a present. You can't. It's not like we're rich people.'

Maybe I can make her understand.

'It's what the money was for,' I said. 'That's why she left it to me.'

'To buy a present for Rita? Oh, don't be so *stupid*.'

Her voice was angry again. She didn't want me to argue, she didn't want to listen to me. She wanted me to do what she said. Tell them I've changed my mind about the spoons. Then use the money for a holiday. A nice *little* holiday, for me and her, because I wouldn't be able to manage on my own, because I'm not very bright.

'So I could learn,' I said. 'Reading, and all that.'

'How do you know? She tell you that? You didn't even know about the money till after she was dead. So how do you know what she wanted? And what's it matter, anyway? She's dead, isn't she? You didn't even go to her bloody *funeral*, that's how much *you* care about what she wanted.'

Oh. Oh, Theresa. I never thought. I never thought, I should have gone. I didn't know, I never even went to your funeral to say goodbye, I never thought. I should have gone to your funeral, and I never thought. I'm sorry. I'm so sorry, Theresa. Please, I'm sorry, I didn't mean not to say goodbye. I didn't mean it. I never thought, I never knew. I never.

'Joanie, don't cry! Come on, lovey, don't cry! I never meant to make you cry. Here, have a hankie. Come on. Have a blow. Don't cry. I never meant to hurt you. It's just, sometimes I have to look after you, I have to help you a bit, don't I? Well, I'm your mum, aren't I? That's what mums are for. Don't cry. There's no harm done. Nobody's going to be angry with you.'

I don't care about that now. I don't care. You're going to be angry with me because I'm going to get those spoons for Rita, no matter what you say. I'm angry. I'm angry with me, because I didn't go to Theresa's funeral. I should have gone, to say goodbye, and to say thank you.

I know this was what she wanted. That was all we ever did really, even though we were polishing the furniture, and cleaning dirty wood with vinegar, and washing glass and polishing silver, all we really did was teach and learn. She was a teacher, Theresa. I never knew it then. I'd thought teaching meant sitting in front of rows of kids and telling them, this happened; that is what you do; learn this; read that; I'm in charge, and you've got to do what I say. Not what Theresa did, saying, right, what have we got now? Bit of old tat, or what? What do *you* think? Is this any good? Not bad, I suppose. What do you think, Joan?

Not bad, I'd said at first, listening to her. Not bad.

But later, old tat, isn't it? All square and ugly. And that wood's yellow. Don't like that.

Right, where did you leave the axe? Mrs Stevens wanted a bit of firewood, now she's got it.

I don't know. Not sure about this. Like the legs. But that top, that's all wrong.

Reckon we could keep the legs and see if there's something nice to put on them? Might find something else with a nice top and lousy legs?

'Feeling better, Joanie? Feeling better now?'

'Yes, thank you, Mum.'

I like that, Theresa. Don't know why, but I do like that.

Joan, I *wonder*. Do you know, I think that just might be Sheraton. On an off day, by his standards, but I think it just might be. I think that goes down to London.

I still don't know Sheraton, I can't tell. But I've got ideas about what's good and what's rubbish. You taught me that, and it's important, and I never even said thank you.

Buying Rita those spoons is a sort of thank you.

'Joan, are you listening to me?'

'Yes, Mum.'

'Good girl. All you've got to do is telephone and say you've changed your mind. Nobody's going to be angry. You could buy Rita another present. Nice box of chocolates, maybe a bottle of wine. Bring her back something from your holiday.'

'No, Mum. Sorry. No.'

'Joan.'

'I don't want to go on holiday. I want to learn to read.'

She hit me. It was years since she'd hit me. She hit me on the side of the face, not very hard, but it stung. I looked at her, and I thought, I want to hit you back. Why should you hit me, and me not hit you back? When she raised her hand again I turned so I was facing her, and my hand was up too. I didn't say anything, but that hand, up like hers, it said it for me. Hit me again and you're in a fight. I'm not a little kid any more, crying and saying sorry. I'm grown up now and I'm angry.

'I'm not going on holiday,' I said, and she was looking at my hand as if she'd never seen it before, she was that surprised.

She didn't say anything else. She went out of the room, and she didn't slam the door.

I'd won.

I felt all empty inside, sort of sad and hungry, and I wanted to cry again. Mum had always been in charge. She'd always told me what to do, and I'd done it, most of the time. This time I hadn't, and it was like the side of the house had fallen down. It was open and free now, but it wasn't safe any more. It wasn't safe, like that.

I hadn't known it would be like this. I'd just been angry with Mum for trying to stop me buying Rita the spoons when I'd known it was the right thing to do, and then for hitting me.

Suddenly it had all got so big. It had all changed, and the way I felt had changed. I was lonely, and I was frightened, and I wished I'd let her hit me again. I didn't want it to be like this, frightening, and on my own. Only a few minutes ago it had been safe, like always, and now it was all different.

Maybe if I said I was sorry it would be all right.

I'd do that. But I'd get the spoons first, and I'd give them to Rita, so it would be too late. And I'd never say I was sorry for doing that, because it was right. Rita would love those spoons. I wouldn't say, they were two hundred quid, but I would say, be a good idea to insure them, Rita. This is what Theresa wanted, Rita. Give them back to me and I'll chuck them in the bin. Being able to read is worth more than the spoons. Sometimes it seems it's worth everything.

I'll buy a book on antiques when I can read. How did you know it was Sheraton, Theresa? How did you know that? Or think it might be? Just a chest of drawers, and I'd thought, that's nice. I hadn't known why. Not too high, not too low. Not too wide, not too narrow, it was all the right shape. The *right* shape.

And those spoons, they were right, too. Venetian, Samantha had said, but I didn't know about that. I'd looked at them, in the case that was new, not made for them, but that didn't matter. Dark blue velvet and the spoons lying on them, and I'd said yes, because they were right. They were right all by themselves, and they'd go with Rita's Rockingham, so I'd said yes.

It felt as if Theresa was grinning at me.

Oh, yes, she'd have said. Oh, yes. I don't think *they* came free with a jar of Horlicks. Let's put the kettle on and have a little gloat.

I'm going to do that, I thought. I'm going to bring them back here, and I'm going to have a wash and put on my nice frock, and then I'm going to make a cup of tea in my mug and put out my special cup as if it's for Theresa, and I'm going to sit up here and look at those spoons, and pretend she's here. I'm going to pretend we're talking about them. Things like, That didn't come free with a jar of Horlicks, I'll pretend we're saying.

I was beginning to feel a bit better. My cheek was still stinging where Mum had slapped it, and I could feel the tears drying. Tears because I was sorry I hadn't gone to Theresa's funeral. I'd been shocked when Mum had said that. It was true, I'd never even thought about it.

One day I'm going to find out where you're buried, Theresa. I've still got that letter from the solicitor, telling me about the money. When I can write, when I can do it myself, I'm going to write and ask where you're buried. Then I'll buy you some flowers, and I'll go there, and say goodbye.

I thought, doing it like that would make it right. I'll buy the flowers with the money I've earned, because it's a present. And I'll write the letter myself, because that's what you wanted for me. That's like saying, look, Theresa. I've done it. I can write. That's how I got here, to where you're buried, because I wrote the letter to find out.

I got off my bed and I found the paper Rita had

written for me, with all her tidy writing in a straight line, and mine underneath it, smudged where I'd had to rub it out, and the dented bit where Sheila had sat on my bed and jogged my arm. I hadn't written anything since then.

Coward, I thought. Coward. Get on with it. Sheila says you're a dumb thicko, so you give up. Take more than that to make *you* normal. Well, maybe you're wrong, Miss think-you're-so-clever Sheila Ferguson. Maybe you're *wrong* then, ever think of that? And maybe Mum's wrong too, with her you're not so bright, have to look after you.

I rubbed out the lines that I'd written. Not good enough, I thought. Not good enough, so do it again. And again and again and again.

Why was I bloody *crying* again?

I don't know.

I went on copying what Rita had written, and I remembered the word I couldn't read. Trouble, she'd written, and I looked at it, and I thought, trouble; trouble. Copy it, and remember. Stupid, to write it like that. Why do they write it like that?

Just because they do, and Joan Ferguson isn't going to change it.

The Empress of the Dark Universe might. She might make a decree. Was that the word? Think so. One day I'll look it up.

Buy a dictionary. Tomorrow. You don't have to wait. Buy it, and look it up. I keep thinking, when I can read; when I can write. I don't have to wait. I can buy a dictionary. I'll buy one tomorrow. Or the next day, maybe.

Anyway, the Empress of the Dark Universe has made a decree. She thinks that's what she's made. She'll look it up later. As from today, the word 'trouble' will be spelt 'trubble'.

Copy it again. Trouble. Doesn't look quite so bad. But the page is all scuffed now where it was smooth.

Write it on another bit of paper, then. Rita only said copy it underneath because it was easier. Maybe I can copy it on to another bit of paper. Maybe I can manage now. I can try. I can always try. If I can't manage I can throw it away and pretend I never did it.

I went on copying until it was time to go to bed. Next day, I had to get the money out of the building society for Rita's spoons. And buy my dictionary. I had to go to Bellinghams to get the spoons, then go to work. Got to allow time for this. There might be a queue in the building society, or the bus might be late. Leave enough time. Mum had always said that. Leave enough time, and you won't have to rush.

'Bye, Mum,' I called out as I went down the stairs, but she didn't answer. She always used to say, Bye, Joan. Have a nice day. Nothing this time. Not a word. Doesn't care if I have a nice day, I thought. Doesn't want me to.

All the way to the building society I thought about Mum being angry with me, hitting me, and me holding up my hand, as if I was threatening her. Now she wouldn't even say have a nice day. She was that angry, she wouldn't even speak to me now.

Don't be angry, Mum. Please don't be angry with me. I hate it when people get cross with me.

Suppose I never can read or write properly? Suppose I can't do it, and Mum stays angry with me? I might not be able to. Sheila might be right.

All the time I was on the bus on the way to Bellinghams I was seeing Rita's writing, so neat, nothing rubbed out, and she'd never even had to think about it while she was writing. Never had to stop and think, is that right?

Even little words, I still had to stop, and look, and think, is that right?

I always asked her, is that right? Is that right, Rita? Have I done it right?

I'd always asked Mum, is that okay?

I can't do that now, I thought. She'd hit me last night, and I hadn't cried and said sorry. I'm sorry, Mum, I'll do what you say. I hadn't said anything, but I'd been ready to hit her back if she did it again, and now I couldn't ask, is that okay, Mum? Because I'd changed everything.

I felt so lonely.

When Dad had gone she'd come into my room one night when I'd been crying. Don't worry, Joanie, I'll take care of you, she'd said. Later I'd gone into her bed, and she'd been crying then. I'd crept in between the sheets and I'd hugged her. Don't worry, Mum, I'll take care of you. She'd laughed, even though she was still crying. Take care of each other, she'd said. You're a good girl, Joanie.

She wouldn't say that any more.

I gave Samantha Bellingham the money for the spoons, and she wrapped them up and wrote me out a receipt. I tried to read it later, but I couldn't manage the first word. The rest of it said 'the sum of two hundred pounds', and I thought, get that dictionary. Why's that a sum? Wasn't any adding up or taking away.

I kept the spoons in my bag, in my locker at work, and I worried about them all day. I'd had to get them. Bellinghams would be closed by the end of the late shift. I kept looking in my bag, or feeling in it to make sure the brown paper parcel was still there.

Those spoons cost a lot of money. If I lose them or somebody pinches them, I haven't got enough to buy any more, not good ones like those. Still got to buy more books, to learn to read.

Stupid, to buy them today, I thought. I should have bought them tomorrow. Tuesday, when I had my lesson with Rita. Should have bought them then. Now I've got to have them here all day today, and all day tomorrow.

But if I'd bought them tomorrow I wouldn't have been able to take them home and look at them. I wouldn't have been able to pretend Theresa was there, and we were talking about them. And I wanted to wrap them up and tie a ribbon round them. Get some nice paper out of the Christmas box and a bit of shiny ribbon, and maybe even write a card. They were a present. I wanted to make my present look nice.

I was on the late shift, so it might be quite a long time before I got to bed. I'd go home and have a wash, and change into my nice clothes. Mum would be home. It was her day off. Would she still be angry?

Please don't be angry.

She would be. When she knew I'd bought the spoons she'd be angry. She'd scream at me, about wasting all that money, about a holiday.

Won't tell her. Not tonight. I'll say, hello Mum, nice day? I'll pretend nothing's changed. Only Joanie, home from work, wants a cup of tea. I won't tell her tonight. I'll tell her tomorrow, when I get back from Rita's.

I gave her the spoons, Mum.

Tonight I'm going to be happy. I'm going to open the box of spoons and put them on the dressing table and have my cup of tea and pretend Theresa's there, talking about my spoons.

What have we got here, then?

I think they might be Venetian, Theresa.

Do you know, Joan, you could be right. I think you could be right.

Brown paper parcel under my fingers. All safe in my bag. I'd bring them to work again tomorrow, wrapped up in pretty paper with a ribbon, and a card if I can find one. Should have bought one today. Never mind, there might be one in the Christmas box.

I wasn't even looking as I came out of the alley, just thinking, with my hand on the paper parcel; thinking about the card in the Christmas box. And then he was standing right in front of me.

The sun was going down, and when I looked up I couldn't see properly, just this black shadow against the sun. Big, and black, and something held up over his head, and he said something.

'No,' I said. 'No.'

And then it was a feeling like being surprised, and standing still, and then going down, and down, and down, until it wasn't ever going to stop until I went to sleep.

And then being asleep.

18

I was in the same ward in hospital when I woke up, but I didn't know that. I felt sick and I couldn't see properly. Somebody leaned over me, asked if I was feeling better now, but I didn't say anything. It was like trying to see through water.

'Going to be sick,' I said, and I was.

Somebody asked me questions, but I went back to sleep instead.

I could see a bit better when I woke up again, but I still felt sick. This time there was somebody ready with a bowl, and she washed my face with cool water.

'You're black,' I said, and she laughed.

'And it don't wash off neither.'

She came back a little while later, and smoothed the hair off my face.

'That is one big bump. Taking you down for X-ray. What happened to you? You remember?'

I didn't remember, not then. I could only remember getting my bag out of my locker, and I thought I remembered going into the alley on my way to my bus stop. Nothing else.

My bag, I thought. Rita's spoons.

'My bag?'

They'd gone. There was nothing in my bag except a packet of tissues and a lipstick.

'I'm tired.'

'Go to sleep then, sweetheart. That trolley ain't no king-sized divan, but it's good enough. Slept on one myself, it can be done.'

I might have a fractured skull, they said, and my right arm was broken. How had it happened?

'Don't know.'

'What's your name?'

'Joan.'

'Joan? What's your second name?'

'Joanie. Dozey Joan.'

There were white coats and blue frocks, and bright lights that hurt my eyes. Questions, how many fingers can you see? Watch my finger. Can you still see it? Don't move your head. What's your surname? Can you remember what happened to you?

I was in a cubicle with curtains, and it was a bit darker. I was glad the bright lights had gone, but when I closed my eyes it felt as if the bed was rocking. I was afraid I might fall off. I opened my eyes and I hung on to the sides of the bed.

'We're keeping you in for observation. Can you remember your name yet? Who should we contact?'

'Mum.'

'What's her name?'

'Mum.'

'Telephone number, then?'

I couldn't remember. I knew we had a phone, but I couldn't remember. We weren't supposed to use it because of the bills. Mum said it was only for emergencies.

'Where do you work, Joan?'

'Fletchers.'

'*Right*. Now we're getting somewhere.'

There were other questions, but I felt too tired to try to answer. They gave up and went away, leaving me in the dim cubicle, and I went to sleep again.

When I woke up I remembered everything. The big shadow of the man in front of me, with the sun behind him so that it looked as if he was on fire, black in the middle with flames all around. His hand was up, and there was something in it. I remembered his voice, and I remembered saying 'No'.

He'd taken Rita's spoons. He'd taken everything out of my bag except a packet of tissues and a lipstick.

'Do you remember what happened?'

It was a policewoman, a young one, looking down at me as if she really was worried about me, not just doing her job and this was one of the boring bits.

'Yes, I remember.'

I said that before I thought, just an answer to her question, and then I was scared. Don't talk, don't talk, I thought. Don't say anything. If you won't tell us we can't do anything. Told you you'd be sorry. What would he do next?

'Just a man,' I said, because she was leaning over me, asking, what happened? What happened, then?

'Did you recognise him? Do you think you'd know him again?'

No. No, don't say. Sun was behind him, all black. All black and cloudy when he hit me, but he looked like he was on fire, flames round the black.

I'd been hit on the head. I'd been confused when I'd woken up. I hadn't even known my own name. How could I be sure? And the sun had been behind him.

Maybe it wasn't him.

I'd never find another set of spoons like that for Rita. I hadn't got enough money in the building society now. With all the books, and what I'd taken out for a dictionary, I hadn't got enough any more. I'd ask Samantha to find me something else, but this time it would have to cost only a hundred. Wouldn't be as nice, but it would be a present.

I wanted them back, those Venetian spoons for Rita.

Another nurse came in and said they were trying to find a bed for me. I'd have to have my arm plastered, but there wasn't any sign of a fracture in my skull, so that was all right, wasn't it? Just a nasty lump. I might have a black eye. Bit of concussion. Bit of confusion. Not to worry.

Then I heard Mum's voice out in the corridor, and she was making a fuss. Why hadn't they found a bed for me, then? What did we pay our National Insurance contributions for? It was disgraceful.

If I hadn't got a fractured skull, why couldn't I go home?

'Oh, *Joanie*. What you been up to now?'

'At least he didn't *do* anything,' I said, but she didn't hear me. The nurse had said there might be a bit of confusion. Shut up, Mum, it's not their fault.

I want Rita's spoons back.

'Where's the doctor? I want to see the doctor. I want to know what he's doing about this.'

'Mum. Mum?'

'All right, Joanie. I'm here now. I'll take care of you.'

274

'You don't need to see the doctor.'

He's done his bit, I wanted to say. He's done his job. Now it's the others, trying to find a bed for me. That's not his job, is it? I've got concussion and a broken arm and a few bruises, and the doctor found that out and wrote it down.

Diagnosed it.

Right. That's another word. I'm getting quite a good collection now.

I want Rita's spoons back.

I want. I am going to try. Very hard. I am . . . *determined*. Made up my mind and I'm going to try very hard.

Another word. Determined, diagnosed, want to remember them. Just, I have to keep thinking before I use them. They don't come out when I want them. I have to think about them.

Practice makes perfect, said Theresa somewhere in my memory. All right, I'll keep practising. And polishing. Silver and wood and words.

Haven't got any silver, those spoons have gone.

I am determined to get them back. Okay? Then I'll polish them.

'Please don't take that tone with me, Mrs Ferguson. I wasn't the one who hit your daughter on the head.'

Oh, Mum. Poor Mum. Only got to snap back at her and she gets so upset. She doesn't mean any harm. Just wants to show everybody. This is me being a good mother. Only the best for my daughter.

'Can't I go home?' I asked. 'I don't feel so bad now.'

'You're *entitled*.' Mum was nearly crying. 'They got to find you a bed.'

'I'd rather keep you in overnight for observation.'

Think of the right words. Keep everybody happy.

'Mum could look after me. She's ever so good. Could have been a nurse.'

He didn't have to look at her like that, like she was some sort of dirty insect. But she didn't see. She was looking in her handbag.

'You're entitled to a bed. I got to go to work.'

He'll sell those spoons. If I don't get after him he'll sell them, and I've got so much to do. Don't even know where he lives. Hope the name's in the phone book. Parry. There might be quite a lot of them. Have to go to them all.

Or, I could phone, say, 'Can I speak to Nicholas?' Then, if I listened to what they answered, I might find out if it was the right family. What would I say, if it was me got a phone call like that, asking for my brother, or my son? And he was locked up because he was mad? Would I hang up? Or maybe I might think, it's not somebody getting at us, being nasty. Might be an old friend, hasn't read the papers, doesn't know he's locked up. 'He doesn't live here any more', that's what I'd say. And then I'd tell them, he's not on the phone at his new place.

'There's a bed in the Intensive Care Unit.'

That was another man, I hadn't seen him before.

'Right,' said Mum, as though it was up to her. 'That's hers, then. Joanie? They've found you a bed, lovey.'

Intensive care, that sounded bad. That should be for people who are really, really ill.

'No,' I said. 'I'm going home.'

I looked at the doctor, and he smiled at me. I didn't need to be in the hospital, that smile said. Not really. I could manage, at home with Mum. He'd wanted to do what was best, but sometimes he couldn't. Intensive care, and suppose somebody came in who might die if they didn't get that bed?

'You're *entitled*,' said Mum.

'So's everybody.'

The doctor went out, saying he'd arrange for us to be taken home in an ambulance because Mum didn't have a car. At least we can do that for you, he said. Come back if you get double vision, or if you're worried, but don't worry about feeling sick, that's natural.

'I got to go to work,' said Mum. 'It's not right, them chucking you out. Should be in hospital.'

Funny flickering feeling in my head. He diagnosed a fractured skull. No, he didn't. He diagnosed a fractured arm. Broken arm. The skull is not fractured. He diagnosed a not fractured skull and I am determined to get Rita's spoons back and polish them. And the words.

'What's that?' asked Mum. 'What you talking about, Joanie?'

'Nothing.'

'It's not right. You're not right, you should be in hospital. Talking like that, doesn't make sense. Oh, Joanie.'

'I'm all right, Mum.'

But she was really upset. All the way back in the ambulance she kept saying the doctor had no right to speak to her like that. No right. I thought, did you have the right to speak to him the way you did? But I didn't say it. I was entitled to a bed, she said. I should be in hospital. Shouldn't have to come home. I wasn't well enough, didn't even know what I was saying, talking funny stuff like that. Who was going to look after me?

'I'm all right.'

Broken arm and lucky to be alive, that big bruise on my head. Could have killed me. Broad daylight, what's this country coming to? Not safe out. Wicked. That's what it was, downright wicked. And then doctors treating you like dirt just because they can't find a bed for you. Good mind to write to somebody about it. Twice, that's happened now. Twice. Kidnapped once, and then assaulted in broad daylight. Wicked.

I wasn't even sure it was Nicholas Parry's brother. What would I do, if he just said it wasn't him? Nothing to do with me, never touched you. Go away.

Got to find him first. Going to get those spoons back. Determined to get those spoons back.

'Who's going to look after you, then? I got to go to work.'

'I'm all right, Mum.'

'Poor Joanie. Poor old Joanie.'

My arm was hurting, and I still felt a bit sick. I wanted Mum to go to work, before Sheila got back. I had to look in the phone book. I had to look up the name, it was going to take ages. Never done this before. There might be lots of them. Then, phone them. Maybe all of them.

Suppose he doesn't even live in this town?

Mum wouldn't let me use the phone. Just for emergencies, that is. You going to pay the bill? You know how much it costs, that thing?

She's not mean, our Mum. If she's got money in her purse she's always kind. Generous? Give you things, anything you want, buy you a present. But she worries about the bills. When she doesn't know how much it's going to be, she worries, and it makes her cross. Turn off the lights, turn off the telly every time you go out of the room, don't use the phone except for emergencies. And the bills come, and she looks upset and opens up the envelope, and then she sort of sighs. Got to save up to pay *that* bloody thing now. Don't know where the money goes.

There never seems to be enough for extras. We've always got food in the cupboard, always got the rent ready, but every time I go shopping with Mum she sees something in the window. Wish I could have that. Wish I could buy that. Wouldn't half like a new three-piece suite.

And when things go wrong, that really upsets her. When the man came to mend the washing machine he said it would be seventy-three pounds for the parts, plus labour, plus VAT. She hadn't got it. She had to phone our Sheila. Sorry, pet, can you help? Can you lend me a bit for a couple of weeks? Pay you back. Even then it was more than she thought. She got that angry later. Gave that bastard a cup of coffee and he sat at my table and drank it and talked about bloody football, and he's put that time on the bill. That's fifteen bleeding quid he's charged me, for drinking my coffee and talking about football. I don't give a toss about bloody Aston Villa, let alone Chelsea. Charging me for his coffee break, good mind to do something about that. Write to somebody.

Every month she sits down at the table with a bit of paper and does sums. That's the rent, and that's the council tax. That's Mrs Niven's club for the new sheets and things. That's the tenner I owe our Sheila.

Forget that, says our Sheila, and Mum gives her a big smile, and crosses it out.

That's from our Joanie, and from our Sheila. That's what's left over for food and things.

If there's enough, she worries. What have I forgotten? There's something I've missed, I know there is. What is it?

And if there's not enough, she worries. Have to ask about a bit of overtime. Joanie, any chance of a bit extra from you? Can you get some overtime? Left me short when the telly went wrong.

Sheila doesn't get overtime. She gets tips. She'll get more money when she's got her diploma. But Mum says she's studying, can't expect to get a big wage when you're still learning.

But Sheila's always got money. That's all right, Mum, forget that, she says when Mum tries to pay her back, and Mum gives her a big smile. Doesn't say thank you, but that big smile, that tells her.

Can you let me have a bit extra? Mum asks, and I think, might get a bit of overtime on Friday, and Sue said she's going to be ill next week because of wanting to go up to Newcastle for that pop concert, so I say, think so, Mum, and she says, you're a good girl, Joanie.

'How much?' asks our Sheila, and then, all right, Mum. Never stops and thinks, can I get the tips? Just, all right, Mum. And gives her the money. She's always got money, our Sheila.

Why isn't there enough? There's three of us earning. Should be able to manage, shouldn't we?

Our Sheila has to look smart for work. She can't go to work in just any old clothes, got to look nice. Hairdressers and people like that, they have to look nice. Mum works in the kitchen at the restaurant, gets an overall anyway so it doesn't matter so much, and me, I get an overall too. Doesn't matter. But Sheila has to use some of her money for clothes.

Mum seemed to have forgotten we'd had that row, when I'd raised my hand to her as if to say I'd hit her back if she slapped me again. I thought, it's a good excuse for forgetting. Me being attacked, and being in hospital. Don't have to think about nasty things. Poor old Joanie, got to be nice to Joanie now, because she's been hurt.

When we got home I went up to the bathroom because I thought I was going to be sick again, but I wasn't. Mum was making a cup of tea. Have it hot and sweet and strong, she said, that's what you need for shock. Hot, sweet tea, she'd learned that in a First Aid class at school.

Suppose it wasn't Nicholas Parry's brother who'd hit me and taken Rita's spoons? Suppose it was just anybody? I'd never get them back then.

Suppose he just says, no, you can't have them back?

Suppose I can't find him?

'Joanie? You want your tea down here, or you want a nice lie down?'

'Down there.'

I don't like too much sugar in my tea, but Mum said it had to be sweet, for the shock. The black nurse had said I had to keep warm. She'd put an extra blanket over me, even though it was summer. You feeling cold, you got to tell me, she'd said. Shock makes you feel cold.

I didn't feel shocked. I thought about it. Funny, that. He'd attacked me, put me in hospital, and my arm was really hurting and my head felt like somebody kept hitting it, only from the inside, but all I wanted to think about was, get those spoons back. Before he sells them. I haven't got enough money to buy any more.

'Wish I could stay home and look after you.'

'I'm all right, Mum.'

'Our Sheila won't be long. Poor old Joanie, always in the wars. Drink up your tea while it's hot.'

My skirt was dirty. Must have got that way when I fell

on the pavement, when he hit me. I wondered how I'd broken my arm. Didn't matter really, but I did wonder. Wouldn't do that just falling over, would you?

Not a bad break, they'd said. Lucky it's your left arm. What are these scars? What operations?

Too tired to explain. What's that got to do with a broken bone? Just put the plaster on.

'What operations?'

'For the tendons.'

'What was the matter with them?'

Why did they have to ask that? They didn't need to know that, did they? They've got the X-rays, it's the bone that's broken, nothing to do with the tendons.

'What was wrong with your tendons?'

Don't want to talk about that. So, look at the man, just look at him. Not in any way, not a *particular* way, but look, until he shrugs, and goes back to the wet bandage and that powder he's mixed up with the water.

He'll think, she's a bit stupid.

The man who came to mend the telly, he didn't ask about my hands. They don't even ask about them at work. But in the hospital, they seemed to think they had a right. I don't think they've got a right to ask, not if it's nothing to do with my broken arm. I didn't ask him, how did you get that scar on your nose?

That black nurse didn't ask. She noticed, I saw her look when she helped me with my arm at the X-ray, but she never said anything. I'd been a bit rude to her, too, when I'd just woken up. When I'd said, 'You're black', that was a bit rude, but she knew it was only because I was feeling funny, just waking up after being hit on the head.

'You feeling all right, Joanie?'

'Yes, Mum.'

'Lovey, I've got to go. They're short tonight, Dizzy's off sick.'

'All right, Mum.'

Go, then. Go on. I'm all right. When you've gone I'll start looking in the phone book. Parry. Have to phone them all. Can I speak to Nicholas Parry? Listen to how they answer. I'll know.

'I'm going, Joanie.'

Sounds like she's sliding off a cliff. I'm going, I'm dying, goodbye for ever.

'Bye, Mum.'

Sheila would be home soon. Have to hurry. Have to look them up. Have to be quick.

I couldn't remember exactly where P came in the alphabet. I knew it was after the middle bit. M,N,O, that was the middle bit. I didn't know why I thought that. I found S, and it was really thick, that bit. Didn't know whether P came before or after S.

Then I found N, and I thought, work on from there. It's after that bit, N, and then where there was an O on the same page. Go through O, up to the end, and there was P.

Nearly there. Hurry up.

P, and A. And then R. That's another letter that comes after the middle bit.

Parker, nearly half a page. Then, is that it? Parry. Got it.

There were lots of them.

Don't count. Just start. Dial the number, and remember to ask, can I speak to Nicholas Parry?

It was a machine. Leave a message after the tone, it said, so I just hung up. It had said the office was closed. It wouldn't be an office, would it?

The next one, no answer. It rang and rang, but nobody answered. Then there was another machine, and then another.

Please, somebody, answer.

The next one they did. A woman answered, sounded a bit funny, like, who on earth's this on the phone?

'Can I speak to Nicholas Parry?'

'There's nobody here. I'm just the cleaner. I don't think there's a Nicholas Parry. There's Mr Norman and Mr Clive. I don't know any Nicholas.'

In the next eight numbers there was only one other answer. A man asked if I was sure I'd got the right number. I hung up.

Machine, or nothing, just the telephone ringing. I couldn't understand. It went on and on, every number I tried. What was this? Most people were at home in the evenings, why were there just these machines?

Then Sheila came in. Mum had phoned her and told her, so she was all poor old Joanie about it, but then she started. What the hell was I doing on the phone? Mum would go mad when she saw the bill.

'I'll have to pay her then, won't I?'

'Using what for money? Shirt buttons?'

That was one of her favourite sayings. I thought, you always seem to have a bit of money in your purse. Why don't I? Just enough for a cup of coffee in the canteen and my bus fares. I reckon I work as hard as you.

Joanie, can you get a bit of overtime next week? Getting the washing machine mended left me short. Got to pay the television licence, can you let me have a bit extra?

So I didn't answer Sheila. I was getting angry. All these numbers, all these Parrys, nobody there. I've got to find him. Before he gets rid of Rita's spoons.

'Who are you ringing anyway?'

'Nobody.'

'Don't be *stupid*.'

'I just want to find out where he lives, that's all.'

'Who?'

It was another machine, so I slammed the phone back down and I wanted to kick something and scream.

'Nicholas Parry's brother, if you must know, Miss Sheila Nosey Parker Ferguson.'

'You reckon he did this?'

Not going to bother to answer. Go away. Please. Just go away.

'You're not going to find him in this lot. This is the business section.'

'What?'

'The telephone directory. You're looking in the business section, dummy. Look, it says here. It's all people like plumbers, and this, this means solicitor. I don't know what that one is. But it's all businesses. It's not private numbers. You want the private section. Residential, it's called. That means private houses. Like ours, that's in residential. It's not in business.'

I listened to her, and I understood what she was saying, but I felt blank, as though the words didn't make any sense. I'd rung all those numbers, and I'd never thought there must be something wrong. Anybody would have thought, after only a few numbers, this isn't right. There aren't so many people with machines, and most people are at home in the evenings. Me, I'd just gone on and on down the list.

Stupid. Because I'm not very bright, I thought.

Sheila had found the residential section in the book. Parry, wasn't it, she asked and I could only nod at her.

I've got a headache, and my arm hurts.

'Go on, then. Don't see what good it'll do, knowing where he lives.'

She went upstairs, and I looked at the new list, and wondered how anybody as stupid as me was ever going to get Rita's spoons back.

'I am determined,' I said out loud, and I dialled the first number.

It was only the third one, and I knew I'd got it. A woman answered.

'Can I speak to Nicholas Parry?'

There was a silence, and then her voice again, all nasty, as if I was doing something wrong. Suspicious, that was it. Suspicious.

'Who wants him?'

I put the phone down very slowly and very gently, as if I didn't want to scare her with a sudden noise, and I was breathing quickly. Got him, I thought. I know where he lives.

How do you know his brother lives there too?

I don't know, but that's all I can do, so I've done it.

Palmer Road, it said. Number eleven.

I don't know where that is. Palmer Road, never heard of it. How do I find it? Have to walk, haven't got any money, can't even get the bus.

And my arm hurts when I move. Every time I move, it's like something's hitting it. Everything I do, even though I'm not using it, it hurts.

It was just excuses, I knew that. I was looking for reasons not to go, but somehow I had to go. Not think about it, or I'd get too scared, just do it. Go on and do it.

'That man, he took all my money,' I said to Sheila.

'Oh, poor Joanie. Never mind.'

Never said, want to borrow some? Not going to ask, then. Not if you don't say, want to borrow a bit? Going off out and leaving me, even though Mum said, stay home and look after our Joanie, she's not well. Going out anyway. So I'm not going to ask, lend me a bit?

Him nicking my money left me a bit short, and getting the telly mended, and he got my passbook from the building society.

'You be all right then, our Joanie?'

'Yes, Sheila.'

Go on, then. Go on out, I don't care. I'm going out myself, see? I am, I'm going out too. I am determined to get Rita's spoons back and polish them.

Going to be sick again, Theresa.

I took some money out of the envelope in the sugar jar, where Mum puts it to keep it safe. She'll kill me if she finds out. I might come back and find the locks all changed, like when Dad left. Stupid, that was, he couldn't come back. But she changed all the locks. She might do that again when she looks in the sugar jar. She's done a bad thing, our Joanie, so she can't come back, change the locks. Done a bad, bad thing.

Taxi driver, he'd know where Palmer Road was, taxi drivers have to know where places are. It was easy after that, as if it was all meant to happen. The taxi down on the rank by the shopping centre, how much to Palmer Road? Not more than three quid, sweetheart. Do it for three for a pretty girl, okay?

What happened to your arm, then?

I fell. Tripped on the edge of the road.

Could get the council to pay for that, the driver said. Get compensation. They've got to keep the pavements right, if you trip, you're entitled.

287

That's another new word, keep hearing it today. Entitled. Entitled to a bed, entitled to, what was it he said? Doesn't matter.

Nicholas Parry's brother, and that woman, who was she? Going to find out. The brother, he hit me, he hurt my head, he broke my arm. Going to see him now. Get Rita's spoons back. Got to get Rita's spoons back, I'll never get another set like that, I haven't got enough money.

The taxi driver was still talking. His friend's mother, she fell over on the pavement outside the bingo hall, got five hundred pounds out of the council just for a chipped tooth. A broken arm and a bang on the head could be worth a lot. Tell them you always get headaches now, never got them before. Might get thousands, they can't prove you haven't got a headache.

Please keep talking. I'm listening to you. While I'm listening to you I haven't got to think, so I won't get frightened.

Head and spinal injuries, he said, as if he'd read it somewhere and was a bit proud of it, they're the most difficult to disprove. You only got to say headache, backache, always in pain, they can't measure it, see? They can't say if you've got a pain or not. They don't know.

Only thing you got to remember, if you say you got a bad back, don't let them catch you doing something you said you couldn't do. There's snoops they pay to watch you. Got to be careful. But you should be okay, saying you got a headache.

What number was it you said?

Right, love, there you are. Don't forget, tell them you get headaches. That's three quid, then, like we agreed.

Nothing to listen to now except thump, thump,

thump, and that's my heart, and I remember that from when I was tied up in that little room. Am I going back to something like that?

Will he be like Nicholas? Will he be mad, too? He hit me, he broke my arm. I must be mad, coming here. I must be mad.

Get Rita's spoons back. I am determined to get Rita's spoons back.

I could hear a telly in the background, and I didn't let myself stop and think, just pressed that doorbell, and I didn't think about it. If I think about this I'll never do it. I touched him once, by not thinking about it, I did that.

Somebody coming. Light in the hall, big shadow on the window.

Oh, I must be mad, coming here.

Standing there with the light behind him again, just a black shape against the light. Oh, yes. It was you. It was you.

'Christ,' he said. 'You got a fucking nerve, coming here.'

19

He walked away from me, but he left the door open, so I followed him. I could only think, I must be mad, and it went on going through my head, I must be mad, I must be mad. Go on saying it so I don't have to think.

I am determined to get Rita's spoons back.

There was a woman sitting in a chair in the room we went into. She was big, a bit fat, and she was drunk. There was a bottle and a glass. She was wearing a dirty frock, black and white, stains all over it. No shoes. Her feet were grey.

'Who's this, then?' she asked. Her voice was loud, and sort of blurred.

'Her. The Empress. Our Nicholas's bit.'

She sat upright in the chair, but she couldn't keep steady. She was rocking from side to side, hanging on to the chair. Her mouth was open.

Never seen anybody as dirty as that, I thought.

'What you want, then? You whore, what you want? Done enough, didn't you?'

'I've come for the spoons.'

He laughed. 'You'll be bloody lucky.'

It was him, then. It was him that took them. Him that hit me, broke my arm.

'They're a present,' I said. 'I got to have them. I can't get any more.'

He did look like Nicholas, but I couldn't picture Nicholas here. Nicholas had been neat and clean, and that woman rolling around in the chair, with her dirty bare feet and the stains on her dress, what was she to him? His mother?

'Fuck off out of it,' she said. 'While you still can. You fat whore.'

She was trying to get out of the chair. She was struggling, trying to stand up, but she was too drunk.

'Fuck off out of it,' she said again, but she gave up trying to stand and she looked back towards the telly and picked up her glass.

'Fuck off.'

'Shut it, Mum,' he said. He was looking at me, watching me, suspicious. That was it, suspicious. Now I know *exactly* what that word means. I've got that one now, that's another word I've got.

I feel sick. I must be mad, I feel sick. Got another word. Got to say something, got to say.

'I just want the spoons,' I said. 'And my building society book, if you still got it. Can't use it, can you? No use to you.'

'Are you wired? I bet that's it. Bitch.'

He moved so fast I hardly saw him coming. One moment he was over by the telly, then he was in front of me, reaching out, and he ripped my blouse open.

'Bitch,' he said again, and I backed away, holding my blouse.

'Don't,' I said. 'Don't do that.'

But he pushed me against the door, and then he was touching me, all over, his hands going all over me, pressing and pushing. I tried to shove him away, I kept saying don't, don't. I was clumsy, with the plaster on my arm.

The woman was watching the telly again, seemed to have forgotten we were there.

He pulled my bag out of my hand, opened it and turned it upside down so everything fell on to the floor. Just the tissues, and my purse with what was left of the money from the sugar jar, and my lipstick.

Mum puts the money in the sugar jar. Nobody would think to look in there, it's all sticky, there was sugar on my fingers. Got it on my blouse now, where he ripped the buttons off.

Got to try to think properly. Got to concentrate. I'm here now. Must be mad, but it's too late. Get those spoons.

He backed away from me, still looking at me, but now it looked as if he didn't understand something. Puzzled.

'Why are you here, then?'

'For the spoons. That's all.'

I pulled my blouse together, held it there with one hand, and I saw him looking at my hand, the way it didn't work properly. The material kept slipping out of my fingers, so I had to keep pushing at it with my other hand, and that was even worse, because of the plaster.

'I am *determined* to get those spoons,' I said, and he blinked, as if I'd hit him, or done something really odd.

'No way. I've got a customer for them.'

He bent down and picked up the things that had fallen out of my bag. He put them back in the bag and gave it to me.

The woman started to laugh. It was something on the telly, she took no notice of us, but she was rolling in the chair, it was a noise like screaming.

'Shut it, Mum.'

He said it as if he didn't mean it, it was just something to say, and she took no notice. She went on rolling around in her chair, screaming.

'Out,' he said to me. 'Out of here. Go on.'

He pushed me through the door, and then pointed up the stairs. 'Up there. Go on, get up there.'

'No.'

Now I was really frightened. That woman was still laughing in the next room, and this man, who looked so like Nicholas Parry, was trying to force me up the stairs. He's going to tie me up, hurt my hands, he's got a knife, he's got a knife.

'No. Please.'

He didn't know what to do. He looked at me, and he looked at the door we'd just come through. He pushed his hand against his head, as if it was something that didn't work, shoving at it.

Start then, head. Go on, start.

'Why did you come?'

'To get Rita's spoons.'

'Rita? Who's Rita?'

If I talk to him maybe he won't push me up the stairs. Maybe he won't get the knife.

'She's helping me with my reading and my writing. I'm not very quick at the reading, she's helping me. I got her a present to say thanks. That's the spoons. Haven't got enough money to buy any more. She's a lady at work, Rita. That's who she is. She's been helping me.'

'You can't *read*?'

Why did he have to say it like that? I'm *not* a freak, there're other people who can't read. Anyway, I can now, nearly. I can nearly read. It's just practice, isn't it? It's just there are words I don't know yet. Not yet. I will, when I learn them. I'll know, when I see them. That says trouble, that says school, that says scornful. Like you, Nicholas Parry's brother. I'll know that word. I've heard it.

'What's your name?' I asked, and I sounded angry, and I sounded like I had a right to know. You answer that question, you. You, man, Nicholas Parry's brother, you answer that question.

He blinked again. That's not like Nicholas. That's just you. You're not all that like Nicholas, not up close.

'Patrick.'

Funny, that name. Patrick. And Nicholas. Nobody ever said 'Nicky', or 'Nick'. Always Nicholas. And it wasn't Pat, it was Patrick. Funny.

'You can't read?'

Not scornful now. Amazed. Never thought of that, had he? And there was something else. Why was he looking like that?

'You're lying.'

'I'm not. Well, I can read a bit. I can nearly read now. Because of Rita, see? Because Rita helped me, that's why I bought her a present. I can nearly read now.'

The woman was quiet again, there was just the voices on the telly.

How had Nicholas come from a place like this? From a mother like that? I didn't want to go back into that room, with that terrible woman, but I didn't want to go up the stairs either. The last time I'd stood at the bottom of stairs like this, feeling frightened, it had been because of Nicholas Parry and his knife. Now it was Patrick, and I couldn't think what to do.

'I want to talk to you,' he said. 'Get up the stairs.'

'No.'

He sighed. He was getting angry.

'She's been on the bottle since they locked Nicholas up. That's down to you. Do you want to go back in there with her? If you think she's bad now, you wait till she comes round enough to know who you are. She'll kill you.'

He'd torn my clothes, looking for something, but he hadn't touched me since then. The way he looked now, determined to get me up the stairs, but not wanting to touch me unless he had to, I could see a likeness.

You're going to do what I tell you, but I don't want to hurt you. Not unless I have to.

'Why did you hit me?' I asked. 'Today, when I was going for the bus. Why?'

He didn't answer. He was listening at the door, his head a bit on one side, just like his brother now.

'She's all right,' he said. 'She's got the bottle again. She'll pass out soon.'

'You broke my arm. They thought you'd . . .' What was that word they'd used? 'Fractured my skull. Fractured it.'

'It's as if he's dead. Worse. If he was dead we could get on with our lives. But we have to go and see him, locked up. Do you have any idea what you did? She never used to be like that.'

'I just wanted you to leave me alone. I never did you any harm.'

'*Are you listening to me?*'

I stopped. I hadn't been listening. Why should I listen? 'No,' I said.

That wasn't the word he'd been expecting. He looked surprised, but then he went on as if I'd said yes.

'You ruined our lives,' he said. 'Not just Nicholas. Bad enough, if it was just Nicholas. Me, Mum, you spoilt everything.'

There wasn't anything I wanted to say. He believed it. How had he made himself believe that? What Nicholas Parry had done to me, was that my fault? What did he think I should have done?

'Go up the stairs,' he said, and then, as if he was remembering something, he said, 'Please.'

I went up, and I could feel him following me. Not too close, but there behind me. There was only one door open at the top, so I went in. A tiny bedroom, even smaller than mine, with clothes thrown all over the place, a real mess. It was clean, or not too dirty anyway, but it was a real mess.

'Sorry about the mess,' he said, and I thought, another one, reading my mind.

That's stupid.

'Who knows you're here?'

'Nobody.'

Then I thought about it. Sheila might guess. If I didn't come back, she might guess where I was.

'My sister, she'll guess,' I said.

He didn't answer. He went on looking at me, and then he thought of something. 'Was that you, on the telephone?'

'Yes.'

That's another word different. Most people say phone, he says telephone.

He sighed. 'That's what set her off. Upset her. We used to get a lot of calls. Sickos, getting at us. Saying things about Nicholas.'

He closed the door behind him, and leaned against it.

'She won't come up here,' he said. 'She can't manage the stairs. She'll pass out down there. I'll put a blanket over her later, keep her warm.'

'Nicholas would have done that,' I said, without thinking.

'Would he hell. Not if I was there to do it, he wouldn't.'

I listened to that, and I thought about it. I had quite a long time to think, because Patrick just stood by the door, watching me, not saying anything. It was as if he was trying to think what to say, and it was important he got it right.

Nicholas wouldn't have put a blanket over his mother if Patrick had been there, because Patrick would do it. Nicholas would think Patrick would do it. Nicholas would *expect* Patrick to do it.

Sheila *expects* me to clear away the tea things, and I do. Mum cooks the tea and puts it on the table. We all eat it. Then I clear it away. Later, we wash it up, all of us, when there's the news on the telly or nothing much we want to see. But it's always me who clears the table after our tea. Never Sheila. That's not fair.

'That time with Nicholas. In that house. Could you read then?'

None of your business, I thought but, after all, I did tell you. It wasn't you being nosey. I did tell you.

'A bit. Just, it takes time. There's some words I don't know.'

'Not now,' he said. 'You're talking about now, aren't

297

you? I mean when you were with Nicholas, or just after that, when you made the statement, could you read?'

'They read it to me.'

'Lies,' he said, but he didn't believe it. It was like when he told his mother, shut it, Mum. Just something you said. You say it over and over again. It was lies. Shut it, Mum. You don't *think* it, you just say it. Turns into a habit.

He believed the next thing he said.

'You made him sound like the devil. It was all bad. There was nothing nice about him in all those pages. He didn't kill you, did he? He didn't do anything bad. Not really bad.'

I held out my hands.

'Look,' I said.

He came over and he did look at my hands, looking down at them as I held them out to him. He looked at the plaster first, and I knew he wanted to ask, did I do that? This afternoon, did I do that? Did I really break your arm?

Then he was looking at my hands, and I could see his eyes moving a little bit, looking at the scars that were nearly white now, like Mr Jenkins had said they'd be. I tried to open my hands out flat, like everybody else could do, and the fingers wouldn't work. Then I tried to close them, and they wouldn't go all the way. I turned them over so he could see the backs. There wasn't anything to see there, but he was looking, so I thought, show him everything. Turn them again.

Go on then, Patrick, Nicholas Parry's brother. Look. Look at what he did. Not really bad?

'He tied me up so I couldn't get away.'

'He didn't mean to hurt you. Not like that.'

It was true, he hadn't. Your poor, poor hands, he'd said. Look what you made me do to you.

Patrick was waiting again, as if he wanted me to say something next.

'He was nice to me,' I said, and he hadn't been expecting that. He blinked, as if something really surprising had happened. As if there'd been a firework, something like that.

'Ever so polite,' I said.

'He thought you were the Empress.'

'The Dark Universe,' I said. 'He told me all about the Dark Universe. He made it sound ever so nice.'

'He believed it,' said Patrick.

I was still holding my hands out, and he looked down at them again, and then went over to the window.

Nicholas had almost made me believe it, too. When I'd been tied up on that third day, counting to try to make the time go, when I'd been hurting, I'd believed the Dark Universe was real. I'd believed that the fat man who came in and found me had come for the summer games. A great prize for the champion, I'd thought when he broke the chain and left me lying on the floor, licking my wrists where the flex had cut them. I'd believed it. It was being rescued that I hadn't understood. There weren't any pavilions, no green grass, no dark and cloudy skies. I was on a floor in a little room with painted windows, and I couldn't understand it, not then.

Straight from the Dark Universe, where I'd been watching the summer games, back to that little room.

If Nicholas Parry had been mad, I'd been mad too, because I'd believed it.

'He said I was a wrestler,' I told Patrick. 'I think he was wrong about that. I never could see me as a wrestler.'

Patrick was looking down out of the window.

'What?'

'Nicholas said I was a wrestler. In the Dark Universe. Could have been in the team for the summer games, he said. But I think he was wrong about that. I don't think I was a wrestler.'

Patrick smiled, as if he was about to laugh. 'I wouldn't be scared if I was matched against you.'

'You think he got it wrong, then?'

He looked at me, as if he was a bit worried. Stupid, I thought. I've been stupid. The Dark Universe doesn't exist, and I'm talking as if it does. He'll think I'm mad too. Maybe he's right.

I felt my face getting hot, and I tried to laugh. 'Can't help thinking about the Dark Universe sometimes. What he said.'

'You look more like a tennis player to me. I wouldn't reckon you as a wrestler.'

A tennis player. That sounded nice. A white dress, and a white hairband, not all sweaty with big muscles. I'd like to be a tennis player.

'They all said Nicholas was the brainy one of the family. Brains and brawn, they used to call us, and he was the brains. They made it sound as if I was the dope, I was only there to do what he said. But he wasn't always right.'

'Didn't you like him?'

'Of course I liked him. *Like* him, do you mind? He's not dead. I do like him, I still like him. He's my twin brother. But he wasn't perfect. People seemed to think he was perfect, and he wasn't. When he went to university, it was as if he'd won the Nobel Prize or something. Nicholas goes to university, Patrick goes to the technical college. You'd think it was written in the stars.'

'My sister went to dancing school and I didn't even get extra reading lessons.'

But it doesn't matter, I thought. That's just how it is, with Sheila. She gets what she wants. I don't suppose Patrick really minds Nicholas going to university and him going to the tech. I don't mind Sheila getting dancing lessons. I do mind her never using them, I mind that a bit. After Dad went, she said she wouldn't go any more, even though Mum couldn't get the money back. The lessons were paid for, why not use them? Be nice, to be able to dance.

'Do you want to sit down?' asked Patrick, and he went over to the bed and started to clear a space, picking up clothes and putting them on the chair. 'Go on, sit down. You can't stand up there all night.'

Downstairs I heard the woman start to scream again. I didn't know if she was laughing, or if it was something wrong with her. Patrick stood up straight and listened, as if he didn't know either, but then he went on moving things on to the chair.

'Sit down,' he said again.

I sat on the bed, and he went back to the window.

'She'll be all right,' he said. 'That's only laughing. You did that to her, made her like that. She never used to be like that.'

That was just something he said, he didn't mean it. He didn't think about it, not usually, but this time he did think, a bit.

'You said they read you that statement?'

'Yes.'

'You agreed it, though, didn't you? You said it was all

right, didn't you? Those witnesses wouldn't have signed it if you hadn't agreed. Didn't you listen, when they read it? Those horrible things they said? It sounded as if he did everything on purpose. As if he deliberately crippled your hands, nothing but cruelty. As if he did it all just to torture you, just because he wanted to.'

He sounded angry again. I didn't want him to be angry. I wanted him to understand. I'd have to try and explain. Try and find the words.

'I wanted to say. I wanted to say about the Dark Universe. What he'd said. You know? I wanted to, but they wouldn't. They said, it doesn't matter, all that. Leave it to the doctors, those psychiatrist ones. Leave it to them, they said. Because he was mad. Well, they said that. Not me, I never said that. I don't know, do I? But they said, he's mad, see? So there's no court case. It's not like it's going to be in court, reading it all out, sending him to prison, not like that. So it doesn't matter. Just sign it. It's only for the files, so it doesn't matter.'

'Who said that?' he asked.

'Policewoman. In the hospital, where I went for my hands. I said to her, it's not right. It's all horrible. She said, if I didn't sign it she'd have to write it all out again. There were pages and pages, Patrick. All that writing. And if it was just for the files, and him not going to prison, not going to be read out in court, it didn't matter, did it? Did it, then?'

'You believed them, did you?'

Scornful again. Why? Why did he sound scornful? I'd been right to believe them. There never had been a court case, so they'd told the truth. Why was he being scornful?

I stood up.

'I've got to go now,' I said.

'Why?'

I couldn't think of a reason. But if he was going to be scornful again I didn't want to stay. He'd been quite nice up to then, not speaking as if I was just stupid, not worth talking to.

'There wasn't a *jury*,' he said, and he made the word sound as if it had a nasty taste. 'I suppose they didn't exactly lie. There was a judge, though, and a whole bloody gang of doctors, and nobody worth mentioning to stand up for Nicholas. Oh, no, there wasn't a court case. What's the point of a court case for a bloody nutter? In a court case somebody might have listened to us.'

He sat down in the chair, so I sat down again too. He was sitting on his clothes. They'd get all crumpled, like that. Maybe he didn't mind, but Nicholas wouldn't have liked it. He liked being neat.

'They read your statement,' he said. 'Those pages and pages she wouldn't write again, so you just signed it. They read it. Now he's locked up. We don't even know when he'll be let out. Mum asked, when they said he'd have to stay in a secure hospital. Don't know, depends on how he responds to treatment.'

I hadn't known that. She'd as good as lied, that police-woman. I would have said, if I'd known, how he'd always spoken nicely. Respectfully. He'd had the knife, but he'd never hit me, never done anything nasty. He'd tied me up and he'd hurt my hands, but he'd been sorry, and I hadn't even put that in the statement.

They'd made me say I'd wet myself, that was in the statement. And they'd all read it. They hadn't said any-thing about the Dark Universe.

'They said he fantasised about killing you. One of the

doctors said it was a masturbation fantasy, a woman asking him to kill her. Sexually stimulating, he said. Nicholas tortured you by tying your wrists with flex so you'd ask him to kill you.'

It hadn't been like that.

But it was just for the files, not going to court, it doesn't matter.

I rubbed the back of my hand against my eyes. I wasn't going to cry, not in front of him. But I was angry, because they'd as good as lied, and I'd been too stupid to know. And I was sad, too.

Dozey Joan. I was never going to be any different. Should have known.

'I would have told them it wasn't like that,' I said, and my voice was all dry, sort of scratchy, so he looked across at me, and he looked worried again. Concerned. Was that the word? I thought it was, but I didn't know for sure.

Look it up.

'I was going to buy a dictionary, and you stole my money,' I said, and then I couldn't stop the tears running down my cheeks. I wasn't even crying about the dictionary, but how could he know that? I want to know, is that the word? Is 'concerned' the word I want?

'You can have Nicholas's dictionary,' he said. 'He doesn't need it. He can spell. Do you want it?'

I nodded.

'I want Rita's spoons, too,' I said, but he just said, 'Don't push your luck.' It was only another thing to say without thinking. Doesn't mean anything. Another one like, shut it, Mum.

He went out, but he came back only a few moments later, with a big book. It was black with white letters.

'What's that?' I asked.

'Nicholas's dictionary.' He looked at it. '"The Concise Oxford Dictionary"', he read.

'What's "concise"?' I asked.

'Short.'

It was a big book, thick and heavy. Short? That wasn't short, that was a big, thick book. Full of words, and what they mean. That many words? Are there really that many words?

'I'll *never* learn all that,' I said. 'I'll never do that. I can't.'

He was still holding the book, and looking at me. He didn't understand.

'Nobody could learn all that,' I said.

'Nobody does. What are you talking about? "Learn all that", what *are* you on about?'

'All the words. I thought I could learn the words. What they all mean and how you read them. I was going to learn them, but I can't learn all them. It's a *big* book.'

Theresa, I thought, I can't. I'm sorry, I can't. Not all that.

'Want a handkerchief?' he asked, and I shook my head. I'd got some in my bag. Not much else, since he'd pinched all the other things.

I opened my bag, and I took out the packet of tissues.

'Do you want a safety pin for that blouse?'

It was hanging open again. I hadn't even noticed. I tried to pull it together, but my hand slipped.

He put the dictionary on the bed and went to a cupboard. He took something out, and held it out to me.

'Too small for me,' he said. 'It'll probably swamp you. We could put two of you in that. Still, it's better than a torn blouse.'

I thought, that's kind. I took the T-shirt out of his hand,

and he turned his back, even though I wasn't really going to be indecent. I did wear a brassière under my blouse, I wasn't going about without any underwear.

It took me a bit of time, because of my arm and the plaster cast, but I did it, and I shoved the blouse into my bag and looked at myself in the mirror.

The T-shirt was blue, a nice colour, and it was like new. It was too big, but it didn't matter.

'You can turn round now,' I said.

'I'm sorry about your blouse,' he said. 'I thought you were wired.'

'What does that mean?'

'A little radio transmitter. So the police listen to what we're saying.'

I'd seen that on the telly, I remembered after he told me. I'd thought it was little tape recorders.

He picked up the dictionary again.

'I've never heard of anybody *learning* a dictionary,' he said. 'You just use it when you need it. You look up the spelling, or see what a word means, or how it developed. You don't *learn* a dictionary.'

How was I going to learn the words, then? Since I'd started with Rita I'd done what she said, listened to the radio, tried to understand. There were always words I didn't know, and some I'd thought I'd known, but then I wasn't sure. They used them in funny ways on the radio, on the news. Didn't make sense. Maybe some words meant different things, depending.

That was one I wanted to look up. Depending. Somebody had said, on the radio, something about it meaning something was hanging from something. Depending. And concerned, was that what I meant, when I thought he looked at me like that? A bit worried?

'Do you want it? Nicholas's dictionary?'

'Yes, please,' I said.

He had a funny look on his face. It was as if he was worried, but he was going to laugh, and he didn't want to.

'I'm giving you his dictionary,' he said. 'I hated you so much I belted you over the head this afternoon, and now I'm giving you this. Funny old world, isn't it?'

He sat down in the chair with the book in his lap, and he opened it.

'What did you want to look up?'

20

He looked up some words for me, and he read them out. He looked up 'depended' and 'concerned', and they did have lots of meanings. More than one, anyway. I was beginning to get angry.

'Why? Why don't they just mean one thing? They're doing it on *purpose*. Just to make it hard.'

'Who are?' he asked, and I didn't know. I thought, he's laughing at me.

'Look up "dog",' I said, and he did. Even that had lots of meanings. I'd been trying to make a joke. Dog, I'd thought. That's easy, that's just an animal. D-O-G, dog. An animal. But he went on reading and reading and reading, there was a mechanical something, and it also meant follow, lots of things.

I'm never going to do it. I'll never manage. I can't.

He looked at me once, as if he'd suddenly thought of something, and he didn't understand it. Almost as if he'd been hit, like a boxer, hit on the jaw and staggering.

'I've hated you for months,' he said. 'Now I'm reading you definitions out of Nicholas's dictionary. I can't believe this.'

'Don't hate me,' I said. 'Don't.'

Nobody had ever hated me before. It hurt, that. Hated me. Didn't like me sometimes, didn't think I was worth much, Dozey Joan, but hate, that was hard. That meant something really bad.

'I don't. I don't hate you. I didn't know you couldn't read. No wonder they didn't have you at that hearing. It never occurred to me you might like him. That's a funny idea. I can't get my head round that one.'

I can't get my head round all these words. All meaning lots of things. I can't do this, I can't.

'Cat?' I asked, and I was trying to make a joke. 'Look up "cat", Patrick.'

My voice wasn't right.

He closed the book, and put it on the floor. He put it down carefully, not just dropping it, because it was mine now, not his to chuck around.

I can read minds, too, I thought.

'Why can't you read?' he asked, and he sounded as if he was interested. Not being scornful. He wanted to know. What went wrong? he was asking.

I told him about my ears, and the operation.

'You were deaf?'

'Sort of. It was all blurry, buzzy. And sort of soft, only I didn't know that until afterwards. Then it was horrible. Only I couldn't say.'

They'd all been so pleased, after the operation. A complete success, they'd said, isn't that wonderful? Her hearing's quite normal now. I'm so pleased it went so well. Joan? Isn't that wonderful?

Yes, I'd said. And, thank you.

Bang, *bang*, BANG.

'You're not like I thought you'd be,' said Patrick.

309

He'd thought I'd be spiteful. He knew it must have been bad for me, what Nicholas had done. Terrifying, he understood that. But he'd thought I must have known it wasn't deliberate. Nicholas was ill. It wasn't really his fault, what he'd done to me. He couldn't help it. Patrick couldn't see why I'd said such dreadful things in the statement. It had seemed as if I was looking for revenge, against a man who was ill.

Nicholas had had to work too hard. The whole family had been so proud of him. He was the first to go to university. The Parrys were working people. His father worked in a glass factory, engraving vases and things. His mother had been in a shoe shop. They weren't stupid, but they weren't the sort of people to go to university.

'Our first school was so bad Mum and Dad moved, to get us out of it. They came here because the schools were good.'

Moved because of that? I thought. Couldn't see my Mum and Dad doing that. Going to live in a different place, just because of the schools? Was it that important, which school the kids went to?

'They had an interview with the headmaster,' said Patrick. 'When Dad told me about it, it was a bit of a joke, but that was years later. Graves, he was called, the headmaster. He wasn't a bad bloke. He told them, children who grow up in houses where there are books to read do well at school.

'So they went out that afternoon and spent all their holiday savings on books. Dad even read some of them. He made a bookcase.

'They were great parents. They didn't give us everything we wanted, but they made sure we had everything

310

we needed. Particularly for school. They seemed to set their minds to it, and they did it.'

There'd been a bookcase down in the room with the terrible woman. Polished wood with glass doors, and the books all neatly in rows on the shelves behind the glass.

All their holiday money on books, because the teacher said so. Moved to a different place for the schools, and all their holiday money gone, and from the way Patrick had said it, I didn't think his mum and dad liked books all that much.

They must have loved those boys an awful lot.

It was dark outside. Patrick had turned on a little lamp on the table so he could see to read in the dictionary. The glass in the window was black.

There was no noise from the telly downstairs. I thought of the woman, so dirty and drunk, with the stains on her dress, not even wearing any shoes. Got the boys everything they needed. Moved house to get them into a good school. Now she couldn't even stand up, she was so drunk, rolling about and telling me to fuck off, calling me a whore.

She never used to be like that, Patrick had said.

'Did you like school, then?' I asked, and he nodded.

They'd done well, both of them. Nicholas had always been better at school, except in sports. He wasn't bad at that, but not as good as Patrick, so people had started to say, brains and brawn.

'Dad was good at football,' said Patrick. 'He used to coach the team I was in. It was fine, while he was there. Nicholas would win a prize for something he'd written, I'd be made captain of the football team. I liked designing things, he liked research. It didn't matter. Then Dad died.'

311

He'd had a heart attack. Only the evening before he'd been on the football pitch, racing about, laughing, strong as a horse, Patrick said. The next day, at work, he'd died. Dead before he hit the floor, one of the men said. It had seemed unbelievable.

'What does your father do?' he asked, and I said, he's dead.

He was murdered, in prison. They couldn't prove it, or they didn't want to. He fell down the stairs, they said. Two lots of stairs. Nobody could say how. He wasn't even supposed to be there, not in that part of the prison. He was supposed to be in a place where they were safe. People who'd done really bad things were put there because the other prisoners might hurt them. It was to try to keep them safe, in a different bit of the prison. But Dad was in the main part of the prison, because there'd been some paperwork gone wrong.

When they came and told Mum, she threw up. Right there, in the living room, sitting in the chair where the policewoman had said she should sit down. She'd never seen him since they'd taken him away that day. Said she never wanted to, not see him, or hear of him, or anything. Never, ever again. Then, when the policewoman said he was dead, she threw up.

Accidental death, it came out in the verdict. Two lots of stairs, and there was ten feet, or near enough, between those two lots of stairs, and they said, accidental death.

'Nobody cared, because he was a pervert,' I said, and Patrick asked, what sort of a pervert?

'Him and our Sheila.'

Patrick didn't say anything. He looked down. Looked at his hands, or his knees, or something. Not looking at me, anyway.

After a little while he started to talk again.

After their dad had died, people said it was up to them now. What their father had wanted was for them to do well. Made it sound like it was sacred, because he was dead. Do well at school, that was what they meant, and it was Nicholas who did best. It wasn't that Patrick was neglected, but George, that was their dad's name, George, he'd always wanted his boys to do well at school, and Nicholas was the rising star. Nicholas was going to university, to study chemistry. Then he was going to do research.

Patrick was going to the technical college to study engineering and design, and he thought George would have liked that. He thought George would have been proud of that, too. You can get degrees at technical college, you don't have to go to university to get a degree. In the end they'd both have degrees.

'University sounds better,' said Patrick. 'Nicholas and I knew it didn't make a lot of difference. It made sense for him to go. I could stay here, with Mum. She still misses Dad. She gets lonely.'

She'd started to drink a bit after he'd died. Not a lot, not really. You might say she had a drinking problem, but you wouldn't say she was a real alcoholic. She drank mostly in the evenings, she used to say she couldn't sleep alone. She used to lie awake, missing George. So she'd get a bit drunk, so she could sleep.

It hadn't been their mother who'd put the pressure on Nicholas. She wasn't the sort to do that. But he'd known Patrick was having a bit of trouble with her, and he'd felt helpless. He was miles away, other side of the country, he couldn't help. And there'd been aunts and uncles, boasting about Nicholas at university, how clever he was, how proud George would have been. Maybe that was it. It was hard work, university, and he did nothing except work. If he couldn't help Patrick with their mother, he had to work. Patrick wasn't having much fun, so Nicholas didn't think he was entitled to any.

Entitled, I thought. There's that word again. Hearing it all day.

'He thought he was falling behind. He thought he couldn't do it. He worked harder and harder, and he wasn't sleeping. That Christmas he wouldn't come out at all, wouldn't come out to parties, wouldn't even come down to the pub for a drink. He said he had to work. He told me there was a library. If he could go there, he'd find the books he needed. He'd manage then. When I asked him, what library? he said it's in the Dark Universe.'

I felt sick. I told Patrick, I feel sick, and he looked up at me. Concerned.

'Concussion?'

He took me into the bathroom, and I leaned over the toilet, but I wasn't sick. I tried to be, but I wasn't. My head hurt, and I felt giddy.

'Lie down on the bed,' he said. 'Do you want a blanket?'

That reminded him about the woman, and he went downstairs. I lay on his bed, and I listened, and a few minutes later he came back. She was asleep, he said.

'Feeling better?' he asked.

'Yes.'

I had my eyes closed, but he turned off the lamp. It was nice, in the dark, but I lay very still, wondering what he was going to do next. Why did he turn off the lamp?

I heard him sit down in the chair again, and I opened my eyes.

'I had concussion once,' he said. 'I fell off a wall.'

'I got hit on the head.'

'I know. I'm sorry. I thought you were a spiteful little tart.'

He'd had hardly any sleep for three nights. She'd been drunk. She'd gone out into the garden, shouted abuse at the neighbours, fallen down and passed out. He'd carried her in, and when she'd come round again she'd gone out into the street and threatened somebody's child. The police had been. Every time he tried to sleep it seemed she got up again, and did something else. He'd hidden the whisky, but she had another bottle.

'I got the idea it was all your fault. I got angry. I went to the bus stop you used. I'd only just got off the bus a minute or two earlier. If you hadn't come I'd have started to walk home. I'd have come to my senses. But you turned up at just the wrong moment. I saw you, and I thought of Nicholas locked up, and Mum back here doing God knows what while I was out, and I thought, this spiteful little tart with her bloody lies, it's all her fault.'

I didn't say anything. I thought about it, and it wasn't right. Even if I had been what he said, a spiteful little tart, I hadn't made his brother mad. It wasn't my fault. If I'd known, when they said I should sign the statement, I wouldn't have done it. I'd have said, no, write it out again, and say what I want, about how he was always respectful. Not all that dirt. And you can leave out about me wetting myself, too. Nobody needs to know that.

'I didn't make him ill,' I said, and I began to feel angry. All this, that Patrick had said, it still wasn't my fault, and he should have known.

315

'It's not fair,' I said.

'I'm sorry. I am sorry, Joan. I truly didn't know you couldn't read. And I wasn't thinking straight. You came round the corner, and I picked up a stone and hit you. I kicked you, too. I think that must have been when your arm got broken.

'God. I'm so sorry.'

I shouldn't have come, I thought, but I'm glad I did. I think this is what was meant to happen, Theresa. This is the other reason. Sort it out, and I think I have.

'Who's Theresa?' he asked.

Been talking out loud? I was just thinking, can you read my thoughts, then? Is that bit of it real?

'Who's Theresa?' he asked again, so I told him. She was kind to me. Didn't think I was stupid, told me about things. Can you tell the difference between cut and moulded glass, I asked, and he said, well, yes, because of Dad. All right, Mister Clever, how do you know if silver's any good?

'Tell me.'

'You look at the shape,' I said. 'Never mind the twiddly bits, look at the shape.'

She died of cancer and left me money, I told him, and when I can write a bit better I'm going to find out where she's buried and buy her flowers and go and say good-bye properly. Writing to the solicitors is a sort of thank you, shows her I did it. I learned, and that was what she wanted.

'Wanted *you* sorted out, too,' I said, and he didn't answer.

I went to sleep for a little while, and when I woke up my head hurt. I tried to sit up, and he came over and helped me.

316

'How do you manage, not being able to read?'

'I don't want to talk about it. I don't feel very well.'

'Why aren't you in hospital?'

They couldn't find a bed, except in intensive care, I thought. I didn't need one that badly. I'm not going to tell you, Patrick Parry. I didn't want Mum doing her act. This is me being a good mother. She hit me yesterday, or the day before, or sometime like that. Yesterday. Shouting at people in the hospital about my rights today. Going off to work. Sheila won't be long. Sheila going out, leaving me alone.

Shouldn't do that, with children, leave them alone at night.

I don't feel very well.

I went out of the house, and I got a taxi here. I shouldn't be here. This man, sitting there in the dark, with a dictionary on the floor beside him, he nearly killed me. Now he's concerned. But I was determined to come here. I was determined to get Rita's spoons. Something depended on it. I nearly had a fractured skull and the doctor diagnosed concussion.

Feeling sick again. All those new words, but I'd got them. I had, I'd got them, I'd thought them. Used them.

I shouldn't be here, not with him. This man, he'd hit me on the head, stolen my things. I didn't think he was a thief though. He'd said he wouldn't give me back Rita's spoons, he'd got a customer for them. He didn't mean it. But he had hit me, and he'd stolen my things. Made it look like a mugging, so they wouldn't know for sure who it was. Might not be him, Nicholas Parry's brother.

'They sent Nicholas to hospital from the university,' said Patrick, when I didn't answer his question about why I wasn't in hospital. 'They telephoned to tell us he'd been taken ill. When I went to see him he was crying. He couldn't stop. They gave him drugs to make him sleep. All the time he was awake, he was crying. He only stopped crying when he was asleep. He told me he had to go back to the Dark Universe, so he could work in the library. He wasn't allowed to go back until he'd found the Empress.'

I didn't answer. It's not my fault, it's not fair. I don't want to hear this.

Nicholas had found a shelf-filler from Fletchers the supermarket. Dozey Joan Ferguson, couldn't even read. He'd made up something about me so he could call me the Empress and say he'd found me.

'He told me he'd found the Empress. That was months later. He was better by then. He was working. It was only a job at an estate agent, showing people round houses, but at least he was functioning.'

'What's that mean?' I asked.

'Working. Like a piece of machinery. When you switch it on, it functions. It does what it's meant to do.'

'Anything else it means?'

He laughed. Yes, he said, a function can be a party. An event. And it's a computing term, too.

I'm never going to understand, I thought. And, I shouldn't be here.

'I shouldn't be here,' I said.

'That's what I thought when I saw you at the door.'

Suppose he won't let me go? Suppose he locks me up, or ties up my hands? Mum might be home by now, but she won't know where I am, and Sheila could be out all night.

'Will they be worried about you?'

'Mum will be.'

'Do you want a cup of tea?'

I did. I was very thirsty. I hadn't realised.

He went downstairs to make the tea, and I sat up on the bed, in the dark, and I looked at the shiny black book lying on the floor. Mine. My dictionary now. He'd given it to me. Concise, that big, thick book.

Everything seemed to be moving. Like being in an earthquake, I thought. Not just because I'm feeling giddy, from the concussion. Things I thought I knew, they're not right any more. Not only words. Dog. Not just an animal, it can mean a bit of machinery, and following. I'd thought, animal. Barks at you, people keep them for pets. Chews bones. But all those other dog word, I'd never known about. If I say dog now, I might mean an animal that barks, or a bit of machinery, or following something. It wasn't right. And Mum wasn't in charge any more, because I'd raised my hand, hit me again and I'll hit you back.

I shouldn't be here. I should have stayed safe at home. Shouldn't have raised my hand to Mum. Shouldn't have asked about the words.

I'd managed before, hadn't I? I'd got by. Got a job, paid my way. Can't all be clever, can we? And Mr Bradwell, saying that about a career in Fletchers if I could read. That couldn't be right.

I wasn't safe any more.

That big, shiny book on the floor, that was dangerous. Words that mean different things, so nothing's safe. Words are dangerous, you never know what they're going to say next. What they're going to *mean* next.

Don't ask. Don't ask questions. It's a secret. A *secret*.

Oh, don't. Don't, Dad. Please, don't. I didn't tell. They

all said not to. They said, if you won't tell us, we can't do anything, so I didn't. I didn't tell.

If it wasn't for words he'd still be there, safe. Safe at home.

Patrick came back. There were two mugs on a tray, and I looked at them, all shiny in the light from the street lamp, and I wanted to cry again. I can't hold them, the handles are too small, but I'm so thirsty.

'Can't hold one of them,' I said.

'Why not?'

Why not? You looked at my hands. I showed you. Why not?

'Because of what Nicholas did to my hands, that's why not,' I said.

He put the tray down on the table, and he stood there, as if he was waiting. Not saying anything, only waiting.

'I can't hold a pen, not properly, can't even pour milk out of the bottle. I drop things. I break things. Your brother, your Nicholas. At least he didn't *do* anything, that's what they all said.'

'I'm sorry.'

'Nobody thought it mattered.' I said. 'It's only Joan. Only shoving boxes around, filling up her cage at Fletchers. Shelf-filler. Different if it was Sheila, all that fiddly stuff working in a hairdresser. Only it was me, so it didn't matter. It never mattered, if it was only me.'

He wasn't looking at me, he was looking down at the floor. He looked just like Nicholas then, with his floppy hair hanging down, but listening to me as if he was waiting for me to do something.

'What do you usually drink out of?' he asked when I'd stopped.

'I got a mug with a big handle.'

320

He went out again, and when he came back he had a thing like a beer glass, only it was metal. It was still wet where he'd washed it.

'I won it, rowing,' he said, and he poured the tea out of one of the mugs into it and passed it to me.

'I never mattered,' I said.

He sighed. 'I knocked two seconds of the record at Henley. Two whole seconds. I had enough drinks bought for me that night to float a battleship. My record still stands. But back here, back in the *real world*, I don't know when that was last polished. I even forget about it myself, sometimes.'

'Did you get your degree at the technical college?' I asked, and I thought, I'm not going to say tech any more. Technical college.

'No,' he said. 'No, I left. I got a job at Stephens, in the electronics department. It doesn't matter. I'll work my way up.'

'It does matter,' I said, and I started to cry again.

He was sitting beside me on the bed, wiping my face with a hankie, as if I was a baby.

'How's your head?' he asked.

'All right.'

'Makes people do funny things, sometimes, a bang on the head. I'm sorry, Joan. I wish I hadn't done that.'

I sniffed, and I drank my tea. He'd made it too sweet, but I didn't say anything. Maybe he thought I had shock, like Mum had said.

'Why did you follow me around?' I asked. 'On the bus, all that? Why did you do that? And that knife, why did you do that?'

'Because I was angry. I didn't know you. All I knew was that statement. It was lies. Nobody could spend three days with Nicholas and believe that about him. That he was a sadist, you couldn't have believed that about him. I didn't know what was going to happen to him. I still don't. Mum was drinking, the neighbours were starting to complain about her, she was shouting at them in the street. She never used to be like that.

'Then I saw you outside Tesco's, and you nearly fainted, and I thought, right. I know how to get my own back on you, you nasty little bitch. I'll scare the shit out of you.'

'Liar,' I said. 'You bloody liar, then. What about the cards? They hadn't done the statement then, had they? When you sent the cards. You're just lying, you are.'

'That was Mum,' he said. 'She was so scared, Joan. For Nicholas. She wanted to stop you saying *anything* about him. She didn't know what you'd say. I think she had the idea she might frighten you into keeping quiet, not saying anything at all.'

We sat in silence for a long time, and then I said, 'I thought I was going mad. Then I thought they'd let him out, by mistake. Paperwork. That was how my dad was killed, and at the shop we sometimes get a delivery wrong, because of delivery notes, paperwork. I didn't know. After that, when I saw you on the bus, I thought, it's the Dark Universe. It's real, and they've sent somebody else to take me back. But I didn't know. I didn't know if I was seeing things. Theresa said I should touch you, see if my hand went through. I couldn't do that. Only, after she died, I thought I'd got to, because she said.'

'Why couldn't you touch me?' he asked.

'You shouldn't touch people,' I said. 'It's not right.'

Everybody knows that, or should do. Davie Evans got sacked for touching. Serve him right. Don't touch people. Keep away.

I don't go out with Carol any more. All those men in the pub, putting their arms round her. And me, round my shoulder. Going to make me lucky, Joan? Just looking down at the floor, thinking, don't. Don't. Don't touch me, it's all wrong. But when I said it, quietly, don't, I'd say, they stopped. Took their arms away. So they know it's wrong. Everybody knows.

He knows, too. Patrick knows.

'You didn't like it, when I touched you.'

'I didn't know you. I was still angry with you.'

He was staring at me. Then he looked down at his hand, with the handkerchief still in it.

'I wiped your face,' he said. 'Shouldn't I have done that?'

'That's different.'

When I looked again he was close to me, leaning towards me. He kissed me on my mouth. He didn't touch me, just lips, nothing else, as if he was being very careful not to come too close when he kissed me.

'Was that wrong?' he asked.

I didn't know. I didn't say anything. I just looked at him, and he kissed me again, and asked, was that wrong? Was *that* wrong? Only he didn't say it. It was on his face, the question. I couldn't answer.

'Did you like that?'

Is it rude to say no?

'No,' I said, and then, 'Well, not very much.'

He went back to the chair and sat down, looking at me.

'They'll be worrying about you now,' he said. 'Your mother, your sister.'

I ought to go home, I thought. And, his mouth tasted of toothpaste.

I hadn't got enough money for a taxi home, but it

wasn't too far. I could walk. Sheila could have given me some.

She's always got money. Whenever Mum asks, when she does her sums, her calculations she says, and there isn't enough, she says, lend me a bit, pet? And she does.

Men give her money.

I love you, Dad had said to her. I love you, Sheila. And she'd answered, that's what he says. And *he* gives me money, too.

I'll give you money.

It was too late by then. He didn't know what to do. I love you, Sheila. Don't go with him. Don't go with them. I'm the one who loves you.

He did love her. He loved her more than he loved me, or Mum, or anything, and he didn't know what to do. So he made that telephone call. Fucking his own daughter, and she's only a child.

Is that you, Joanie? Say a word about this and I'll cut your tongue out.

I never said anything, and he still didn't love me. It was always Sheila.

'Will you be all right?' I asked Patrick, and he didn't answer.

No, he wouldn't be all right. It couldn't be all right for Patrick now. Three nights with no sleep because of his mother being drunk all the time, shouting at the neighbours. Left the technical college before he got his degree, got a job at Stephens. Work his way up, he'd said.

He and Nicholas, they'd known it didn't make much difference, a degree from a university or one from a technical college, but he'd had to leave. Just work his way up, and try to cope with his mum, and not get enough sleep. Nicholas was his brother, his twin brother, locked up, and nobody knew when he'd ever come out again.

He got me Rita's spoons and my purse and my passbook, and he gave me Nicholas's dictionary, and he phoned for a taxi to take me home.

Don't come back, he said, and he didn't try to touch me again.

THE BLACKSMITH
Jenny Maxwell

There had been a forge at Anford for about a thousand years, but not until the twentieth century was the blacksmith a woman.

From a childhood and adolescence scarred by rejection and loneliness, the forge became Ann Mayall's sanctuary, and the traditions of its craft brought her success, security, and the tentative beginnings of friendship.

But the new owners of the neighbouring manor see her presence as a threat, although she doesn't know why. She rejects their increasingly large offers to purchase her inheritance. Hostility and intimidation fail to move her, so they revert to more violence; if she will not leave, she must die – but they have not reckoned on Ann's formidable physical strength.

ISBN 0 7515 1804 2

THE BLACK CAT
Jenny Maxwell

Glory is as different from her blacksmith sister as it is possible to be. Stylish and graceful, she is described by more than one man as the most beautiful woman he has ever seen. Her career as a theatre designer takes her from condemned structures in blighted urban towns to the Shakespeare Memorial Theatre in Stratford, and everywhere the casts and staff call her their lucky black cat. But away from the stage Glory is a victim of perversion and abuse, experiences which have dangerously damaged her mind.

Then her sister is threatened by the same breed of men who have ruined her, and Glory is prepared to sacrifice her own life rather than allow them to destroy Ann.

ISBN 0 7515 2009 8

THE IRON SNAKES
Jenny Maxwell

Ann Mayall is in love with a man she cannot have.
Blacksmith at the historic forge of Anford, sister to the
successful theatre designer Glory, she finds a kindred spirit
in the shape of Swedish professor Arno Linssen. But Arno
is already married, and tragic news forces him to return to
his homeland. In a moment of despair, Ann settles for the
lesser charms of stable owner Jake Brewer.

Almost immediately, it is clear the marriage is a mistake.
Jake's wedding gift is a share in his business, one crippled
by financial mismanagement and illegal gambling debts.
Ann's forge is threatened, yet despite pleas from family and
friends she refuses to dissolve the partnership. She has
made a promise and is determined to keep it, even if it
means losing the livelihood she loves.

ISBN 0 7515 2905 2